THE PACT

OF

Freedom

Risen Halo Publishing
The Pact of Freedom

Copyright
© 2024 by M. L. Bull
All rights reserved worldwide. No part of this publication may be reproduced, distributed, or transmitted any form or by any means, without prior permission of publisher or author.

Scripture quotations are used from the Holy Bible, King James Version ®KJV ® Copyright © 1611

Author's Note: The Pact of Freedom is a work of fiction. However, slavery, the Fugitive Slave Law, and the Underground Railroad network, were all real historical events that took place in America during the antebellum era in the South between 1815 to 1860 prior to the Civil War. Any resemblance to people, living or dead, companies, locations, institutions, or locales is completely coincidental.

The Pact of Freedom/ M. L. Bull
ISBNS: 9798303325494 (KDP Paperback), 978-1-7333248-5-4 (Ingram Spark Paperback), 978-1-7333248-6-1 (Hardback), 978-1-7333248-1-6 (E-book)

Cover Designed by M. L. Bull
Cover Image from Pixabay.com
Portraits made in Portrait app
Edited by Diana Sharples from CritiqueMatch.com and M. L. Bull
Map Designed by Nikola Jankovic, a map designer from Serbia.
Find him on Fiverr.com
Printed in the United States of America

DEDICATION

For Family & Friends

Also By

Eva's Promise

THE PACT

OF

Freedom

M. L. BULL

Risen Halo Publishing

NORTH CAROLINA, USA

Mildred "Millie" Crabtree: The narrator. She is the eighteen-year-old daughter and only child of Charlotte Grace and Wade Crabtree. Her dream is to become a children's author, a rare pursuit among white women in the South.

Master Wade Crabtree: Millie's papa. He is the mean-spirited and inhumane slave master and owner of Crabtree Plantation who threatens his slaves by misusing the Holy Bible and desires to have a son to pass on his plantation.

Missus Charlotte Grace Crabtree: Millie's mama. She is the sickly housewife of Master Crabtree who has suffered multiple miscarriages due to her poor health. Being a loving mother, she regrets her mistreatment toward the house slaves under her husband's supervision.

Pearl: Millie's best friend. She is a nineteen-year-old, mulatto house slave who was brought to Crabtree Plantation when she was nine. She and Millie formed a blood pact to be sisters and always look out for each other.

Dula: Pearl's grandmother. She is an old house slave who was Millie's mammy that helped raise her from childhood to her young adulthood. She is sweet, warm, and golden brown, her character described as "a baked apple pie."

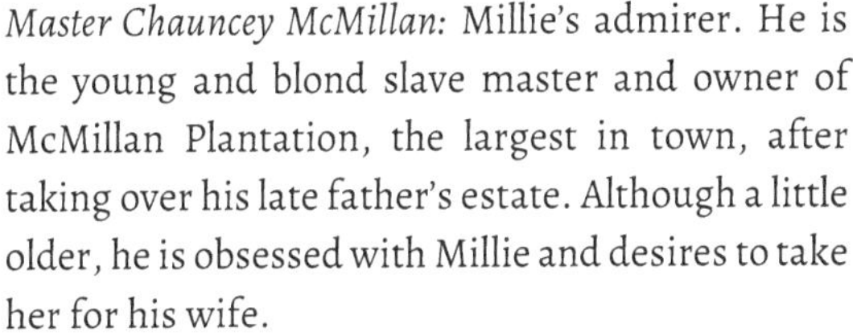

Master Chauncey McMillan: Millie's admirer. He is the young and blond slave master and owner of McMillan Plantation, the largest in town, after taking over his late father's estate. Although a little older, he is obsessed with Millie and desires to take her for his wife.

Randall ("Randy"): Pearl's lover. He is a young field slave on Crabtree Plantation. He is often seen as a troublemaker for his spite toward Master Crabtree and rebellious behavior.

Noah Shepherd: Abolitionist. He is a Canadian violinist and conductor for the Underground Railroad network, known for his curly, red hair described as "rolls of shiny, red ribbons," short stature, and ruby frock coat. He and his musical comrades, Arthur and Hubert, assists in transporting slaves North for freedom.

Arthur Wagner: Abolitionist. He is a Canadian pianist and conductor for the Underground Railroad, known for his wired eyeglasses, thick, ridiculous mustache, and blue frock coat. With Noah and Hubert, he assists in transporting Millie and slaves to Windsor, Canada.

Hubert Duncan: Abolitionist. He is a cellist and conductor for the Underground Railroad, known for his deep voice, rosy cheeks, and yellow frock coat. With Noah and Arthur, he assists in transporting Millie and slaves to Windsor, Canada.

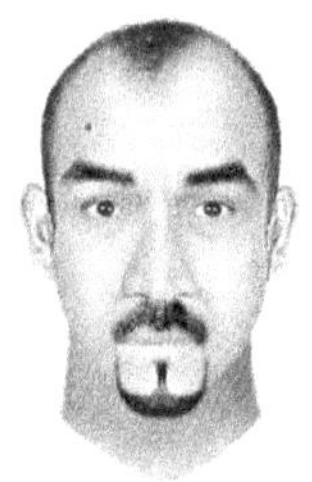

Joseph ("Joe"): Field hand. He is a middle-aged slave who works on Crabtree Plantation. His parents were sold by another plantation owner when he was four, so he barely remembers them.

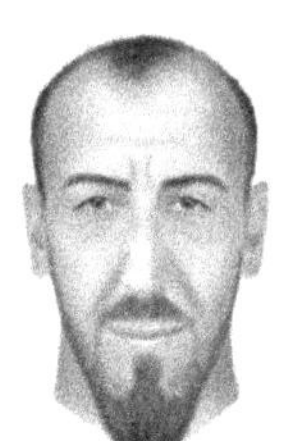

Mr. Feldman: Station master and Beatrice's husband. He is a lanky, hunchbacked man with a long, gray beard and thin, salt-and-pepper hair. He attempts to ride Millie and others to Lexington, but gets shot and killed.

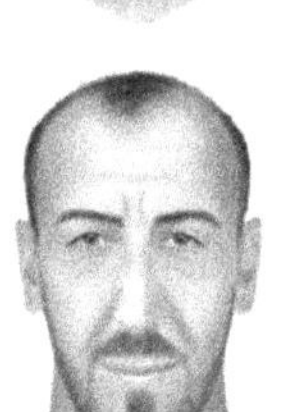

Mrs. Feldman: Station master and Matthew's wife. She is a middle-aged, pudgy woman with honey brown hair who's a housewife and helps work on a farm with her husband.

Louisville ticket collector: A grouchy, white man who collects train tickets and works for the Louisville and Nashville Train Station. He has a unibrow and bad breath from chewing tobacco.

Mr. Hughes: Station master. He is a slender man with a bushy, western mustache who works as an undertaker. To avoid suspicion, he harbors Pearl, Anna, and Marge in coffins in a boxcar during their train ride into Cincinnati, Ohio.

Savannah Hughes: Station master and Mr. Hughes' daughter. She is a blonde, shy little girl about twelve or thirteen years old who assists Millie with hospitality while she and the others freshen up for their train ride to Cincinnati, Ohio.

Lewis Poindexter: Station master and Clarissa's husband. He is a young, mulatto businessman from Detroit, Michigan who runs a boarding house. He also owns a small ship named "The Odyssey," which he uses to transport runaway slaves across the Detroit River to the Canadian border in Windsor.

Clarissa Poindexter: Station master and Lewis' wife. She is a pretty, redhead woman originally from Canada who helps run a boarding house and shelters fugitive slaves with her husband who seek refuge through Detroit to freedom. Her parents live in Windsor, Canada, often worrying about her and Lewis' safety due to their interracial marriage.

Ophelia Vaughn: Station master. She is a free negro woman who lives in Sandwich, a neighborhood within Windsor, Canada. For a while, she cares for Pearl like a loving mother, letting her stay in her home back in the woods.

Cecil: Blacksmith. He is a free negro man who helps Ophelia around her house. He and Pearl befriend each other and later get married.

| OTHER IMPORTANT CHARACTERS |

Margaret ("Marge"): House slave. She is a middle-aged, ebony-skinned house slave who enjoys cooking and is always ready to help in the kitchen. She knows how to make all kinds of different soups.

Master John Weiss: Slave master. He is a fellow neighbor in town and close friend of Millie's father.

Anna: Field hand and Ozzie's little sister. She is a tall, youthful, deep-brown-skinned slave woman known for wearing a blue shawl around her shoulders.

Ozzie: Field hand and Anna's big brother. He is a powerfully-built slave on Crabtree Plantation, and Master Crabtree's best and strongest field hand. He and his sister are very close, sticking together like "salt and pepper," as they lost their parents during a slave auction when they were little children.

Miss Winifred Perkins: Station master. She is an old, Quaker woman with circle, wire-framed eyeglasses, a pug nose, and silver curls of hair covered with a sheer white bonnet tied under her chin. She is the first "station master" to take Millie and her slave friends into refuge, lives alone in a small house entangled by pink rose vines, and walks with a cane.

Jack Crenshaw: Bounty hunter. He is a tall, red-skinned man who resembles an Injun with slick, jet black hair. He wears an all-black outfit, which includes a cowboy hat, a long-sleeve shirt, a leather vase, pants, boots, and gloves. On his hip, he has a holster loaded with a gun. He and his partner Sal are hired by Millie's papa to capture and return her and the runaway slaves from Crabtree Plantation.

Sal: Bounty hunter. He is a stout, negro man that wears a tan bowler hat, a white dress shirt, a brown-and-cream gingham vest, dark brown trousers fastened with braces ("suspenders"), and light brown leather boots. Like Jack, he carries a revolver in a holster.

Mrs. Penelope "Penny" Talbot: Station master. A young, country housewife with ash brown hair and green eyes who stays in Kingsport, Tennessee with her husband and son. Her husband is a pro-slavery supporter, convinced slavery is best for the nation.

Henry Talbot: Penelope's five-year-old son. He likes to read and wants to be a doctor when he grows up.

Mr. Paul Kilgore: Station master. A yeoman farmer and Irish immigrant who runs a potato and livestock farm and resides in Scott County, Virginia. His beloved wife Greta died from influenza, having suffered a terrible fever.

Mr. Ezra Hadley: Station master. An elderly Quaker man with a long white beard who loves playing spiritual hymns on the piano. He provides refuge and food for Millie and her slave friends after a long, treacherous journey to Lexington, Kentucky.

The Murphy Sisters: Two slave women who were threatened to be sold "down the river" from Master Chauncey McMillan's large cotton plantation, but escape to freedom with Ozzie and other fellow slaves.

Nina & Gerald: A middle-aged African American couple from Kettering, Ohio after Millie and the others take an unplanned rest stop during their journey to Toledo, Ohio.

Grandma Hughes: Station master. She is an elderly woman known as Savannah's grandmother who assists Pearl, Anna, and Margaret before their train ride into Cincinnati, Ohio.

Waldo Finley: Station master. A free negro man who's Ophelia's cousin and lives in Toledo, Ohio. He ran away from Louisiana after his master died and sought safety and freedom in Ohio as many others negro people before him; but as promised, he uses his former master's surname who never had children.

Mrs. Caroline Simmons: Lady cook. She's a witty, middle-aged woman with dark hair and a paisley shawl who assists with feeding and harboring fugitive slaves in the secret hideout of the Wendell Bookstore in Cincinnati, Ohio.

Mr. Willie Fisher: A dirty-faced white man who works at the railroad and wears a sea cap. He helps transport Pearl and Margaret in wood crates during their journey from Cincinnati to Toledo, Ohio.

Mr. & Mrs. Carlson: Clarissa's parents who live in a neighborhood called Sandwich in Windsor, Canada.

Noah's Map

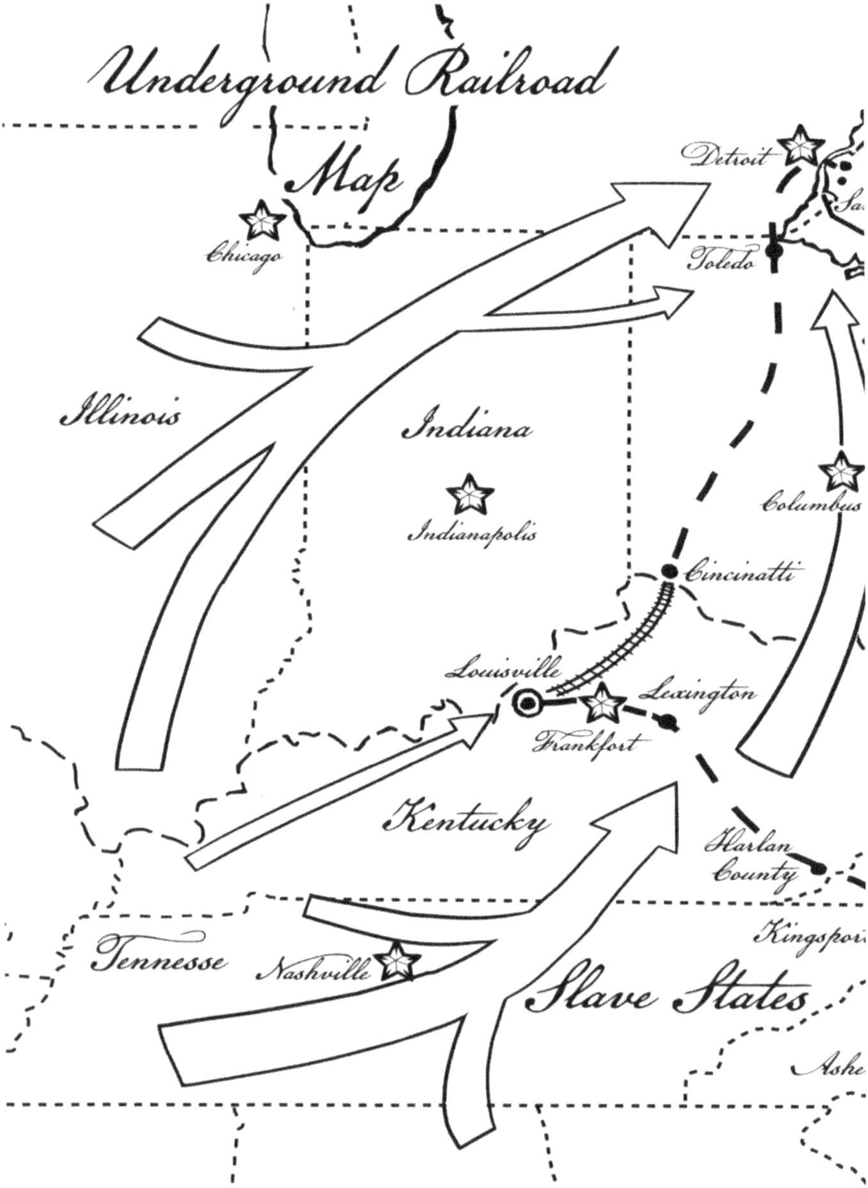

Underground Railroad Map
Detroit
Sa.
Chicago
Toledo
Illinois
Indiana
Columbus
Indianapolis
Cincinatti
Louisville
Lexington
Frankfort
Kentucky
Harlan County
Tennesse
Kingspor
Nashville
Slave States
Ashe

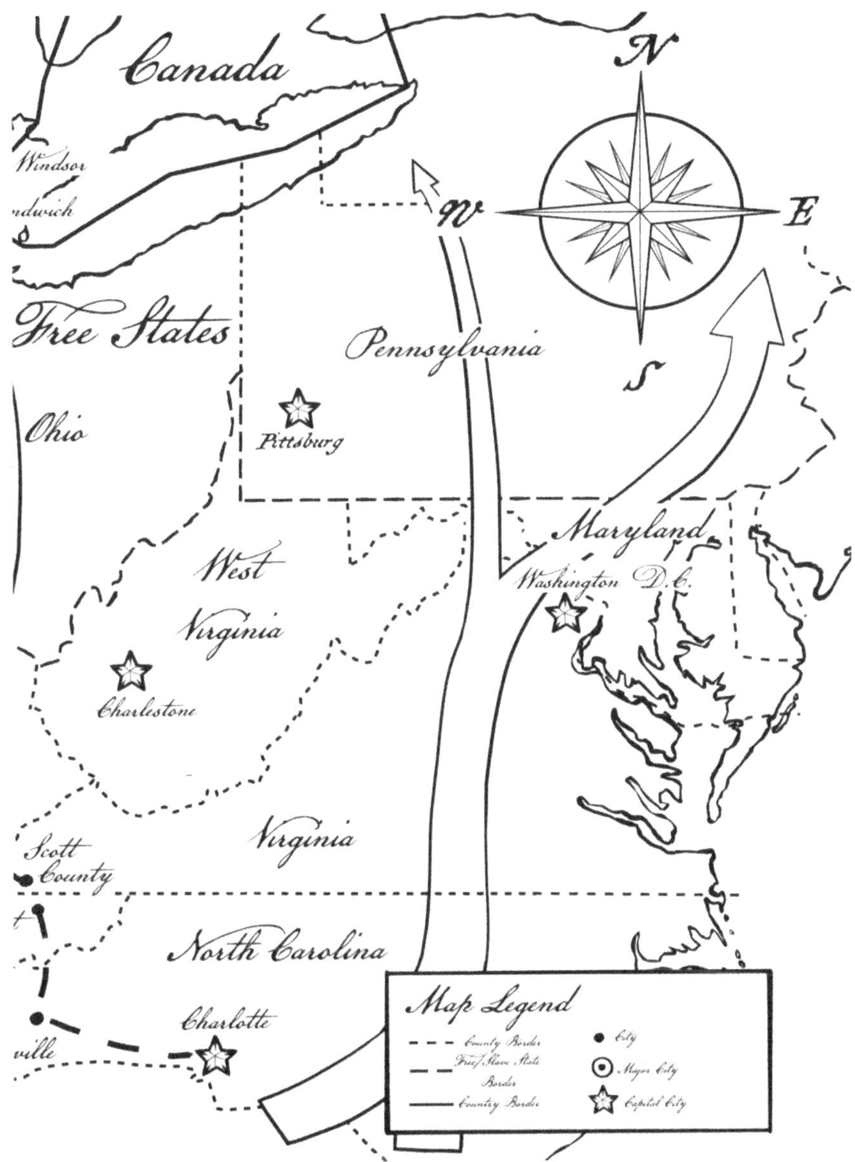

Canada
Windsor
ndwich
s
Free States
Ohio
Pittsburg
Pennsylvania
West
Virginia
Charlestone
Virginia
Scott
County
t
ville
North Carolina
Charlotte
Maryland
Washington D.C.
N
W
S
E
Map Legend
County Border
Free/Slave State
Border
Country Border
City
Major City
Capital City

EPIGRAPH

"Love thy neighbor as thyself."

Matthew 22:39

1 *Curse of the Family*

July 1852

CRABTREE PLANTATION
Charlotte, North Carolina

MOST FOLKS IN TOWN called me Millie, but my Christian name's Mildred. It means, "gentle strength." Of course, I never thought it suited me well. There's nothing *gentle* about a breech birth, and as my Papa always said, "Any child born feet first was a curse." Since I was born, Mama struggled to reach full-term, leading to her inadequacy and depression. Every white woman's value in the South rested on two things: her husband's status and her ability to bear him a son.

I was a disappointment to my father, the curse of my family's roots. Papa said my mind was dark to the ways of the world—that I was a naïve walker, and maybe it was true. Fear and insecurity lived within me like haunting spirits taunting my soul. *What could I do to make my parents proud? How could I accept the traditions of the South?* Once my best friend Pearl and I formed our sister blood pact as little girls, I felt as much in bondage as the slaves on my father's plantation. Rather than accept life as it was, I wanted the freedom to explore the world, live my own dreams, and grasp the pleasures of life, liberty, and happiness.

But in the South, this felt like a fantasy—an elusive dream, as I lacked the courage to execute it. Maybe my statements were inconsiderate in a nation that favors the white race, but I saw slavery as inhumane and nothing more than a pit of hell. Having opposing views made me a branded traitor to my own flesh and blood. "Slaves aren't *friends*, they're *servants*," Papa often emphasized.

But I saw things differently, or maybe I was too ignorant to grasp the expectations of a slave master's daughter. As a young, female child, I didn't know what slavery was. But when I grew older my eyes opened to the dark truths of the mortal sin of my family. Papa, like most slaveholders, criticized the Yankees for their fight for abolition and saw nothing wrong with slavery.

Mama claimed she didn't either, but her hard shell was a facade to cover her guilt from owning slaves. Her countenance exposed the shame buried in her heart. Like most wives, she did whatever her husband told her to do, which made her no better than the house slaves she ruled in our mansion home.

Constantly, I prayed to God I'd somehow escape the corrupted institution in the oppressive South. But things worsened, and I learned witnessing the brutality of slavery was only the start of my misery. Being the wife of a slave master held its privileges, but also its trauma and loneliness. Those who gave a male heir to their husbands were the most treasured. Unlike others, my mother was a sickly, weak woman—unable to meet my father's desire for a son to pass on the land and bear his name.

After me, she miscarried every other child she had. Perhaps it wasn't God's will for them to live a life of sin. Lying on her bed, something changed in Mama's eyes, a sparkle of remorse as Dula tended to her needs, her cold bitterness no longer there. Dula was an older house slave and the grandmother of Pearl. After I turned one, she was my mammy, who Mama placed the duties of motherhood on to keep watch of the other house slaves.

Though Dula worked for us, she was also a good friend of mine. She was sweet, warm, and golden brown, like a baked apple pie. Somehow, despite living on Crabtree Plantation, she had a joy kindled within her like a steady, burning fire. I reckon it was how she coped with her aches and pains from her chores and whenever she overheard Papa or Jed, the overseer, flogging one of the field slaves.

"It's a curse . . . it's a curse, I tell you," Papa fussed, during Mama's fourth miscarriage.

On the bright, humid morning, the tension in the sitting room was so thick one could chop it like wood with an axe. Within the unbearable silence were Mama's deafening screams and low moans as she fought with her pain. *Dear God—why was this always happening to her?*

Reclining in his big chair, Papa stroked his black, full beard, in deep thought. *Was I to blame?* From his steady glare, his intimidating words echoed inside my mind, "Any child born feet first was a curse . . ."

Ashamed, I looked away from my father through the curtained window. Shifting my eyes across the snow-white, cotton field, I tried to make sense of and find an escape from the current situation. Somehow, there had to be some kind of explanation other than me, right?

"Mama's . . . Mama's a thin and fragile woman, Papa. She needs time to heal and build up her strength." I fluttered my eyelids and exhaled a shaking breath. "I'll . . . I'll go see about her."

Walking past my father, I sighed and entered the big room to check on my mother in bed.

"Dula . . . Dula, please, get me some water," Mama said. "I feel like a wilting plant. I'm . . . thirsty." She panted and wiped her hand across her sweaty forehead.

Dula nodded. "Yessum, I be right back." She grabbed the glass from the nightstand and glanced at Margaret, one of the younger house slaves. "Marge, you stick with her. Doc should be here shortly."

"Yessum." Margaret gulped and stood at the foot of my mother's canopy bed, clutching the brass frame bars like a prisoner in a cell. Her ebony face wore a look of terror as she watched my mother and Dula left to do her errand.

I sat in a chair next to my mother's bed and held her hand. "Good morning, mama."

Mama smiled tenderly, but tears twinkled in her eyes. She patted the top of my hand with her free one. "Mildred . . . my dear Millie. You look lovely today, darling. I'm sure you'll turn the heads of every man in town the day of your birthday party."

My mother was hanging between life and death, and all she could think about was me getting a husband? Looking in her moist, brown eyes, I struggled to accept her compliance while trapped in a male-dominating system of gender roles and proper place. But it had gone on for many years in the South, so it was most expected of us.

I hung my head, ashamed and dismayed.

"Millie, dear? Millie, please, don't blame yourself. Your Papa's claims are wrong. You have nothing to do with my health issues. Cheer up, now, I don't want you to be sad on your special day."

"I'll try, mama." Moisture blurred my vision as I gave a weak smile.

Mama squeezed my hand. "Good, that's my girl. Be sure to wear your best dress . . . and make sure you mind your manners."

I knew what that meant. She was asking me to keep my Christian notions and unfavorable views of slavery to myself, so as not to offend our invited house guests.

"Yes, ma'am," I said and glanced down, but I wasn't confident I'd be able to hold my tongue about Papa and the townsmen's slave dealings.

Dula returned with a glass of water and walked around the opposite side of the canopy bed. "I brought you water, missus."

"Help me sit up, girls," Mama said.

Dula put the glass on the windowsill and then she and Margaret helped my mother sit into an upright position, one of them placing her pillow behind her back.

Then Dula handed my mother the glass.

"Thank you, Dula." Mama sipped the water and ran her fingers through her chestnut-brown, wavy hair.

Dula stepped back and kneaded her white apron with a nervous look. "Anything else you need, missus?"

"Just the doctor," Mama joked, "but at least the worse is over." She laughed faintly, and then winced, rubbing her hand to her chest. "My heart aches. This one put a strain on me." Her cheeks turned crimson, glancing up at Margaret. "I'm deeply sorry for ruining the linens, Marge. I know how hard you clean them."

Margaret wore a weak smile. "It's all right, missus. You couldn't help it. Just a part of nature, that's all."

Horses neighed outside, followed by the sound of hoofbeats and squeaking wheels.

I stood and peeked out of the window. "The doctor's here, mama. He came up to the house."

"Thank God." Mama drank from her glass of water again. "One of you girls make me a warm bath in the basin, please."

"Yessum. Maybe Doc will give you medicine for your chest pain," Margaret said.

"Breakfast must be served. I'll check on Pearl in the kitchen. The girl's got lots of learnin to do," Dula said. She and Margaret left in separate directions, one to the washroom and the other to the kitchen.

Pearl was as pretty as her name, and what folks in town called a mulatto. Her high yellow complexion could make her pass for white. After birth, her former slave master sold her mother before she knew her well enough, lest her mama disgraces him. I didn't know what happened after that, but when she was nine, Papa bought Pearl and three others from a slave trader.

For a while, she was like a lamb led to the slaughter, so scared she couldn't speak. It wasn't until I noticed she had an interest in storybooks that she opened up and talked more. Without Papa knowing, I helped her learn the alphabet and read, and let her borrow some of my books. Little by little, we became friends—like close sisters.

Ten years ago, I took one of Mama's pink roses from the bush and we each punctured our forefingers with a thorn, forming a secret blood pact. Since that day, we promised to look out for each other, and I consented I'd help Pearl get her freedom someday. One summer morning, we were playing hide and seek during harvest time, and Pearl had gotten into trouble with my father and Jed, the overseer.

As Papa instructed, Jed took a branch switch to her for not harvesting cotton as the other slaves did. The overseer tied her small wrists with a rope around the trunk of the same tree where I had counted to ten and beat her until her shoulder blades were bruised. We thought Jed would never stop. Every time Papa said, "Again," the switch slashed her little body. My father hadn't long bought Pearl, but she told me this day was her wake-up call to slavery. As a slave in the fields, there was hardly a time for play, just work, work, work.

I felt like I had broken my promise. Nonetheless, Pearl forgave me. Ever since Mama's third miscarriage, Pearl was brought into our white mansion from the fields to work as a house slave. As an only child, I was distressed by the loss of my siblings, as was my mother. Being friends and a year apart, Papa said her in the mansion was to help me cope and feel better, and it was one of the nicest things he's ever done. But every day he liked to watch Pearl, and I worried about his true intentions.

Part of me thought he was keeping her from Randall, another slave who worked in the fields. It wasn't a secret Randall and Pearl were fond of each other and had hopes of someday escaping to freedom as many slaves had before them. They had already asked for permission to leave twice, but Papa made it clear he owned his slaves, and no one would leave his land without getting caught. Crabtree Plantation, which Papa said had been in our family since the late seventeenth century, had a long and terrible history.

Since then, not one slave was known to ever get free.

There was a knock at the door.

"Come in," Mama called.

Dr. Grayson, the town doctor, peeked around the door. "Good morning, you two." He entered the big room, holding his derby hat and black valise. Then he walked to the bed and looked at my mother. "I'm sorry, Missus Charlotte."

"Nothing to be sorry for, doctor. Like Marge said, 'It's a part of nature," Mama said in a sad, weak voice.

Dr. Grayson placed his derby hat on the nightstand and opened his bag on the bed. "I suppose, but four times? How are you so strong about this?"

"Just prayer and faith, doc. The good Lord said He'll heal the brokenhearted, didn't He?" Mama said.

Dr. Grayson inched up a little smile. "Indeed, He did, Missus Charlotte." He took out his stethoscope. "Let me check your heart." He plugged his ears and moved the drum over my mother's chest, listening intently. "Your heart sounds slow, but it's strong." He smiled and linked the earpieces around his neck.

Mama smiled. "Thanks, Doc. You got anything in your

bag for my chest pain?" She studied the doctor as he rummaged through his valise.

"I've brought some laudanum, but it's about all I can do, I'm afraid. With your condition, you should get plenty of rest, and wait a year or two before, well . . . any more *physical activity*. That's what your body needs. Perhaps then you'll have another successful delivery."

"I told Wade, Doc. But . . . he's getting older, he's worried it'll be too late," Mama said.

Dr. Grayson sighed and filled a spoon with laudanum from a glass bottle. "Well, it's that or your life, ma'am. I'll talk with him outside. Open wide for me, please."

Mama opened her mouth and took in the spoonful.

"Feeling better?" I asked.

"Yes, dear—" Mama grimaced and smacked her lips— "but it's the *nastiest* stuff I've ever tasted, and I feel filthy as a pig in slop. I can't wait to freshen up and take a bath."

Dr. Grayson chuckled. "I'll leave this bottle here for you. Based on your reaction, I reckon I don't have to worry about you taking more than one spoonful per dose." He tucked the cork back in the bottle and placed it on the nightstand. "Are you ready for me to examine you?"

"Sure, doctor," Mama said with a nonchalant shrug. "Do what you have to do." Bending her knees in an upright position, she propped up her legs.

After losing so many babies, I suppose the process of examination wasn't too big a deal to Mama anymore, but

I'd never been in the room during one of them. Thus, I didn't know whether to stick around for support or leave to give her and the doctor privacy.

"I could use some extra light," the doctor said, surveying the bedroom.

A kerosene lamp rested on the armoire.

"Oh, I can help you." I stood and came over to the oil lamp. A few matches were near my mother's hairbrush. Some oil was already in the lamp, so I took out a match and struck it on the box. Raising the glass globe, I lit the wick and replaced the globe over the burning flame. "Where would you like it, doctor?"

"On the edge of the footboard will be fine. Thank you, Millie." Dr. Grayson moved from aside the bed and stood in front of my mother with his valise.

As I placed down the lamp, he glanced at me over his wired eyeglasses, unbuttoning and raising his long sleeves up his hairy forearms to his elbows. "Uh, Millie, you can leave if you want." Perhaps he saw the fright on my face, but I'd wanted to be brave for my mother.

"That's right, dear," Mama added, "I'll be fine."

Dr. Grayson cleared his throat. Then he took out two strange, metal instruments from his bag that looked like a pair of large eating utensils.

I gulped and tensely looked at my mother, squeezing her hand again. "Are you sure?"

Mama smiled and nodded, patting my hand. "Yes, dear. It's not the first time. Besides, you look like you're about to faint." Well, my mother was right—I *was* about to faint. Going out to calm my nerves and relax my shallow breathing seemed like the remedy I needed at the moment.

"All right, I guess I'll go outside then. I love you, Mama." I kissed my mother's forehead and left the room. Stepping onto the front porch, I warmed my face in the sunshine and inhaled a couple of breaths of fresh air.

Papa was getting a morning shave from Harold, one of the male house slaves. He grimaced and slapped a *Carolina Watchman* newspaper on the small table beside him, resting in his outdoor rocking chair. "Who does that boy think he is? If he's got a problem with white folks celebrating the birth of our country, why doesn't he go back to where he came from?"

I turned to my father. "Who are you talking about?"

"That runaway fugitive Frederick Douglass," Papa said. "He had the audacity to make an anti-slavery speech in Rochester, New York and everybody's talking about it."

I picked up the paper and skimmed the front page. Sure enough, printed on the cover was Mr. Frederick Douglass' photograph and a passage about the event. The title of his news article: *"What to the American Slave is the Fourth of July?"* An eloquent black man speaking against the injustice of slaves and the ills of slavery irritated my father, but I admired him and would've liked to have met him one day.

I know you don't like him, Papa," I said, "but you have

to admit he's got power and heart." I placed the paper back on the round side table.

"But slaves get work and taken care of in slavery. Negroes shouldn't be causin no trouble," Harold said, sharpening his blade, "it disrupts the peace, Miss Millie. Seems to me that youngster Frederick Douglass is tryin to steal away his own people's rights."

"You're a smart one, Harold." Papa smirked and perked his elbows on the arms of his rocking chair, getting comfortable. "I wish my daughter had your common sense."

I frowned. How could Harold take sides with an evil man like my father? Maybe he was too scared to speak against Papa's blunt notions. After all, the best way to survive for the slave was to be submissive to whatever was required of them.

Placing my hands on my hips, I sighed and tilted my head, concerned. "Aren't you going to check on Mama?"

Papa snorted and remained seated. "By now, your mother's a natural at handling physical pain. It isn't the first time she's lost a baby, no thanks to you."

Resentment arose and burned within me. "It's not my fault! Mama said the same thing."

My father grimaced and leaned forward, clenching his large, rugged hands on the arms of his chair so hard his knuckles turned white. "You can believe that if you want, but I *know*—I know the truth!" He sat back and rocked himself, lowering his tone to a whisper. "You don't realize how bad it was . . . she nearly *died* when you were born."

Loss of words, my lower lip trembled as I gulped, turning away my attention. What could I say? It was true my arrival into the world wasn't an easy one, but at the same time, no one ever asks to be born or come here, right?

Facing the front yard, the slaves worked in the cotton fields, Jed's indistinct orders and whip echoing in the distance as he pranced around on his horse. From sunup to sundown, they worked tirelessly in the hot sun, picking cotton from the bolls and putting it in baskets and sackcloth bags like millions of pearls.

In the South, there wasn't a more pleasant sight than a full-bloom, cotton plantation, a wide field of fallen snow. It was the way of life for Southerners and meant an incoming profit—a white emblem that gave slave holders and masters a sense of high reputation and power.

Cotton was wealth, raiment—everything. It was the reason my Papa and other slave owners were so keen and relentless about their slaves following through with their expected pounds per day and getting their duties done. My father called his cotton "white gold" because his plantation was like a goldmine. He was proud and bragged about it, but the wealthiest plantation owners in Charlotte weren't my family—it was the McMillans.

On the dirt trail between the cotton fields, a blond gentleman rode in a buggy with a pretty brown horse toward our mansion home. It was Chancey McMillan.

His father had fallen gravely ill, but he'd made sure Chauncey inherited his massive estate before he passed away.

Chauncey pulled his reins and stopped in front of the house. "Whoa, boy." He tipped his dress hat to my father. "Hello, Mr. Crabtree. I came to wish Miss Millie a happy birthday and to give her some flowers."

"How nice of you, son," Papa said, but I was more annoyed than anything else.

Chauncey leaped from his buggy. He took off his hat and handed me a bouquet of white lilies with a grin spread across his narrow face. "For you, Millie, dear."

I glanced at his hand, and then at his face again. His pointy chin made his face the perfect shape of a triangle and was so unattractive and a nuisance to me. "I don't want them."

"Millie, dear. Don't be rude. Take them," Papa said.

I drew a breath and grudgingly took the flowers.

"You should have one of the slaves put them in water to keep them fresh," Chauncey said.

"I'll handle them myself," I replied.

"Very well." Chauncey eyed me and smiled. "I can't wait to see you during your birthday party. Perhaps you'll become smitten with me."

"I doubt it," I blurted.

Chauncey snickered and tipped his hat to me.

"Goodbye, Miss Millie." He rode away.

I watched him until I couldn't see him down the road

as the distant heat waves jittered on the blistering summer day.

Papa sat up with shaving cream on his wide chin. He raised his brows, stunned. "I'm surprised you don't like him. You ought to be glad to get Chauncey's attention. He's a rich, young man who could have any woman he wants."

"Well, I'm not." I grimaced at my father, clutching the stems of the lilies in my hand by my side. "I wouldn't settle for Chauncey McMillan if he was the last man on earth!" I turned away my face and strutted toward the front entrance, almost bumping into the doctor. "Oh, sorry, Dr. Grayson."

"You're fine, Millie." He smiled and pat my shoulder.

"How is she, doc?" Papa asked, reclining in his chair.

"Charlotte's doing well. Nothing a little medicine and proper treatment couldn't cure; but please, ensure she gets some rest before Millie's birthday celebration." He sighed and looked at my father. "Most of the tissue from her miscarriage has been removed, but the rest will have to discharge naturally. And, please . . . wait longer and let her body *heal* before . . . well, you know."

"Of course, doctor. Anything you say." Papa gave a nod, rocking in his chair.

"Good day, Mr. Crabtree." Dr. Grayson placed on his derby and climbed into his carriage with his valise. He struck his reins and drove in his carriage of gray horses down the long dirt trail between the cotton fields.

"Your mama's gonna be fine, Millie. She'll be *just* fine," Papa said casually, rocking in his chair.

Uneasiness filled me. I glanced from my father in his chair to the flowers in my hand, pondering whether to place them in water.

I wasn't sure I wanted them to die.

2 *Happy Birthday, Millie!*

TURNING EIGHTEEN WAS TO be one of the best times of a young girl's life, but for me, it was utterly frightening and dreadful. I stood in front of the full-body mirror as Pearl tied my corset and put layer after layer of clothing on me. Figuring out what to say in the presence of all the young gentlemen and making an impression was an obligation given to me by my parents.

Within the South, love wasn't much concern when it came to marriage. Families blended together for wealth, status, and money—rarely for love. It was how we lived from generation to generation. Proof of this was my parents' marriage. Papa was eight years older than my mother, as she married him at the tender age of nineteen for his wealth and a stable life.

I wasn't thrilled to be the center of attention, but after her written requests, Mama hoped I'd meet my future husband. Like me, she didn't take too kindly toward Chauncey and thought he was too skinny and annoying as a chirping cricket. But I had other plans, which didn't involve becoming a wife to a wealthy plantation owner.

Since I was a little girl, writing always fascinated me. Although my dream was to become a children's fiction author, Papa said all the talented writers were men, and I partially believed it. After all, the only authors I knew were men, as writing was hardly seen as a profession for women. Many barriers hindered the publication of their work.

Mama thought my fairytale stories were interesting, but a pastime and would never amount to a stable living. In a male-dominating world, women were only meant to be cooks, laundresses, or housewives—not published authors. Because of this, sometimes it felt like I was fooling myself into ever becoming one.

Pearl wore a wry grin, pulling back the silk ribbon straps of my ruffled, baby blue evening gown. "You look terrified."

"I am," I said, "it's my birthday, but I already feel like I'm getting hitched. What if I say something foolish?"

Pearl chuckled and smiled. "You're good with words. Relax and just be yourself." She tied the straps into a bow behind the small of my back. "There, you all done. This dress brings out your deep-blue eyes."

I smiled shyly at her reflection behind me. "Thanks, Pearl."

Pearl was nineteen, but her motherly nature and wise heart sometimes made her seem so much older. We were about the same height, but she was much thinner than me. She wore a burnt orange turban, a twisted part of the scarf around the front of her cranium. Her long, sandy brown twists dangled loosely alongside her oval face and shoulders. Comparing my evening gown to her dull brown, orange-patterned calico dress and white apron made me a little sad but grateful. With her slimmer frame, I felt as if Pearl should be wearing my gown.

I frowned and turned sideways, examining my somewhat stocky figure in the mirror—hence, why I was wearing a corset for support. Having inherited my father's bodily build, I didn't know what Chauncey saw in me, but he must've been blind in one eye.

Unlike myself, his younger sister Clementine had a graceful form, which was more appealing to most of the young fellows of town. If any of them besides Chauncey approached me, it'd be an startling surprise—ironically, appropriate for a birthday celebration.

Pearl turned me around and hugged me. "Happy Birthday, and have a nice time." She grinned and held me at arm's length. "I reckon we should go downstairs, so not to keep 'em waiting. Let's go."

We giggled and walked side by side out of my bedroom in a friendly, one-arm embrace, and then we turned the corner.

Pearl shooed me off in the middle of the hall, urging me to go downstairs alone.

Overhearing the chatter of countless voices, I bit my lip and sheepishly glanced back at her.

"Go on, Millie. They're waiting," Pearl whispered.

I drew a long breath and inched up a smile, coming out into public view.

"Happy Birthday, Millie!" the crowd announced.

Cheers and applause greeted me as I held the wide skirt of my blue gown in my white-gloved hands and descended on the hardwood staircase, taking one step at a time.

"Thank you, everyone!" I said, bending my knees to courtesy.

My mother stood in the center of the crowd of guests, arrayed in a beautiful, white evening gown, appearing as a bride adorned for her husband. Her brown hair was pulled back in a double-twisted arrangement with a low bun at the nape of her neck.

Mama grinned and kissed my cheeks. "You look magnificent, dearest."

"Thank you, Mama." I hugged my mother. "So do you."

Pearl came downstairs and stood on my right side with her hand on the banister. Then Harold and George, the two male house slaves, presented the refreshments on a serving cart before me. On it was a large birthday cake lit with candles, and a silver punch bowl with cups and a ladle. They grinned, suited in their pale yellow, two

—buttoned vests and white gloves, standing shoulder to shoulder with a significant height difference.

"For you, Miss Millie," they said in unison.

"Eighteen candles, same as your age," George added with his wide smile across his elongated, ebony face.

"Thank you very much." I smiled and blew out the candles.

Everyone cheered and applauded me again.

One dark-haired young man in a burgundy frock coat wasted no time in stepping forth. He took off his top hat, a big grin stretched on his bearded face. "Your evening dress is lovely, Miss Millie, but much more stunning are your eyes." He took my left hand and planted a kiss.

Unexpected chills washed over me like a tidal wave, and I was terribly embarrassed. I smiled shyly and blushed. "Ooh, uh . . . thank you—" It was the first time a man kissed my hand out of courtesy and admiration.

Chauncey sneered and slid in front of the dark-haired man, making me feel like I was a golden trophy on display for competition. But were they after me, or just my family's wealth? I had my doubts; at least, all except for Master McMillan.

"Miss Millie, would you like to dance?" he said.

Pearl and I glanced at each other with teasing smiles.

I wrinkled my nose. "I'll pass for now, Chauncey."

Standing aside from me, Mama placed a hand to her mouth and giggled.

"Fine, but I'll be waiting, darling," Chauncey said, giving me a smug look. He served himself a cup of punch and walked off into the spacious parlor with a group of others.

I likewise scooped myself a cup of punch with the ladle and followed Mama and Pearl into the sitting room, who entered after Chauncey.

Guests and slaves talked, laughed, and waltzed around to Mozart's piano concerto No. 21, played by the three musicians. The three performers wore frock coats, forming the primary color scheme. One of them was a middle-aged, bald pianist in a blue frock coat. His posture was straight as he bounced his skinny fingers on the ivory and ebony keys, but his thick, wild, black mustache I didn't think complemented him well.

Another was a fat, clean-shaven cellist in a yellow frock coat. He held his bow and focused on his sheet music stand, plucking his strings, which added volume and depth to the waltz music. The third was a young, handsome violinist in a ruby frock coat. He strummed his instrument and read his notes, his violin singing the lead before harmonizing in a duet with the cello in the musical piece.

While playing, the violinist glanced at me and the dancers with a crooked smile. He nodded subtly at me and focused back on his sheet music. For the first time in my life, a burst of intrigue toward a man filled my spirit.

My mouth hung slightly in speechless awe of his charisma and talent. Something I couldn't explain drew me to him, a certain magical allure I couldn't pull myself away from.

He was at least average height, a small man, but not thin and feeble. His curly hair was like rolls of shiny, red ribbons, and his eyes were the color of cognac liquor. He had creamy buttermilk skin and a small, fuzzy red mustache under his nose, trimmed and neat. His face was a combination of youth and experience, like a teenage boy.

I sighed and sipped from my cup. First coming in the parlor, I didn't expect interest to strike me, but it did the moment I saw him. Were we the same age, or was he older than me? I wasn't for certain, but I hated being attracted to him—a young man who, as all the others, likely supported the brutality of slavery or a slave owner himself.

Turning my attention away from him, I faced the mantel of the fireplace and took another sip from my cup. On my far left of the rectangular room, Randall, one of the field slaves, was standing by one of the lace-curtained windows. His face brightened with a smile when Pearl held out her hand and approached him in the parlor. Like many of the others, they waltzed together in the room.

Centered in the room across from me, Papa sat ankles-crossed in his hard leather chair and nibbled his smoke pipe. His steel-blue, piercing eyes watched their every move and spin as if he were figuring out a private mission.

Mama took him by his hand on the armrest. "Come Wade, let's dance."

"What about your heart condition?" Papa asked with a disturbed gaze, observing Randall and Pearl twirling by him among the other dancers orbiting the room.

Mama placed her hands on her hips. "My health is fine, Wade. I've rested well for three days. Besides, I've already taken my medicine. Come now, it's Millie's birthday." She tightened her lips, glaring from Papa to Randall and Pearl. "What are you sitting there staring for?"

"Nothing." Papa smacked his lips and sighed with a groan. "Oh, all right, let's dance."

I watched from a corner of the room as he stood from his chair, took her right hand in his left hand, placed his right on her back, and danced with her along with the others.

Chauncey approached me with his tin cup. "So, Miss Millie, exactly why don't you like me?"

"Are you sure you want to know?" I said.

Chauncey lifted his brow and shrugged it off. "Sure, I can take it."

"I'm opposed by your loyalty toward slavery."

Chauncey smirked and lifted a shoulder, nonchalant. "Well, cotton production is extremely important in our country, and slavery has been around for hundreds of years. Isn't it a normal way of life in the South?"

I frowned and turned from him. "It doesn't mean slaves shouldn't be treated like humans." Swiftly, I faced him again with a disturbed look. "I mean, would you condone someone severely whipping your horse to break him in?"

"Why, no," Chauncey said, casually, "that's no way to properly train a horse."

"And it's not the way to treat slaves either," I added.

Chauncey gave me a long look of disapproval. "That's different, Miss Millie. Slaves are property and must be disciplined to obey their masters."

"Perhaps, they would, if they weren't so threatened. Chauncey, you call yourself a Christian, don't you?"

"Of course, Miss Millie," Chauncey said.

I studied him, inquisitive. "And you believe you'll be saved while owning slaves?"

"Why, certainly," Chauncey said, irritated, "my soul belongs to God, and I don't appreciate you judging my salvation." He tossed up his cup, taking another drink.

I bit my lip, a little ashamed. "I'm sorry. I was merely expressing my concern and notions."

"Well," Chauncey began, "I advise you keep them to yourself. They aren't welcomed among the guests." He glanced at the other standing visitors who overheard and curiously watched us across the room. "So, are there other reasons you don't like me besides slavery?" His eyes met mine again.

I inclined my head, staring at him. "Actually, there is. Your face is shaped like a triangle and you're an arrogant cockerel."

He blinked and stared, unmoved. "Well . . . that's unfortunate for you to think that. Can we still dance?" He placed his cup on the mantle of the fireplace.

I sighed and made an eyeroll. "I reckon I should. You'll be asking forever if I don't." After finishing my punch, I placed my cup beside his.

A smile grew across Chauncey's narrow face as he took my hand.

But while I danced in his close embrace, I stayed captivated by the violinist behind him. My eyes followed the redhead man wherever we turned and twirled around, watching him play his instrument. Applause roared when the musicians finished the classical piece. Then a faster song started, which sounded like music for a square dance. Some of the house slave women clapped or patted their white aprons to the upbeat.

Worry gnawed me, hoping I don't step on Chauncey's toes. Luckily, he carried me along like a rag doll and did all the footwork. Even though I hadn't expected to, I actually laughed and had fun with him.

"Charlotte!" Papa caught my mother in his arms.

Everyone turned their heads with awe and looked at my parents as the music stopped.

My father dragged my limp mother over to the sofa in the center of the room. Gasps of shock and commotion from the party guests filled the parlor as Dr. Grayson and I approached the scene.

"She's fainted," Papa said.

Dr. Grayson slapped the ruby cheeks of my mother's flushed face. "Madam Charlotte, can you hear me?"

Mama's eyes were stretched wide, her mouth slightly open, gasping for a breath of air. Then she fluttered her eyelids and closed them.

Panic throbbed in my chest. "Mama?" I choked on a stifled sob.

The doctor turned his head and surveyed the crowd of bystanders surrounding him. "Someone get my bag from my wagon. Hurry!"

Mr. John Weiss, another slave master and friend of my father, rushed out and returned with the doctor's black valise. "Here you go, doc."

"Thank you, Weiss." The doctor took his stethoscope from his bag and checked Mama's heartbeat as Papa, I, and everyone else fearfully watched him. He knitted his bushy, gray brows and twisted his mouth as he shifted the drum over her chest. His expression weakened, slowly removing the tips of the stethoscope from his ears. "Dear God, she's . . . she's dead."

"No! No, Mama, please . . . no, no, no!" Moisture blurred my vision, desperately reaching out to hug my mother's motionless corpus lying on the sofa.

Papa took me away in a tight embrace and covered my head with one of his large hands.

I sobbed and gripped on his velvet jacket, unable to contain myself. Heaviness weighted upon my heart and seemed to collapse my whole body. My beloved mother was gone—the beautiful, sentimental woman who carried me nine months and bore the excruciating pain that brought me into the world.

In an instant, everything had changed—my birthday would never be the same again.

3 *Mama's Burial*

MONDAY, JULY 12
CHURCH CEMETERY
Charlotte, North Carolina

EARLY IN THE MORNING, the gloomy sky shed tears I couldn't release from my eyes. I felt like I was trapped in a figment of my imagination. My mother—*dead*? How could that be? A youthful, exquisite brunette woman full of poise and life. I refused to believe it until I had no choice but to accept it as my reality. During her viewing the other day, my mother lay pale and motionless with her eyes closed, appearing as if in a deep sleep.

"Mama," I called, but she didn't speak and wouldn't answer ever again. Today, everyone gathered at the church's cemetery, dressed in dark suits and dresses to show their respects to my mother's death. In a state of shock, I stared at Mama's closed wooden casket in the heart of the earth.

"Let us pray," Preacher Tompkins said, hugging his black Holy Bible against his thin chest.

Everyone bowed their heads with sorrow for a silent

moment of prayer. Some of the town women from Mama's quilting circle sobbed and sniffled with their dainty hankies. Thunder rumbled amid the mournful whispers and mumbles.

I glanced up at the blanket of smoky clouds as the cool rain sprinkled on my face, praying for my mother's pardon. She apologized to the slave women for her years of slaps and bitter remarks during her last days. From then on, I saw repentance in her eyes.

Would God have mercy on her? I hoped and prayed the Lord wouldn't burn her soul in hell after judgment for the sins of my father, but trusted He was a righteous God. Slavery was one of the worst of sins. Reading the scriptures, I realized the hypocrisy slave owners used to deceive slaves and justify their greed and prosperity.

"Slaves, obey your masters," Papa said, one day to Randall, before giving him a whipping. Randall was the most stubborn of my father's slaves, and I felt as though rightfully so. Some of the other slaves feared my father would shoot him down. However, Randall was also one of Papa's best field hands, so he'd have to be a fool to kill off Randall during the summer harvest season.

Silence ceased as Preacher Tompkins took a long breath and began Mama's eulogy. "Today . . . we are here in respect of Madam Charlotte Grace Crabtree. Charlotte was a beautiful and good wife and mother. She loved life and sought to enjoy it with lighthearted humor and laughter. But her time came to an end, and she'd gone to meet her Maker. Although she suffered poor health, she wouldn't let it slow her down, which should be a lesson for us all . . . to live every day like it's our last. She'll be missed greatly by her husband, her daughter, her friends, and everyone who knew her. May her soul rest in peace."

Some of the women sniffled and stifled sobs.

Preacher Tompkins opened his bible. "For Jesus promised to prepare a place for us . . . that where he is, we may be also." He read from the book of Revelation as he always did during burial ceremonies. *"And God shall wipe away all tears from their eyes; and there shall be no more death, neither sorrow, nor crying, neither shall there be any more pain: for the former things are passed away...."*

A tear rolled down my cheek as I swallowed a hard lump in my throat. Intense sobs consumed me so much I couldn't speak.

Chauncey glanced across the gravesite at me with a somber expression, holding his top hat.

I bowed my head, too ashamed to look at his face. Since Mama died, I was sure he thought he had an advantage over me. My broken heart and vulnerability made me more insecure about myself than I already was.

After the burial, everyone comforted themselves with sugar cookies and chamomile tea served by the house slaves over at our mansion home.

I hugged a giant stone column of the front porch and stared at the cotton field peeking through the thick fog.

Footsteps clacked and approached behind me. Glancing over my shoulder, I sighed with dread when I saw it was Chauncey.

He licked his lips, still holding his hat. "I'm deeply sorry about your mother, Millie."

Fighting back tears, I looked away and banged my fist on a column. Words couldn't express my worrisome thoughts, nor the mixed emotions stirring around in my heart.

Chauncey sighed. "Her death must devastate you. It isn't every day one's mother dies on her birthday. I know what it's like to lose a parent to sickness. I'm here if you need someone to talk to."

"Thanks, but no thanks," I said, watching Pearl and Randall whispering aside the house.

Troubled, Pearl glanced at me and then turned her attention back toward Randall. Something secretive was going on between them and I had a hunch I knew what it was, but I hadn't known for sure until night came.

STILL THINKING OF MAMA, I struggled to write more of my children's fairytale short story. Pearl was my most faithful reader and always encouraging me. Of course, she never read in Papa's presence. He would be furious if he knew I had taught her to read. Pearl thought my fiction stories were entertaining, but I was a harsh critic of my masterpieces. Tonight, she read my medieval tale about the enchanted prince and princess. I sat patiently and nibbled my lip as she read the last lines.

"Oh, thank you, great prince. You saved me," Pearl said dramatically, her hand over her heart. "I shall live peacefully with thee forever. And the beautiful princess and charming prince lived happily ever after. The End."

"Well?" I asked, arching my brow.

Pearl shrugged and smiled. "It sounds all right to me. Children will love it."

I grinned. "Thanks, but the opening could use more work. Maybe I'll work on it some more tomorrow night." I took my story back from her and turned in my desk chair. Placing the cap on my inkwell, I glanced at Pearl's reflection in the wall mirror.

She kneaded her hands and relaxed her shoulders with a deep, shaking breath.

"Is something wrong, Pearl?"

Pearl rubbed her arm. "I-I . . . it's Randy."

"What about Randall?" I turned around and faced her in my chair.

She sighed and tuck her hands in her white apron's pockets. "Nothing, it's just . . . I love him. He's fixin' to run away tomorrow night. He wants me to go with him. And well, he asked me to ask you to write passes for us to flee North. Since you're friendlier than your Papa, he reckoned you'd do it."

I turned away from Pearl. My heart skipped a beat. "I can't do it."

Pearl's face fell. "What? But why? You promised to help me get my freedom when we were little girls. Now's your chance to do that."

I shifted and faced Pearl again. "I'd write the passes, Pearl. You know I would, but what can I do? My father's name would have to be on them."

"I know," Pearl answered. "You could peek in the ledger in his office and forge his name."

I gulped and nodded slowly. "All right, I'll sneak in his office and copy his signature Saturday night. I'll write the passes."

As her sunny smile grew on her face with relief, Pearl leaned forward and hugged me instantly. "Thank you, Millie. Thank you so much."

I tried to smile, but sadness ached in my heart and a ton of worry dropped in my stomach. Although she was happy for freedom, I was losing my best friend, and there was no guarantee she and Randall would make it safely. I'd read the horrific stories and money ads in the newspapers.

Fugitives were searched for different priced rewards for their returns. Some got attacked and eaten by wild bloodhounds, others got caught by bounty hunters or sold at auction farther South. Some slaves were found dead from starvation and pure exhaustion. And others killed themselves rather than get brought home by their masters into captivity. I hoped to God Pearl and Randall would make it to the Promised Land. But since Congress passed the Compromise of 1850, which included the Fugitive Slave Act to satisfy white slave owners, I feared they'd get hurt or caught and sold farther South into auction.

After I changed into my nightgown, Pearl brushed my dark chestnut brown hair slowly, talking about all the plans Randall had for them: having a proper church wedding, building their own house on their own land in Canada, and having their children born free.

Unshed tears filled my eyes, listening to all of her hopes and dreams. Being tied to a childhood promise and having a *good* friend place so much expectation on me weren't easy positions to be placed in. How could I move on without Pearl? And how could I disappoint my dearest friend?

My bedroom door flew open, startling Pearl and I.

Papa stood in his robe, smoking his pipe. He eyed Pearl and jerked his head. "Go to the sack, girl. I have to talk with Millie privately."

"Yes, sir," Pearl answered and placed the brush on the vanity. Shamefaced, she held her apron and eased by my father through the door as he watched her leave the room.

"What is it, Papa?" I asked.

My father closed the door. He took his pipe out of his mouth, exhaling a cloud of smoke. "I think you know,

Millie. Slaves aren't your friends anymore. They never *were* your friends."

"That's not true! Pearl's my—"

"Enough!" Papa interrupted. "From tonight on, the slaves are only your *servants*. I'll expect you to be stricter and tougher on all of them, including Pearl. Do you understand?"

"Yes, sir," I answered without looking at him.

"Don't stay up too late. Get some sleep. Good night." My father stepped out and shut my door.

I knew what my Papa was implying, but I didn't want to accept it. As Mama's dying fate, I was to be the miss who ruled the home while he kept watch of the field slaves.

This was my destined life.

 A Promise to Keep

Saturday Night, July 17
CRABTREE PLANTATION
Charlotte, North Carolina

A STREAM OF MOONLIGHT flowed through the draperies of the windows in my father's office, glowing across the surface of his centered, mahogany desk. It was the only light in the room, the other furniture hidden in the dark shadows from the starry night. My father's leather ledger was always on the top surface of his other roll top writing desk against the wall next to his bookshelf. Within it, he recorded the slaves' names, how much they were worth, and the slaveholders from whom he bought them. Whatever I did, I had to do it quickly. Papa had eyes like an eagle and could tell whenever someone touched his things or meddled around with his belongings.

I walked across the hardwood floor and groped his writing desk for one of the side drawers. Opening the middle drawer, I took out his small pack of matches. I struck one of them for a flame and lit the wick of the kerosene lantern resting on the compartment shelf of his writing desk. I glanced over my shoulder toward the entrance. Everything was pitch-dark and Papa's loud snoring rattled from his bedroom in the midst of the night. Glancing heavenward for a split second, I exhaled a long breath of relief. Then I bent down, lifted the imported rug where he hid a brass key, and unlocked the shutter of his writing desk.

Later, I would have to ask God to forgive me, but at least I was doing something for a good cause. I moved the lantern from the shelf to the lower flat surface of the writing desk aside from my father's ledger and sat down. When I opened the ledger, on the first page was his signature below the words "BELONGS TO" and above a straight underline. I took a thin sheet of paper from my robe pocket and grabbed one of his pencils. Carefully, I copied my father's black signature, every curve and slope of his messy handwriting to the best of my ability.

Behind me, the floor of the hallway squeaked.

My heart pulsated in my throat and my hands sweat, hurrying to get the signature without making a mistake. The hairs on my neck stood as a voice called me.

I abruptly blew out the lantern.

"Miss Millie, you all right?" Dula asked.

Leaning back in Papa's chair, I let out another sigh of relief. "Yes, Dula. I'm fine. I was just . . . doing a little writing." I glanced back and saw Dula holding a lit lantern. She was standing in her white nightgown, her coiled, thick, silvery-gray hair protruding around her ruffled nightcap.

She frowned and cocked her head. "Rooster be crowin soon, Miss Millie. I got concerned 'bout you. You weren't in bed. I know you miss your mama."

"Yes, very, but I'll be fine," I said. "You can rest up. I'll be in bed shortly."

Dula nodded and started to leave the room, but rustled toward me with quiet steps. She whispered in my ear. "Pearl told me she and Randy are fixin' to run. You can trust me, Miss Millie. I won't tell your papa Massa Crabtree nothing." Then she left.

I tucked the paper I wrote my father's signature on in my robe pocket, closed the ledger, slid down the shutter, and locked the desk. Afterward, I hid the key back under the rug and tiptoed out of my Papa's office, hoping I hadn't left a trace of my presence. I had the means to write the passes now and wrote them in ink at my desk, one for Pearl and the other for Randall.

Then I dragged myself into bed and went to sleep.

"MILLIE . . . MILLIE?" A HAND TOUCHED my shoulder.

Warm sunshine hit my face as I fluttered open my eyes the next morning. My drowsy vision cleared to Pearl sitting in a wooden chair beside my bed. For a moment, I felt like my mother. Missus of a plantation home? The household ruler to a group of subservient slave women and men in the absence of my father who followed my every command? It wasn't what I'd always wanted or dreamed of, but an overwhelming burden on my back seen as a privilege to the majority of the white society. Looking at my dearest friend, I wondered, how could we sever the ties of our close friendship?

Pearl smiled and cocked her head. "Good morning, queen."

"Good morning, Pearl." I blinked at the sun's glare and pushed myself up in bed. "I wrote the passes."

"You did?"

I yawned and nodded. "They're in the drawer of my desk."

Pearl's eyes teared up a little. "Thank you so much. Randy will be glad."

After climbing out of bed, I took the passes out of the drawer of my desk and handed them over. "Here, but you mustn't let anyone see them, and don't leave until nightfall."

"We won't. I promise." Pearl stood and hid the passes in the pocket of her work apron.

Dula knocked and peeked into my bedroom, her blue turban partially in the door frame.

I smiled. "Morning, Dula."

Dula glanced at her granddaughter and wrinkled her face. "Pearl, whatcha doin standin dere? You should be gittin' Miss Millie ready. Mr. Jed done already hitched the team."

Pearl and I looked at each other, startled. How could we have forgotten about Jed, the overseer? He lived in a cabin on a hill not far from the slave quarters and kept watch of the field slaves during the day. It was obvious we needed to keep a lookout for him when Pearl and Randall went running tonight.

"I am, nana. We were just talking," Pearl said.

"All right, now." Dula left.

I sighed and rubbed my hands down my face. "Dear God, I forgot about Jed."

Pearl placed a hand on my shoulder. "Don't feel bad. I didn't think o' him either."

"Listen, we're going to have to be careful of him. You won't be able to go through the front door, so I'll stall for you."

Worry formed on Pearl's face. "Are you sure you can? Maybe Randy and I should sneak off after church service today. It'll be packed anyway. Nobody will notice us."

"No," I said quickly, "it has to be tonight while Papa's sleeping. It's safer, and you and Randall will be able to get a head start if you sneak off without Jed noticing y'all. Mama's pink rose trellis is outside my bedroom window. Maybe I can keep him busy inside with a game of checkers or something while you sneak and climb out of the window."

"All right, I'll let Randy know." Pearl opened my chest closet. "Come, let me help you get ready."

"HOLD THOU THY CROSS *before my closing eyes; Shine through the gloom and point me to the skies. Heaven's morning breaks, and earth's vain shadows flee; In life, in death, O Lord, abide with me . . .*" the congregation sang with their open hymnals.

Miss Gertrude Copperfield, a gray-haired spinster, played the pipe organ beside the wood pulpit. She struck a melody of harmonious chords as the blended voices of the congregation echoed toward the ceiling, ending the last verse of the song.

Preacher Tompkins gripped his hands on the pulpit and nodded. "You may be seated."

All the white townspeople sat on the creaking pews, but the group of slaves stood above on the balconies.

I glimpsed up at Pearl with a sad smile and she smiled timidly back.

Since I was a child, I wondered why we couldn't sit together. After all, we were in the House of the Lord, a place of worship that welcomed and accepted everyone no matter their race, color, or creed. Of course, the only part I enjoyed about church was singing hymns. From a little girl to a young woman, I learned some things said about slavery were wrong and I became uncomfortable. I had read the forbidden Old Testament, and based on my secret findings, God was clearly against the violent oppression of people. Sadly, the church was a place of power and manipulation, but why wouldn't it be? Like most of the white men in town, Preacher Tompkins was also a slave owner himself.

"Good morning, church," the preacher said.

"Morning," the congregation replied in unison.

Preacher Tompkins grinned. "It's wonderful to see everyone on this lovely, Sunday morning. I'm delighted we have a packed house in the pews and balconies." He glanced up at the standing slaves. "In today's time, we are living in a horrible mess, folks! It's written in the newspapers across our nation. All over the South, plantation owners are suffering loss . . . loss of land and faithful workers, but it's to be expected, right? The rich always afflicts the poor, amen?"

"Amen," some of the congregation echoed.

"The Northerners want to change our Southern way of life . . . to dismantle our *good traditions* and make us sin against our beloved, Lord and Savior—" Preacher Tompkins turned and gestured his hand up at the white imitation of Jesus on the stained-glass window above him— "but thank God Almighty for the Compromise of 1850, amen?"

I hung and shook my head. Good traditions? Did he honestly believe chaining men, women, and children like animals, splitting up their families, and selling them on auction was the best way to handle negro people? How dare he say such a disgraceful thing!

"Why, if it wasn't for us kindhearted Southerners, the negroes wouldn't have a home and be wandering vagabonds with no place to go!" Preacher Tompkins chuckled and lifted a hand in his elaboration. "George Fitzhugh, an honorable theorist, plainly states slavery as a benefit to care for slaves, and by God, I can't agree more." He cleared his throat. "Today's sermon will be from Colossians three verse twenty-two." He opened his holy bible and read the verse. "Servants, obey in all things your masters according to the flesh; not with eyeservice, as menpleasers; but in singleness of heart; fearing God, and whatsoever ye do, do it *heartily*, as to the Lord, and not unto men . . ."

While listening to the preacher, my stomach flipped. I thought I was going to be sick from his frivolous talk as I struggled to contain myself. My soul stirred from his misuse of God's Word, taking the scripture enforced by Apostle Paul as an excuse to justify slavery and fulfill his greed.

I gripped the pew in front of me and jumped up from my bench seat. "What about the children of Israel who were set free from bondage?"

Some of the members mumbled and whispered behind their hands.

"Why don't you read that?" I asked, staring at the preacher.

"Millie, sit down!" Papa's face was flushed red as a tomato, nervously scanning the angry men and women sitting around him.

Disturbed by my intrusive question, the preacher shifted his eyes and cleared his throat again, clutching the pulpit.

"She's a Jezebel!" one cranky man scolded, pointing toward me.

A woman shouted behind me. "Banish her from the church! Let her soul burn in hell!"

Other members arose with her and ranted against me, pounding their fists in the air.

Preacher Tompkins lifted his hands at the noisy gathering. "Quiet, everyone! We're in God's House, not a courtroom!" He grimaced and looked over his glasses at the tip of his hawk nose as the commotion died down. "Sister Millie, I'd appreciate if you listen to your father and the congregation and sit down. For it is written, in First Corinthians chapter fourteen, "Let your women keep *silent* in the churches; for it is not permitted for them to speak!"

Some members from behind urged me to be quiet.

I held the preacher's glare with my own and slowly took my seat.

"Now, shall I go on?" the preacher said calmly.

I pursed my lips and studied him without another word. Surely, Preacher Tompkins had a good side, as I believed most people did, but I refused to accept his corruption. Some things in life were morally wrong, and I believed a part of loving our neighbors as Jesus said was treating everyone as equals and with respect. No matter how we looked on the outside, we *all* were God's creations, whether male or female, black or white.

The church bell dinged, signaling the end of Sunday service.

While in the sanctuary, the preacher and my father discussed matters and glimpsed in my direction from a short distance. The preacher whispered and shook his head and Papa nodded, as if in agreement. I assumed they were talking about me, but if I got banished from the church, it wouldn't have bothered me much at all.

As a believer, I had already accepted God as my Lord and Savior, but not the god that stained the church windows and hung inside the townspeople's homes. Who was he? Why had people trusted in these images when the Lord condemned the worship of idols? To me, these were pictures and figments of a white European man's imagination painted on a canvas or molded into clay. They were symbols used to manipulate slaves and justify slavery and their selfish ways.

Once Dula said, "singing comforts her soul." Witnessing slavery firsthand, I understood what she meant. Having a brutal, unpredictable life, their faith and hymns were the only things slaves had to hold on to for hope. Maybe others saw the White Jesus as an innocent portrait of our Savior. I must admit, even I did at one point. But as I grew older, I read the contents of God's Word and had gotten another perspective.

Papa and others criticized me for my beliefs, but the Word of God condemned idolatry and graven images. And honestly, nobody knew what He really looked like. Although it's known he was a Jew, what mattered most was the character of Jesus Christ, not his skin color. Since then, my mindset changed. Thus, I wanted to stir up the minds of the slaves for justice and the saving grace of God—that in His eyes we all were created equal and loved the same.

"Millie," Pearl called, walking through the massive congregation talking and milling about outside of the church.

I turned my attention to her and sighed heavily.

She held me at arm's length, glanced around, and pulled me behind a big oak tree. "You had me scared for a moment."

"Sorry," I whispered back, "something came over me. I felt like I had to speak up."

Pearl spoke quietly again. "I know you're strong-minded, Millie, but you should stop those outbursts before you get into serious trouble." She glimpsed at the congregation and then looked back at me. "But, is it true?"

"Is what true?"

Pearl cocked her head. "What you said during church service? Is it?"

"Yes," I answered quietly, "it's in the Book of Exodus. God sent the prophet Moses to free the Israelites from the bondage of the Egyptians. He worked through Moses to split the Red Sea and lead the Israelites from Egypt toward a new land called Canaan."

"Canaan," Pearl said, thinking deeply, "sounds like Canada."

My father approached over and stood in front of us, looking suspicious. "What you girls whispering about?"

"Nothing, Papa."

My father clasped his hands behind his back and puffed out his barrel-like chest. He scowled at Pearl, eyeing her like a hungry scavenger. "Get in the wagon, girl. The others are waiting."

"Yes, sir." Pearl folded her hands in front of herself, barely looking at his face. With her shoulders hunched, she scurried across the grass past him, as if bracing for a quick slap.

A little smile inched on my father's lips as she left, but quickly faded into another frown. "That was a terrible thing you did today, Millie." He pointed his forefinger at me. "You upset the preacher, and brought shame to me! I won't tolerate it from you again."

"I'm sorry, Papa . . . I'm sorry you're ashamed of me!"

Anger thundered in Papa's voice, startling some of the congregation. "Millie, come back here! Millie!"

On the verge of crying, I held the skirt of my dress and fled toward the wagon, ignoring my father's calls.

5 *Goodbye, Pearl*

SUNDAY NIGHT, JULY 18
CRABTREE PLANTATION
Charlotte, North Carolina

AFTER NIGHTFALL, I PEEKED out of the curtain of Papa's office window at Jed, the overseer, and my father on the front porch of the house. The two men could talk for hours, laughing and joking about nonsense. While they were outside, I left to meet with Pearl and her grandmother in the attic.

Before Papa went outside, Pearl pretended to go to sleep at her usual time where Papa had checked in on her, but she snuck out of bed when he left. As I entered, they were fixing the bed with extra pillows under the blanket to trick my father into thinking Pearl was still sleeping there.

"Dis oughta do it. Massa Crabtree caint see well in the dark nohow." Dula pulled the blanket over the pillows and tucked it into the mattress.

I stood by the opened doorway. "Papa and Jed are outside on the porch, Pearl. You'd best come to my room while you still can."

"Yes, I reckon so." Pearl shared a final look with her grandmother and embraced her.

Dula smiled through her tears, hugging her. "The Lord be with y'all. You take care of Randall and yourself, gal. You hear?" She planted a kiss on Pearl's forehead.

Pearl sobbed and nodded. "Yes, nana. I will." When she first arrived at Crabtree Plantation, she showed Dula the pearl cameo brooch her mother had. Being separated from her daughter years ago, Dula counted getting united with her granddaughter a miracle. It was hard seeing Pearl say goodbye to her grandmother. But she and Dula knew getting freedom was a chance of a lifetime—and so did I.

"I'll look out for Papa and Jed." I hurried downstairs to my father's office and peeked out of the curtained window behind his wide desk again.

Neither one of them was on the porch.

"Whatcha doing in here?" Papa's deep, raspy voice throbbed through my body, startling me with a quick gasp.

I swiftly turned away from the window. "Oh, I just—" I glanced at his bookcase and thought of a quick explanation— "wanted to get one of your fiction novels, if I may?"

Papa narrowed his black, thick brows and eyed me. "All right, but make sure you put it back when you're done."

"Yes, sir." Grabbing Moby Dick from Papa's large bookshelf, I glanced over my shoulder at the short overseer sitting in a chair next to him. "Mr. Jed?"

"Yes, Miss Millie?"

I licked my lips, thought a moment, and chose my words carefully. "I've . . . been lonely since mother died. You wouldn't mind playing a couple rounds of checkers with me, would you?"

Jed grinned and drew a slow breath, gripping his buckle belt. "No, ma'am. You know I *love* checkers."

"I'll be back shortly." I smiled and exited the office, but my stomach flipped at his blushing admiration and eagerness for my company. Like Chauncey, I had a feeling he had his hopes of someday taking my hand in marriage too. But there was no way I was going to settle for a dirty, rotten-toothed, stinky horse-breaker, even if my life depended on it.

When I entered my room, Pearl was inside, waiting for me beside the window nearby my brass bed.

I rushed over and held her hands. "They're in the house."

"I know. I saw when they came in," Pearl whispered.

"Do you have the passes I gave you?"

Pearl pulled them out briefly. "Yes. I kept them in my apron pocket since this morning. Thank you, Millie. I'll never forget you for this."

"I'll never forget you either." Sorrow clouded my vision. "You're the best friend I've ever had. I know you must go, but I wish you could stay here in peace."

"Me too." Pearl took a white, floral hankie out of a pocket of her apron and unfolded it, revealing her pearl cameo brooch. She opened my hand and placed the brooch in my palm, folding my fingers over it. "Take this to remember me by. It was my Mama's. Her master gave it to her. I promise I'll ask for you later up North. We'll be sister friends for life."

I sniffed and stifled a sob. "It's beautiful. I'll cherish it forever."

We shared a long hug and held each other at arm's length.

Fear suffused my whole being, and after sneaking around, forging Papa's name, and writing the passes, I just had to ask one last request . . . one last promise.

"Promise me . . . promise me, you'll get away." Waiting for Pearl's response, I searched her hazel-brown eyes and sniffled again.

Uncertain, she hesitated, her chin bobbing. "I-I don't . . ."

"Promise," I urged, slightly shaking her.

Pearl sobbed and spoke in a trembling voice. "All right, all right, I promise."

As we hugged one more time, Papa's heavy footsteps trudged upstairs to the second floor of the house.

"He's coming. You should go now. Hurry, and be careful!" I lifted my window and looked outside below. Shifty-eyed and keeping a watchful lookout, Randall was standing under the big maple tree, panting and fidgeting with his small wool hat.

Owls hooted and hound dogs howled in the night.

Pearl raised the skirt of her tan calico dress tied with a white apron, snuck outside, and climbed down the trellis to her love. The two of them shared a tight hug and ran off into the wooded forest, holding hands.

I shut the window before my father pushed back my bedroom door.

"Don't stay up too late with Jed, you hear? George will keep a watch of you two while you play, just in case. I'm going to sleep. Good night," Papa said.

"Night, Papa."

My father shut the door.

I laid across my bed and released a loud sigh. From the way it looked, everything worked out fine, but I could only imagine the pain Dula was feeling of losing another loved one.

While we played checkers, I offered Jed some shots of Papa's whiskey, getting him drunk before he realized it himself. George, however, knew something was off and purposely going on from his suspicious facial expressions. Thankfully, he wasn't a talebearer like Harold, the other male house slave who told my father everything. As he entered and departed, straightening things and cleaning my Papa's office, he thought better than to speak against my intentions. By our fifth game, Jed was completely intoxicated and drifted in and out of sleep.

"It's your move." I propped my head on my hand, feeling faint myself.

"Forget it. I quit," Jed slurred, "you won da-game." He yawned, dropped his head on the small square table, and snored so loudly my late mother could have heard him in her grave.

I snuck away from the game table in the sitting room, placed the bottle of bourbon in the wine chest, and snuck off to bed. Before I fell asleep, I prayed Pearl and Randall would somehow get to Canada. They had the written passes they needed for safety against slave patrols, but they had a long journey to go. I hoped some kindhearted people would help them along the way in their pursuit of a better life.

Their departure meant a lot and inspired me and my dreams. If they got away, I figured I'd have the courage to flee to the North too. Instead of surrendering to my family's southern traditions, maybe I'd take a chance of striking it out on my own in the city and to do what I wanted to do with my life.

Become a published children's author.

HOURS LATER, A VIOLENT rattle of my doorknob snapped me out of my sleep. I gasped and tugged up my multicolored, quilted blanket close to me, trembling with fear. My eyes stretched wide as I stared at the fiery light seeping under my door through the darkness of my bedroom. *Who was coming at this time of night?*

"Millie! Millie, girl, wake up!" Papa said. "Open the door right now!" He knocked impatiently and rattled the knob again.

Knowing my father was angry and disturbed, I gulped and hesitated whether to obey his command. *Had he found out about Pearl and Randall? Did he know they ran away? What would I say if he asked me where they were?*

Clothed in my long, white gown and nightcap, I stepped out of bed onto the cold hardwood floor, hoping on my way over, a bent, loose nail wouldn't pierce my bare feet. My palms sweat and my heart quaked in my chest as fast as a hummingbird flutters its wings. I could barely catch my breath. Since I was a little child, my father always scared me so much when he lost his temper.

"I'm coming, Papa!" I sauntered toward the door as my father continued knocking like a madman. With his irritated urgency, I thought he would kick the door open before I got to it. I gripped the iron knob and felt a skitter dance through my heart.

Before I opened the door well enough to see his face, Papa barged inside and pushed it back against me.

With a gasp, I stumbled backward and almost lost my footing, but caught my balance before I fell.

Like a furious, wild animal, Papa stood before me huffing and puffing, holding a kerosene lantern in one hand. His sweaty face reflected the light from the lantern. "Pearl and Randall are gone! They ran away!" He scowled at me. "You know anything about this?"

My chin bobbed, struggling to find words. "N-no, Papa . . . nothing." *But why would he believe me—me, of all people? His sympathizing daughter?* I hardly expected him to.

Papa grabbed my face in one of his large hands and shook me. "Don't you lie to me, girl! Lying is a sin. You know about this, don't you?"

Panicking, I tried to shake my head in his firm grip.

"Don't you?" he urged, glowering.

"No, sir!" I hated myself for lying, but I was too frightened to admit anything, and what else was I supposed to say in a life-and-death situation?

Papa growled. "Honest to God, if they get away, I'll give you a thrashing you'll never forget! Nobody leaves my land without my permission!" His heavy boots thudded out of my bedroom as he left and slammed the door.

I whimpered and rushed over to the window above my bed, looking at the slave quarters. Some of the slaves had awakened with lanterns in their hands, watching Jed, the overseer, harnessing two of the horses from the barn.

My heart sank within me.
They were going after Pearl and Randall.

6 *Broken Promises*

MONDAY, JULY 19
CRABTREE PLANTATION
Charlotte, North Carolina

HORSES SNORTED AND THEIR hooves stomped as a wagon came to a squeaky halt. Dula, the other house slaves, and I breathed and froze in the kitchen, listening to the outside commotion. My heart banged in my chest—and then Pearl screeched. It was all Dula needed to hear, the unfortunate terror of recapture. The old woman beat her fists on the table and threw her head back, wailing a cry so potent, it vibrated off the walls and seeped into my soul.

"Noooo, Lord . . . oh, dear God!" She buried her face in her wrinkled hands and sobbed, fleeing from the kitchen.

Collapsing in a chair at the center table, tears slipped down my cheeks. *They've been caught. Oh, God, they've been caught.* I couldn't believe what happened. Perhaps it was me again—the dreaded curse that followed me as my shadow since the day I was born.

"I'm tired of beating you, boy!" Papa said, "Jed, Ozzie, hold him!"

Racing from the kitchen, I stood on the front porch of the house. "Papa, don't!"

Randall was shirtless, squirming to break loose from Ozzie and Jed's hold.

Pearl was crying, her white apron and dress soiled with dirt and fragments of dried leaves from their short voyage. Anna, Ozzie's little sister and one of the other field slaves, held Pearl back in her arms from interfering with Randall's punishment.

Papa clenched his jaw and studied Randall. He stuck out his barrel-like chest as a gorilla and placed his hands on his hips. "I bet you wish you died, huh. We found an old negro dead and stinking under a tree back in the woods, flies all over him." He chortled. "How many times do I have to tell you, boy?" He snapped the whip in his hand on the ground. "Slaves must obey their masters in everything. It's not a choice, it's a principle!"

Randall grimaced and spat in my father's eye.

"Gah!" Papa turned aside and wiped his hand over his left eye, and then used the same hand to slap Randall across his face. "That's it! Bring him to the ground! I've had enough of his rebellion. It's time to teach this boy a lesson! Jed, Ozzie, grab his arms and legs."

Ozzie knitted his brows and looked as though he didn't want part in the matter, but followed suit with the overseer. He and Jed wrestled Randall to the dirt ground and held him facedown, one by his arms and the other by his legs.

Papa tossed his whip on the ground. He smirked and yanked Randall's head by his black, coiled hair, speaking in his ear. "You're never gonna forget this. Maybe you'll think twice before you run away from me again." He chuckled and released Randall's hair. Then he took a branding tool with what looked like a horseshoe at the end of it from a crackling fire pit. The metal shape at the end of the iron instrument glowed bright orange and faded to black, thin smoke from it vanishing in the morning breeze.

"No!" Pearl screamed. She tussled to break loose from Anna, trying to defend Randall.

My father scanned the other field and house slaves, witnessing the torment and standing around him. "Let this be a warning to all of you. You all belong to me! And I mean all of you!" He placed his huge boot on Randall's back and moved the tool to his bare skin.

"Papa, no! Please, don't do it!"

He glared at me. "Silence! I've heard enough coming out of you, girl. I'm teaching this boy here a lesson, and if you can't accept it, then hush and go inside!"

Moisture blurred my vision as I glanced from Pearl and the other slaves to my father. Covering my ears, I whimpered and ran into the house, rushing upstairs to my bedroom. But it didn't suffocate Randall's painful, deafening yell echoing from the outside. Sobbing, I slid down against the door, convinced everything was all my fault. I was the Miss of the house and already failing at my authoritative position. Against Papa's will, I allowed Pearl to talk me into writing passes for her and Randall. Slavery was a part of our lives, and there seemed to be no way for me or my fellow friends to escape it.

Sometime later, I came out of my room and walked down a few stairs. I stood with my hand on the banister as Papa entered the house. He closed the door and hung up his hunting rifle on the side of the wall.

"What about the ninth verse, Papa? Why don't you tell them that one?"

Papa sighed wearily. "What are you talking about?"

"From Ephesians chapter six," I said, "the one you like to quote all the time. Have you read the ninth verse of the scripture?"

"Yeah," Papa said flatly.

"Well, why don't you tell them then?" I asked.

There was a long silence between us, my father staring down, his back turned toward me.

I licked my lips and started quoting the citation. "And ye masters, do the same things unto them, forbearing threatening: knowing that your—"

"I know what it says!" Papa interrupted, facing me. He pointed at the front door. "But they don't need to know it. You don't understand anything. They have to be taught to obey."

"How do you expect them to when you treat them like animals?" I said.

Papa glared and stepped up to the staircase. "Don't you try to rebuke me. I'm the head of this household and what I say goes, young lady. Go to your room!"

"What'd you do to Pearl?" I studied him. "Did you punish her too?"

Papa's voice grew louder. "I said go!"

Trotting upstairs to my bedroom, I wished Pearl and Randall hadn't gotten caught. Although slavery was an important asset to how the South raised its money, I couldn't understand the cruel punishment that existed with it. Slaves weren't instruments or things to misuse; they were people with hearts, souls, and feelings. But this was difficult to explain to people like my father who cared solely about getting rich than loving their fellow neighbors and the welfare of men.

FOR MOST OF THE day, Pearl and I hadn't spoken to each other. I stayed cooped up in my room, trying to forget the harsh reality of my everyday life. Immersing myself in my imagination, I sulked and wrote another chapter of my children's story.

Then a knock tapped on my door.

"Millie, can I come in?" Pearl asked in the afternoon.

"No! You promised you'd get away and you didn't," I said, heartbroken. "Oh, Pearl, why'd you have to get caught?"

Pearl spoke to the closed door. "I can explain, Millie. Please, let me in."

"All right." I sighed and unlocked the bedroom door. Then I sat back at my desk again.

Pearl entered and closed the door. She knelt beside my desk as I distractedly wrote on my paper. "We were trying, Millie. We really were. Don't you believe me?"

I paused and glanced at her weary expression. "I guess so, but what happened?"

Pearl wilted her shoulders. "We found Eldon, Randy's gramps from Master McMillan's plantation along the way and that slowed us down. He was dead under a tree, like he was sleeping. Randy thinks he had a heart attack. He wanted to bury him, but we had to keep moving."

She paused and continued. "When we reached the middle of the forest, he tripped over a thick root and sprained his ankle. That's where your Papa and Mr. Jed found us. Randy told me to keep running, and I tried to, but your Papa fired a rifle and threatened to shoot us if I did. You see, I couldn't let that happen. And I couldn't leave Randy behind either, so I stopped and stayed behind. I'm sorry I broke my promise. Can we still be friends?"

"I don't know if we should be." I bowed my head, ashamed.

Pearl frowned. "What are you saying? Of course, we can."

"I'm a curse to you, Pearl. I was to Mama too, like Papa said." I buried my face in my hands and sobbed. "Everything's my fault. I wrote the passes for you and Randall. I got you in trouble again." I shook my head. "I'm not made to be a missus of a plantation. I'm sorry about my father and everything, Pearl."

Still kneeling, Pearl placed a hand on my shoulder. "It's all right, Millie. I know you ain't like him. It's not your fault. Besides, Randall and I chose to run away." She sighed and inched a weak smile, but her eyes were wet. "I'd better help my nana with the laundry."

I nodded and blinked back my tears.

As she started to leave, the thought of Papa's reaction to Pearl's defiance came to mind, but she exited before I could ask what happened to her. Nonetheless, because he was so fond of her, something told me Pearl was chastised a little less than Randall and for more reasons than one. I dropped my pencil, bowed my head, and prayed there in my chair for a miracle to happen; for someone to come to the rescue.

Someone who knew how to help slaves escape to Canada like the brave, good-natured people I'd read about in books and the *Carolina Watchman*. People like William Garrison, John Brown, and Harriet Tubman who dared to stand up and set free their fellow men. I didn't expect a quick reply from God, but when night fell, I beheld a surprise outside my bedroom window—my prayer was answered.

STARING OUT AT THE full moon blanketed in shadowy clouds, there wasn't a star in sight, except the North one. It shined steadily like a diamond, glowing at me from above the cotton fields. Although we were in the middle of the summer harvest, plenty of white, fluffy bolls still remained, so there was quite a bit left to pick off the stems. Fewer slaves meant a longer process and more work to do. In fact, sometimes Papa worked in the fields along with the field hands.

I gripped a wood pole of my headstand and sighed hopelessly. *God, please, help us . . . help me rest in peace.* If I died on an evil plantation, I thought my family's sins would stain my soul throughout eternity.

After I tucked in bed and closed my eyes, something tapped on my window. Was it a bird or a raindrop? I awoke and heard it again—louder than the first time. Tugging down the blanket and getting out of bed, I looked outside below the second floor of the mansion house. There was a small man in a gray fedora and gray cloak. He took off his hat, revealing a head of red curls that glistened in the moonlight.

Peering at the gentleman, I gasped in disbelief. The violinist from my birthday party? What's he doing here? I wasn't expecting to see him again.

I raised my window. "Sir, why have you come here?"

"Shh," the redheaded man whispered, placing his forefinger to his lips. "Not so loud. Meet me aside from the house. I'll explain everything there."

Suspicion formed on my face as I closed the window. Could he be trusted? Or was he an ally to the rest of the slaveholders in town? From the time I first saw him on my birthday, I knew there was something significant about him, and I hoped it was for the common good. Grabbing the *Moby Dick* book, I snuck out of my room into the dark hallway and went downstairs. In case Papa woke in the middle of the night, I brought it with me as a good excuse for being awake.

I exited the house through the kitchen's back door. "What's going on?"

"Is your father asleep?" the young man asked in a whisper, kneading the brim of his dress hat.

I closed the door slowly. "Yes, I believe so. Is there something you want?"

"Yes," he said, "I overheard the commotion earlier this morning while spying from behind the house. You sounded upset with your father hurting Randall."

"Yes, I was, but I'm partially to blame." I hung my head. "I wrote the passes for Pearl and Randall."

I walked closer to him alongside the house. "What is it you want, sir?"

"I've been sent to fulfill a private mission, Miss Crabtree," he said. "I was hiding out in the woods and saw them running together—Pearl and Randall. You're the only one I feel I can trust."

I frowned and inclined my head. "Trust about what? Who are you?"

He checked up at the house and faced me again. "I'm Noah—Noah Shepherd, ma'am, an abolitionist from Canada of the Underground Railroad. My colleagues and I have heard of the dreadful history of Crabtree Plantation and others nearby. I've been sent to help as many slaves as possible who are willing to run and flee for freedom to Canada."

Joy blossomed within me. "Abolitionist?" From my newspaper readings, I was aware of abolitionists, their political and religious views on slavery, and what many of them did to free slaves. But I had never met one before in person, so I was honored and flattered by his visitation.

"Yes," Noah answered, "but you mustn't tell your father. He'd have me shot or hung if he heard what I said."

"Oh, no," I said, "I won't tell him. You have my word."

"Let the slaves know about me. Tell them they should meet me in the first slave quarter on the right tomorrow night. They should answer me by the code word, 'A friend of friends.'"

"All right," I said. "I'll tell them tomorrow."

"Thank you, Miss Millie. You're quite a young lady. A wealthy slave master's daughter? You astound me."

Noah looked askance at me. "Why are you different from the others?"

I gave a half-shrug. "I don't know. I guess because I'm a curse to my family."

Noah gazed in my eyes and smiled gently. "No, that's what your father would want you to believe, Millie. You're a special human being—a woman with a heart for all mankind, which reminds me . . . I've heard of a young woman similar to you who left her family's plantation in Charleston, South Carolina. She and her husband wrote a book about slaves' testimonies a few years ago."

"Yes, Angelina Grimke," I said, intrigued and aware of the lady and her husband he was referring to. "I read the book *American Slavery as It Is: Testimony of a Thousand Witnesses* by her and her husband Theodore Weld. It was quite disturbing, but their bravery inspired me because I also would love to become an author."

"Is that so?" Noah folded his arms and studied me. "What do you write?"

"Children's fiction," I said. "I want to leave the South to pursue my dreams in peace, but Papa said all the good fiction authors are men."

Noah shook his head. "Not so, Miss Millie. There are many women fiction authors; some of which live right in Canada. Never let anyone crumple your dreams, Millie. There's a whole world outside the confined South." He glanced upward at my bedroom window above again. "You best go inside before your father wakes and gets suspicious."

"You're right," I said. "Good night, Mr. Shepherd."

"Good night, madam." Noah adjusted his fedora back on and took off running through the blackness into the wooded forest aside from the house.

For a split second, I stood in the moonlight and stared at the black forest with a smile across my face, mesmerized and uplifted by our private conversation. Unlike Papa's deep, hoarse tone, I could've listened to Noah speak all day.

His voice was as smooth as a jasper stone, and to me, sounded British, which made me wonder which region of Canada he was from. No one—and certainly not any man—had ever encouraged my pursuit of becoming a children's writer. It inspired and drove me to run after my dreams while I had the chance to. When the time came, I would go North with all the others.

I sighed and relaxed my shoulders. After I returned to the house through the kitchen door, I tiptoed to Papa's office to place the book *Moby Dick* back on his bookshelf. When I entered the upstairs hall, there was a squeak.

Startled, I swiftly looked to my right at a large, shadowy figure.

My father had come down the attic stairs in his long nightshirt. He paused with one hand on the side wall and stared at me. "Whatcha doing up, girl?"

"I returned your book in your office." Frowning, I glanced from the stairs behind my father to him again. Dread gnawed within me, and my heart kicked in my chest. I could've asked him the same question after coming from Pearl's room in the attic. He didn't usually walk around at night without his housecoat, but I didn't want to believe the wild thoughts suffocating my mind. I was too frightened to question him. From his alarmed expression, I think he suspected I knew exactly what he'd secretly done.

"Good night, Papa," I said humbly with downcast eyes, passing him into my bedroom. Once I closed my door and tucked myself in, I covered my ears with my pillow and closed my eyes for a second before opening them again.

Intuition startled me. For the rest of the night, my nerves were shattered as I fought to fall asleep, trying to understand my troublesome emotions. Some hours later, I stirred in bed and lay flat on my back with tearful eyes, staring at the high-vaulted ceiling. *Dear God, why am I afraid?*

7 *Dark Secrets*

PEARL ENTERED MY BEDROOM and helped me get dressed, but today something felt different. Her countenance was like still waters, and she was quiet as the day we first met. I studied her emotionless face in the vanity mirror as she slowly brushed my hair. A part of her being was missing. Now the spirited friend I once knew was nothing more than a compliant house slave.

Her liveliness had become a sunset on the horizon as if she had died from her everyday world. Nothing I said she responded to or laughed at, and neither could I cheer her mood. Her present fate was the only thing that seemed to matter to her, the thing fixed on her mind.

Unshed tears flooded my eyes as I stared at her dull reflection. "Pearl, you worry me. I can't bear your steady quietness—not this much. I know you're upset about what happened to Randall. We can talk about it if you want to."

Pearl tilted her head and paused with the brush in one hand and my back-length, brown hair in the other. She sighed, said nothing, and then continued brushing again. Her hazel eyes welled up with tears. She pressed together her lips, refusing to speak.

Releasing my hair from her grasp, I turned and faced her, gripping the back of my chair. "Pearl, please . . . please, talk to me."

Pearl sniffled and stifled a sob. She placed down the brush and fled from my bedroom, shutting the door.

Certainly, Papa was to blame, as I sensed Pearl's startling reaction had more to do with than her and Randall getting caught and brought back into slavery. At breakfast, I sat in miserable silence, watching the house slaves serve my father and me around the long dining table. A pin could be heard dropping on the floor—it was so quiet. The house slaves wore pensive faces and whispered to each other with shifty eyes as if they knew something—a dreadful secret I didn't know myself.

Dula waddled to me and spooned eggs onto my plate from a serving dish.

"Thank you, Dula," I whispered.

Papa continued eating his oatmeal like any other day, scraping his spoon in his glass bowl. How could he eat peacefully after all his horrible dealings with the slaves?

"Gimme more bourbon," he told George, holding up his wine glass.

With a stiff face, George walked over with the bottle and filled my father's cup. As he poured, he gave me a sidelong glance. "Good morning, Miss Millie."

"Morning, George." I munched on a strip of bacon and studied my father, contemplating when to ask him why he was coming from the attic last night, but he spoke on another subject.

"Jed will watch the field slaves. I've gotta take care of some business, so you keep things orderly in the home while I'm gone." Papa guzzled his bourbon, dabbed his mouth with his napkin, and stood from the table.

A carriage galloped outside and stopped.

"Dear God," Papa grumbled under his breath.

"Who is it?" I asked, frowning.

"It's the lender," Papa said.

"Lender?" I nearly choked on my food, clanking my fork on my plate. What was he coming to our plantation for? Were we in debt? Had my father owed him some money?

Papa turned from the curtained window and glanced from me to some of the house slaves. "You stay in here. I've got business to take care of."

My heart sank. Surely, money was little after Mama's medical bills; not to mention, my eighteenth birthday celebration. Would we lose our home for collateral? Where would we go? I blinked in disbelief and hung open my mouth as my father exited and spoke to the men about business.

The front door slammed shut.

"Oh, Lord, no, we in trouble." Margaret kneaded her white apron, panicking. "Your Papa gonna sell some of us. I know's it! I know's it! He would us before the field hands."

Dula grabbed Margaret in a tight embrace and shook her to her senses. "Get a hold of yourself, gal! It ain't for certain. Now, I been a house slave all my life. I been on Crabtree Plantation even before Miss Millie was born, and he said he'd never sell me or any house slave if his life depended on it. 'Field hands are more expensive,' he said."

"There's always the first time," Margaret said weakly.

Worry engulfed me as I glanced from Margaret to Dula, and then at Pearl. Unlike the other slave women, Pearl's expression had lifted from hearing the possible news, as if from a sense of relief.

We gathered around the slightly open window and watched Papa talking to the lender and a slave trader, eavesdropping on the men's conversation. The lender was a pudgy, elegantly dressed man with rosy cheeks and a cane. To me, he looked like a fat penguin in his top hat and black suit. The slave trader was a rustic-dressed, tall, slender man wearing a brown wide-brimmed hat and yellow kerchief on his sunburned neck. He wore a smirk across his lips, standing with his arms crossed.

"I'm afraid I can't extend your payment period, Mr. Crabtree," the lender said. "Now, if you can't afford to pay out of pocket or give your home for collateral, the only sensible thing to do would be to sell some of your slaves in exchange for your loan."

Standing on the porch out of the sun, Papa jammed his hands in his pockets and sighed. "I reckon you're right."

The slave trader chewed and spat a wad of tobacco on the ground. "Any suggestions on who can cover the cost?" A little smile played on his lips, chewing.

I frowned and bit my lip. That man already knew the slaves on our plantation because he sold them to my father. I could tell he was eager to take them back into his custody again.

"Yeah, I got some," Papa said unwillingly. He raised his head and spoke abrasively. "But Pearl, the mulatto . . . she stays for now. Nobody's getting her."

Pearl and I shared a look of despair. She grimaced, placed a hand to her stomach and walked away from the window, disgusted by my father.

Of course, Papa wouldn't sell her, and Mama knew it too. If there was a slave who could soften his stony heart, it was Pearl. Fearing him greatly, she always strove to please him and stay on his good side. Papa always admired her since she was a child, saying she was prettier than the darker-skinned slave women. He'd even given Pearl her own room, unlike the other house slave women who shared the hallway bedroom across from mine.

"I'm disturbed by your stinginess, Wade," the slave trader said and chuckled, "but I can't say I blame you. She's grown up into a fine one—mighty fine. I'll be back to take whoever you sell bright tomorrow morning."

"It's a deal." Papa shook the trader's hand. He signed a form the lender handed him and offered it back.

The lender stuffed it in the chest pocket of his vest. "Nice doing business with you, Crabtree. Best wishes for the summer's harvest." He winked.

The slave trader helped the lender into the carriage, and then he struck the reins and they drove off.

We scattered from the window as Papa entered the house and returned to the dining room, disheartened.

"It's been settled," Papa said, glancing at Margaret, Dula, and the other house slaves. "I'll be selling one of y'all with a few field hands. There's nothing else I can do." He walked back out of the room, lighting up his smoke pipe.

Margaret hugged Dula and whimpered.

I looked at them after my father and the male house slaves left and whispered, "Don't worry, help is on the way."

Margaret sniffled. "Whatcha talkin' bout, Miss Millie?"

"Someone has come to help," I said.

Dula frowned. "Who?"

"Mr. Noah Shepherd," I answered quietly. "He's the redhead violinist who attended my birthday party. I'll explain more later. You should meet him in the first slave quarter on the right tonight and answer him by the code, 'A friend of friends,' but be careful."

Margaret and Dula looked inquisitively from me to each other and hugged again.

With a disaster on the rise, tonight was the night. I needed to talk with all the slaves, but first I wanted to settle matters over with my father. Obviously, there was a big problem between him and Pearl, and I was going to figure it out one way or another.

"WHAT'S WRONG WITH PEARL, Papa?" I crossed my arms and waited for my father's response.

Sitting in his white rocking chair on the front porch, Papa sipped a glass of lemonade and placed it on the side table. He fanned himself with his wide hat and looked at me, squinting from the afternoon sun as the field slaves worked together in the cotton field. "What makes you think something's wrong with her?"

"She hasn't said a word all day," I said. "It's not like her. What did you do?"

Papa's thick brows drew together. "Well, Dula *did* say she hasn't been feeling well. What is it to you? I'm your father and the boss on this plantation. Pearl might be your *friend*, but she was my *slave* first, you got that? I do whatever I please and with whoever, girl."

Speechless, I shook my head and stepped away from him. I reckon I had always known what happened, but I couldn't bring myself to believe it until I had no choice. Fury burned my face. "How . . . how could you?"

"How could I what?" Papa asked. "Why else did you think I brought her in from the fields? I've got to keep the plantation going . . . to pass it on after I'm gone. What did you expect me to do? Your Mama failed me and was a sickly woman losing children. If she's with child and people question me, I'll say it's my niece or nephew. Besides, with her complexion, nobody will know anyway . . . once she's sold." His tone dropped.

Hot tears blinded me. "I hate you, Papa! This is why you didn't want us to be friends, isn't it? You're the most selfish man ever—breaking up a friendship for your own advantage! I hate you!"

Holding the skirt of my gray, white-dotted dress, I marched into the house and slammed the door. Now I understood everything. My father was taking advantage of my best friend and her light skin for his selfish benefit and our family's tainted name. But as soon as she bore him a son, Papa would ship her off in a wagon like one of his cotton sacks, as what happened to her birth mother. I had no idea how long their relations had been going on, but I knew there was a close friend who I had loved hurting with bitter pain and shame. If there was ever a time for me to keep my promise for her to escape to the North and get her freedom, it was right now.

I rushed upstairs to the attic and knocked on the door urgently. "Pearl, it's Millie. Open up!"

"Go away," Pearl said weakly.

"I can't," I replied, "I have to talk with you about something. It's important."

"Go away," Pearl urged irritably, her voice rising.

I sighed and slumped my shoulders. "But I have good news. You can get free."

"I said go away!" Pearl threw a hard object and glass shattered on the inside floor of the attic, startling me. Her heartbreaking sobs and whimpers pierced through behind the closed door. Then there was dead silence.

"I . . . I know what happened," I said. "My father let me know what he's done."

Blinking back unshed tears, I placed my ear to the closed door. "Pearl?"

She said nothing.

"Pearl . . . please?" I called again.

Quietness remained her response, and there seemed to be no hope for reconciliation. What could I do to help Pearl feel better? How could I heal her pain when my blood father was the one to blame? I didn't want to cry, but what else could I do? At that moment, there were no words of comfort or advice I could give to help her cope or make her situation easier to handle. Her innocence was stolen from her, and she could never get it back again.

I clenched my fists on the door and fell to my knees. "Pearl, I'm . . . I'm sorry. I'm so sorry." Unable to suppress my emotions any longer, I sobbed and hung my head. Maybe I could've done something to stop my father. Maybe if I hadn't gone outside the other night to Noah, I could've intervened the incident.

Tears ran down my cheeks and chin. I took the pearl brooch out of my skirt pocket and looked at it in my hand. It was one of Pearl's most precious belongings and I didn't think I deserved to keep it anymore. After all, I was the problem—the cause of my close friend's heartache like when we were little girls and she got in trouble and was beaten for playing hide-and-seek with me. I didn't blame her if she hated me.

Sniffling, I placed her brooch on the hardwood floor and pushed it under the door.

"Pearl?" Once more, I listened for her reaction and hoped she'd let me in or answer, but she did neither again.

Clutching my dress in my hands, I closed my eyes tightly and tried to dissipate my tears. But as I lowered my head, I couldn't stop myself from weeping again. Being confident I had lost my best friend, it seemed all our happiness, smiles, and laughs had disappeared. There was only grief and emptiness, the sin of slavery severing our sisterly ties. Now the special bond we shared together was gone. Like a broken contract, my father had torn our friendship to shreds.

8 *A Fair Exchange*

AS PAPA, JED, AND the field slaves loaded cotton sacks into my father's rig, I checked my father's ledger to discover which slaves he'd chosen to sell to the trader. Hearing footsteps in the hallway, I glanced over my shoulder a moment as one of the male house slaves passed the entryway. Relieved, I exhaled a slow breath and slid my forefinger down the list of names, skimming their prices across those encircled in black ink. Whenever Papa sold slaves, he always drew circles around their names. There were three of them, a house slave and two field hands:

Margaret...$500
Pearl...$1000
Joseph..$700
Anna...$600

Beside the ledger was a short notice scribbled with a name:

Master Sylvester LaDuke from Lexington, Kentucky

My heart dropped at their names and where they were likely being sent to from North Carolina. *Oh, no . . . it can't be true.* I closed the ledger and hurried to inform the others upstairs in my bedroom.

Dula and Margaret were folding clean towels and linens and putting them into the trunk by the footboard of my bed.

"It's three of them," I said after entering the room. "There was also a piece of paper written with the name Master Sylvester LaDuke from Lexington. I think the slave trader's planning to bring them in Kentucky to a slave pen site."

They gasped and paused, looking at me with blank faces.

"Who they be?" Margaret grimaced and flared her nostrils, breathing heavily as she waited for my dreaded response.

Not wanting to confess the devastating news, I tightened my mouth and fluttered my tearful eyes. "I'm sorry, Marge. You're one of them."

Margaret placed her hands on her hips and shook her head.

"Who's the others?" Dula asked.

"Joseph and Anna, Ozzie's little sister," I answered.

Dula placed a hand to her mouth. "Good Lord, Anna and Ozzie have never been separated since they were children. The news will crush their hearts."

"Marge, you must leave tonight with the others," I said.

"I reckon so." Margaret glanced from Dula to me. "But what about Pearl? She should come too."

"I know," I said, "and I've tried talking with her, but she won't open the door. She's angry at me. She doesn't want to hear anything about getting free again."

Dula shut the lid of the trunk and nibbled her lip. "Humph, looks like I'll have to talk some sense into her myself then." She and I left my bedroom.

We went upstairs to the attic, and then Dula knocked on the door.

"Pearl, it's your nana. Open the door."

The door remained shut.

"Pearl, open the door, gal. I ain't sayin it again," Dula demanded.

Her granddaughter opened the door and peeked at us through the crack with tear-stained cheeks. "What is it, nana?"

"We got to talk with ya," Dula said.

"About what?" Pearl asked.

Dula turned sideways and glanced at me. "Miss Millie will explain everything."

Pearl opened the door wider and let us into the dimly lit attic. "Very well, what's the news?" She closed the door.

"An abolitionist is in town," I said, "and possibly more than one. His name's Mr. Noah Shepherd. He's a conductor of the Underground Railroad. That's what I was trying to tell you."

"Stop funning me, Millie." Pearl frowned and crossed her arms and walked by, staring out the small window streaming with sunlight by the headstand of her bed. "Nobody gets off this wretched plantation until your Papa gets tired of us."

Dula and I moved forward toward her.

"I'm not funning you, Pearl. I'm telling you the truth. He wants to meet all the slaves in the first quarter on the right tonight who are willing to run for freedom," I said.

Pearl glared at me. "Randy's got a C scarred on his back, and you're talking about running again? You think this man can lead us safely to Canada? What makes him different from anybody else around here?"

"He's an abolitionist," I answered, "he knows the way North from here better than me; and honestly, I have good feelings about him."

"Has he ever helped anyone else escape to Canada?" Pearl raised her brow.

My smile weakened. How was I supposed to answer her? I hadn't a clue if he helped any slave to Canada. There wasn't proof whether Mr. Shepherd had ever accomplished such a challenging task and dangerous mission. Nonetheless, taking a chance was better than staying on a God-forbidden cotton plantation.

I held out my hands and shrugged. "I . . . I don't know, but it's worth a try, isn't it?"

"Maybe," Pearl said, "but I just can't be disappointed again. I'm . . . I'm too scared." She buried her face in her hands, shaking her head. "Please, God . . . please, not again."

Dula joined the conversation. "Now you listen, gal. Look at me."

Pearl slid her hands from her face.

Her grandmother spoke on with an intense stare. "You and I know what Massa Crabtree tryin to do. Don't wait till it's too late." She grabbed Pearl at arm's length. "Run, child. Leave dis hell and run for your life! They be headin North tonight."

Pearl's eyes went round. "That soon? What about Massa Crabtree?" Shamefaced, she looked at her black, laced shoes and wring her hands. "He may search for me."

"He'll just have to search," Dula said and shrugged.

"What about you, nana?" Pearl asked, looking up. "Aren't you coming?"

Dula wore a wistful smile and cocked her turban-wrapped head. She placed a hand on Pearl's cheek. "I'll stay here, dear."

Disappointment fell in my heart. As Pearl had, I also wanted so much for Dula to leave for the sweet land of

Canada. From what she said, she'd been a slave all her life since birth and she'd never seen the light of freedom shine upon her face. Saying goodbye to a loving woman who'd helped raise me was as hard as if she were my grandmother.

"At my age now, there ain't much left for me to do," the old woman said, "but you . . . ya got your whole life ahead of ya. Don't worry about me. I got my freedom from Jesus. You remember me and take the Good Lord with ya on your journey. And if'n ya come across your mama along the way, tell her I love her and said hello."

Tears pooled in my eyes, watching Pearl sobbing and hugging her grandmother.

"Where will I go?" Pearl unembraced and glanced at both of us. "How can I escape from my disgrace?" She closed her eyes and wept on her grandmother's shoulder again.

"Be patient and take one day at a time. Your heart will heal, dear. Let the Lord free those shackles of sadness," Dula said, consoling Pearl. "Don't let Massa Crabtree hold your soul captive twice."

"You can sneak in the cellar. Papa never goes down there. He's scared of ghosts and thinks it's haunted. I'll come for you later before bedtime tonight. Just do your house chores like usual until then."

Pearl dried her cheeks with her long sleeve and giggled. "All right, I sure hope things work out this time. I promise I won't say a word about this."

I smiled and hugged Pearl again, reassuring her. "Hold on, you're going to get out of here. I promise."

Dula sighed. "Well, I best get back to work myself." She and I exited the attic and I closed the door.

WITH SOME OF THE slaves at risk of being sold, things became worse when Chauncey visited our home. Word spread around town about our financial troubles, and the young, cocky plantation owner came to make a "fair exchange" with my father.

Standing against the outside wall of the parlor, I peeked through the entrance, eavesdropping on their discussion.

"Please, have a seat on the sofa," Papa said, gesturing a hand.

Chauncey nodded, holding his felt hat. "Thank you kindly, Mr. Crabtree." He sat and crossed his thin legs.

"So, what brought you over here?" Papa took the cap off his decanter of brandy and filled a glass on a side table.

Chauncey caressed the brim of his hat and curled his upper lip. "Nothing unusual. I can't stop thinking about your daughter, sir."

"I see," Papa said, smiling, "you're smitten with my Millie, are you?" He snickered and drank from his glass.

"Yes, sir. She's the one—" Chauncey smirked and chuckled— "and I'm confident she's into me too. Sure, she's headstrong, but I like a young woman with a little stubbornness, and I'll have her melt in my arms and under my control before your rooster crows cock-a-doodle-doo." He sat up and looked at my father. "That's why I've decided to offer you a special proposition in exchange for her hand."

"Really?" Papa said, intrigued. "What's the deal?"

"Well, my estate is larger than yours," Chauncey said, "and I'm a young man who needs financial assistance in running my cotton plantation. My late father dropped it in my lap without much explanation. I've got two good overseers, but they're not the smartest fellows in the world when it comes to solving figures. But you . . . you've been bookkeeping for years and I could use your help in a business partnership, if interested?"

"Why are you coming to me?" Papa said. "I'm not in a better position than you are."

"Yes," Chauncey admitted, "but you're smarter and within a partnership, building my finances could also help restore your credit. Mr. Crabtree, it's like killing two birds with one stone."

"Two birds with one stone, huh?" Papa said, contemplating. He sipped from his glass and glanced out the window behind his centered mahogany desk.

"That's right," Chauncey said, "I'm offering a down payment of two hundred and fifty dollars. That alone will help clear more of your debt."

Papa scratched his beard, thinking again. "Two-fifty, huh?"

"Yes, sir," Chauncey said. "Do we have a deal?"

Papa grinned. "You know, why not? We've got a deal. Millie's all yours." He patted Chauncey on his shoulder.

"Much obliged, Mr. Crabtree. I promise Millie will be in good hands."

The two men laughed and shook on it.

Shock paralyzed me. First, it was the slaves, and now me. Wealth and money were more important to my father than his own daughter's happiness. I was a token used for his greed and the financial success and sake of his guilty, blood-stained plantation.

As they said their goodbyes, I dodged from the wall and hid out of sight behind the door of one of the first-floor bedrooms. After Chauncey left and the front door closed, I came back out from hiding and walked into the sitting room.

"I reckon you're selling me too?" I said, devastated.

Papa turned around to me. He wiped his sweaty face with a kerchief. "What do you mean? You're always complaining about what decisions I make. Besides, it was him or another fellow from town we don't know well. It was strictly business, and it'll be a great asset to both you and me in the future."

I narrowed my eyes and shook my head. "You can't make me do this."

My father slammed his empty glass on the side table. "It's too late. I've given my blessing for him to marry you."

"Well, I won't do it." I turned and started walking away from him.

"You must and you will!" Papa said in a stern tone.

I glared over my shoulder. "No, I won't, and you can't make me!" Humiliated, I fled from the sitting room and hurled upstairs to my bedroom. As always, Chauncey took charge and meddled around like a flying insect, being an absolute pest. Now I had no choice but to force myself to face my deepest fears. It was the only way to avoid the shackled chains of a miserable marriage; a marriage of slavery, unhappiness, and restraint.

Becoming Mrs. Chauncey McMillan.

9 *The Secret Escape*

BAWLING WITH TEARS, I popped open the latches of the trunk at the footboard of my bed, took out my carpetbag, and placed it on top of my bed mattress. Then I took a few clothes out of my armoire: two pairs of pantalettes and a pair of white stockings. As I folded the items in my trembling hands, I thought to myself.

What did I know beyond my life of luxury and the cotton plantation? How could I survive in the great outdoors? I didn't know the first thing about how to make it out there. Ever since I was born, slaves had always done everything for me and I didn't have to lift a finger to do one thing.

By leaving home, I was placing myself in a different situation where I would have to fend for myself. It made me realize how runaway slaves felt when they took the risks of departing the only homes they knew too. But the heavy plight of my current situation left me with few options, and I refused to follow my father's demands.

I stuffed my pantalettes in the bag.

"Where do you think you're going?" Papa's voice suddenly spoke behind me.

I froze and turned around to him. "I can't stay here anymore. I'm going North, Papa."

"Over my dead body," Papa said, inching forward, "you aren't going anywhere unless I say so. You're not my wife, but you're my daughter, which makes you my property."

My brows drew together. "I'm not a possession, Papa. I'm a person."

"You've been reading too many of those feminist short stories and Women's suffrage articles in the newspaper. You should get your head out of the clouds, especially all your writing and imagination. It's a waste of time. Why can't you be satisfied with your proper place in this world, like other women?"

"Because I'm not *just* any woman, Papa," I said. "I want to do more with my life than get married and have a family. Why can't you understand that?"

Papa disregarded my question and turned away. "I've invited Mr. Chauncey McMillan over for dinner. Make sure you wear one of your nice dresses tonight." He walked off down the hall.

My stomach churned. How could I eat anything?

With the arranged marriage forthcoming, I wasn't looking forward to seeing Chauncey again. Before he came, I already pictured his narrow face, his sharp, pale-blue eyes, staring me down like a plate of hors d'oeuvres during mealtime.

SOMEONE TAPPED THE KNOCKER as I was sitting in the parlor with my father.

"That should be him. Get the door, George," Papa said.

"Yes, sir." George walked and answered the door, greeting Chauncey as he entered our home. He led him into the parlor room with a polite gesture of his white-gloved hand.

As they arrived, my father opened his decanter and poured two glasses. I hated whenever he drank, but it was customary for the Crabtree men to serve drinks to welcome guests.

"Hello," Papa said, "make yourself at home. Dinner will be served in a few minutes. How about a drink?"

"Thank you, Mr. Crabtree." Chauncey looked at me on his way over to my father. "Hello, Miss Millie. You look wonderful."

"Thank you, Mr. McMillan," I mumbled, kneading my silk, yellow evening gown and sheepishly looking at him. My heart raced in my chest.

Watching Papa and Chauncey tap glasses and swallow their drinks, chills of fear from this evening's dinner covered my whole body.

Harold stood in the arched entrance of my father's office. "Massa Crabtree, the kitchen women said dinner is ready."

"Very well, Harold," Papa said.

Chauncey grinned and rubbed his hands. "Boy, I can hardly wait. I'm starved."

We entered the dining room and sat at the long table with a dinner of roasted turkey, sweet potato pudding, okra soup with white rice, and fresh bread from the oven. Although the food looked good and delicious, I lost my appetite when Chauncey sat across the table in front of me.

My flesh boiled and warmth spread through my chest, feeling his intense, starving gaze.

"So, how are things on your plantation?" Papa said.

Chauncey averted his eyes to my father. "Oh, they're well so far, besides a few runaways."

"Runaways?" Papa's eyes widened, leaning back in his chair.

"Yes, the Murphy sisters. They disappeared a couple days ago after my field hand Old man Eldon was found dead." Chauncey unfolded his napkin and tucked it in his collar.

Papa snorted a laugh. "What's the matter? Your overseers can't control your slaves either?"

"Nah, word has it there's some trifling abolitionists in town stealing slaves off of folks' plantations," Chauncey said.

Startled by the rumor, I raised my head but remained quiet and continued listening to the conversation. With the sudden departure of the Murphy girls from the McMillan plantation, Noah or his colleagues had to have something to do with their disappearance.

"Abolitionists?" Papa screwed up his face.

"Yeah," Chauncey said, "Mr. Weiss also said three of his went missing in broad daylight last week, but losing two kitchen helps doesn't make a difference for me. Besides, I can always get more of them." He smirked and glanced at my papa. "I'm sorry about your financial issues, Mr. Crabtree. Let me know if there's anything else I can do to help."

Papa nodded. "Thanks, Chauncey. You're a good, young man. Your father would be proud of the job you're doing on the McMillan estate."

"Thank you, sir." Chauncey stole a look at me. "I wish your daughter felt the same way as you do. But she will within time."

"I doubt it," I said blatantly.

Chauncey plastered on a smile and laughed at my reply. "Oh, Miss Millie, you're a delicate flower, but as stubborn as an ox, aren't you? We could be so happy together if you gave me the chance."

"I already danced with you during my birthday, Mr. McMillan," I said. "That's enough."

Chauncey smirked and leaned back in his chair. "And so, you did, and as I recall, you enjoyed my company. Did you not?"

Guilt pierced my stomach as I placed my napkin on my lap. "It was a mistake."

He chuckled. "Whatever you say, Miss Millie." He raised his brow and looked at my father. "Would you like me to say grace, sir?"

Papa shrugged. "Sure, if you'd like."

We all bowed our heads and Chauncey said a quick blessing, adding at the end for God to help me come to my senses and accept his marriage proposal.

"Amen," the two men said.

I said nothing and stared at my empty plate as my father and Chauncey served themselves a portion of everything. After taking small portions, I ate silently, picking over my food as the men changed the subject to the upcoming hunting season in the fall and shooting deer for venison. When dinner was over, Papa asked me to show Chauncey out of the house, but as an arranged couple, I knew it was so we could be alone.

THE FULL MOON HUNG in the cloudless, blackened sky like a silver dollar. Chauncey and I stood outside on the porch at night, listening to the chirping crickets. For a while, we were quiet and looking up at the moon shining on us.

"Well, Miss Millie, I guess this is goodnight," he said with a wry smile.

I sighed and wore a straight face. "Yes, I reckon it is. Be careful in the dark." I tugged at my tan knitted shawl and started walking back inside, but Chauncey grabbed my arm.

"Now, come on, Miss Millie, that's hardly a proper goodbye." Chauncey turned me toward him and held my arms tightly, planting a firm kiss on my lips. He gave a smirk, releasing me. "There, that wasn't so bad, was it? Goodbye, Miss Millie."

A lump caught in my throat and tears formed in my eyes, glaring at him. My dignity had been stolen away without me having a say in it, making me powerless. Stunned and terribly embarrassed, I felt as if he had stripped me naked in public. I had always pictured my first kiss to be with a polite gentleman, not a pompous imbecile. Now I knew a little about how Pearl must've felt with her secret encounter with my father—lost, helpless, and violated.

Chauncey rubbed a hand over his blond, parted hair and placed on his felt hat. He hopped in his carriage and rode down the dirt trail that led to our home.

I wiped my mouth and walked back into the house.

"Is he gone?" Papa asked from his centered desk in his office, smoking his pipe.

"Yes, and I hope you're happy!" I raced upstairs to my bedroom. Despite the dinner, my plan was still on. The only choice was to follow through with my intended journey. Chauncey had kissed me as he'd always wanted to do, and there was no stopping him until he had me for life.

Sobbing at my writing desk, I wrote a heartfelt letter, a farewell note to Papa. Although I hated his evil deeds and we couldn't agree, he was my father and I still loved him for that sake. When I finished the note, I placed down my pencil and skimmed my written words:

Dear Papa,

I'm writing this letter to say goodbye, but my prayers are with you. Though you and I don't agree on slavery and my writing dream, I still love you. But my affection isn't a gateway to comply with your will for me. I won't be a trade-off to increase your wealth or marry a man I don't love. I told you I was moving to the North, and that's exactly where I'm going. Please, don't try to find me. Just let me be and live my own life. I'm a young woman and not a child anymore. Trust me, I'll find my way and be fine. Please, don't be angry and forgive me.

Your beloved daughter

Millie

I folded the letter and placed it under my lantern. Then I gathered a few extra things I wanted to take, including my journal, a few pencils, and a small string pouch of coins. I tucked these things into my carpetbag, said my prayers, and changed into my nightgown and robe.

While my father worked on his figures in his ledger, I snuck upstairs to the attic for Pearl.

I knocked on her door. "Pearl, it's me Millie."

She opened the door with a startled look. "Millie?"

"Come on and follow me. You should go to the cellar. Papa's on the first floor, sitting at his writing desk in his office." I led Pearl out of the attic and downstairs toward the hallway.

I glanced behind me at her. "Let me check the hallway first." Peeking around the corner, George was standing on the embroidered carpet runner in the middle aisle, dusting off a wall shelf. He placed a vase of pink roses on the shelf and walked off to another room with his gray feather duster.

"It's safe. Hurry!" I whispered to Pearl.

She ran with me around the corner into the narrow hall by the cellar.

"There's a secret trap door under the center rug. You can hide in there until you leave with the others," I said, opening the door.

Pearl hugged me. "Thank you, Millie. I appreciate this." She entered the cellar, closing the door.

Because the door didn't lock, I wasn't completely confident my father wouldn't find her in there, but I didn't want Pearl to worry herself. Before I went to sleep, I prayed Papa wouldn't become brave and check the cellar. If he was desperate enough to find her, there was no telling what he would do, or where he would search for her.

THE MOON WAS HIGH in my window when Papa barged into my bedroom.

"Where's Pearl?" he said. "She was resting in her attic room a few hours ago."

I sat up and looked at him as he placed his lantern on my writing desk and approached my bed. His large shadow loomed behind him across the wall like a black, deformed monster.

"Where is she? I can't find her!" Papa stood over me.

My chin bobbed, staring at his wide-eyed, full-bearded face. "I . . . I don't know. Maybe she went to the outhouse."

My father knitted his brows. "She's gone running again, hasn't she?" He slapped me and cradled my face in his large hand, shaking me violently.

"Hasn't she?" he urged for my response.

"I don't know!" My heart thumped so hard I thought it would burst to my death.

"Jed and I are going after her. You stay here, you hear me?" Papa warned. "Don't you step a foot outta this house! Not one!" He marched out of my bedroom and slammed the door as he had before.

I stood on my knees on my bed and peeked out of my window.

Papa's horse was ready to go, and Jed was pulling his saddled horse out from the barn with a lantern in one hand. Over at the row of slave quarters, there wasn't a flicker of light lit in one of the wooden cabins, but a few of the brick chimneys puffed with smoke. By the looks of it, everyone appeared asleep in their cots. My father and Jed mumbled and fussed about Pearl. They rode their horses down the dirt trail in the distance between the two cotton fields.

I watched them until I couldn't spot them past the nearly bare stems of the fields.

Now was everyone's chance—it was time to go.

Seeing my father had become a maniac, he and Jed would be out searching for Pearl until sunrise; at least, that's what I suspected for a slave worth a thousand dollars. As the most expensive slave, Pearl held great value in my father's eyes. Hence, another reason why he cherished her so much above many of the other slaves.

Leaping out of bed, I changed out of my nightgown into my blue-and white plaid day dress. Then I pulled on a pair of cotton stockings and tied on my leather, patent boots. Lastly, I pinned my hair in a simple bun and tied my white cloth scarf around my neck. Staring at my reflection in the mirror one last time, I took a deep breath and released a nervous exhale, relaxing my tensed shoulders. *You're a young woman, Millie. You can do this. It's time to live your own life.* Canada was hundreds of miles upon miles away from North Carolina. We had a long, rugged journey ahead, but I was ready—prepared to run for freedom and fight through whatever battles and challenges were thrown at us along the way.

Carrying my heavy carpetbag, I rushed out of my bedroom to wake the others. First, I woke Margaret, who went downstairs to quickly gather some food for the journey. While she was in the kitchen, I entered the cellar to get Pearl.

Beside a stack of firewood, there was a gray circle rug spread on the floor. I removed the rug and opened the trap door. "Pearl, are you still there?"

"Yes, I'm here," Pearl answered, looking at me from below. "Your Papa came inside and searched the cellar, but he never thought to look under here."

"Good." I gestured my hand. "Come on, you have to get outta here."

Pearl blew out the lantern she had lit and climbed up the ladder out of the secret trap door. "Why are you dressed and holding your bag?"

"I'm coming with you and the others," I said, closing the trap door.

Pearl fluttered her eyes in disbelief. "You are?" She tilted her head and placed her hand on my shoulder.

"Are you sure you should? You could get in a lot of trouble for this, Millie."

"As long as I can get away from Chauncey, I'll be fine, Pearl," I said. "Besides, I promised to help you get your freedom, didn't I? I want to keep my promise, and assisting Noah is the way I can do that. Now, let's go."

We left the cellar and entered the kitchen where Margaret tied a bundle of apples and biscuits into a checkered cloth. Afterward, I grabbed my father's gold compass and his Navy revolver from the drawer of his centered, mahogany desk.

As a Christian woman, I wasn't entirely comfortable carrying a weapon, but I suspected it was necessary with our lives in danger. I tucked them into my carpetbag in case we needed them. All of us gathered into the first slave quarter on the right as planned with some of the other slaves.

A fire danced and crackled in the brick furnace, and another lantern burned on a small square table. Randall was lying on one of the bottom wooden cots, resting his sprained ankle. Anna and Ozzie sat beside each other on an adjacent bottom cot from Randall. Joseph was sitting at the table with the lantern. As we entered, Pearl sat on the floor and quietly conversed with Randall.

Randall inched up a smile and lovingly stroked her cheek.

I closed the door and surveyed the small, dimly lit room.

During the summer night, it was moderately warm inside with a comfortable chill in the air. Cool wind seeped through the cracks of the wooden boards of the walls, flickering the glowing, red-orange flames in the fireplace.

"All right, what's da big secret?" Joseph said, irked.

"My papa's planning to sell you, Anna, and Margaret to clear our money debt, but you don't need to worry. An abolitionist is coming soon."

"Abolitionist?" Ozzie wrinkled his wide forehead.

"Actually, it's more than one," I added. "Papa and Mr. McMillan talked about it during dinner tonight. Many slaves are leaving their masters' plantations, running for freedom to Canada, just like in the papers. One of the abolitionists met with me one night. He's the redhead violinist who performed at my birthday party. He's on his way here."

"When?" Joseph folded his arms on the table.

"He should be here any minute," I said, "but we shouldn't answer the door unless he says the proper code word."

"What's the code word again?" Margaret asked.

I thought a moment and recalled the phrase. "He said it's 'A friend of friends.'"

Anna held her blue shawl around her, shivering. "I sure hope he comes soon."

"Me too." Margaret knelt near Anna and her brother on the hard floor. "Sitting around here too long, Massa Crabtree's fixin to find us."

Some branches snapped outside and everyone fell silent.

Anna flinched and grasped her big brother's arm. "Oh, God, what waz dat?"

A knock came from outside and startled us more.

Ozzie, a tall and powerfully built man, hushed the group of us whimpering and took charge of everyone's protection. He stepped to answer and gripped the knob, placing his ear to the cabin's door. "Who is it?"

"A friend of friends," a young man said.

Ozzie glanced at everyone from the distance and carefully opened the door, standing behind it.

The slaves gasped and looked at the short gentleman.

"Hello, dear friends," he said with a smile, removing his hat and catching his breath.

It was Noah.

10 *Running for Freedom*

RELIEF SETTLED WITHIN ME from Noah's presence. The time was short, so everything said in the secret meeting was quickly explained as Pearl and the others needed to go on their way. Noah had brought his violin case, but there were other things he had hidden inside it. He joined Joseph at the small table, placing his case on top of it.

"My father and the overseer went looking for my friend Pearl," I said. "Marge, Anna, and Joseph will go first along with her. They're are in danger of being sold tomorrow morning. Please, you must help them."

"All right, Millie. I'll do my best." Noah turned his attention to the others and exhaled a slow breath. "I'm deeply sorry for the bondage you've all suffered, but there's hope. However, before we leave there are some things you should know. So, please, listen closely to everything I say."

Everyone gathered around the table as Noah opened his case and took out a tan, square paper, unfolded it, and laid it out over the table. It was a map of the United States, marked with trails across the Southern and Midwestern states and arrows pointing up to cities of Canada.

Noah shifted his eyes, focused and determined. "The way to Canada from here is a long, tiring, and perilous journey. So, it's crucial for those of you accompanying me to follow my instructions. For your safety, we'll travel at night or early morning while it's still dark." He explained the route. "First, we'll need to go through the wooded forest and Willow Creek. The water of the creek is deep, so you'll need to be careful when crossing it. Once we've passed these, we'll follow a dirt trail through a grassland and walk across a large meadow. Then we'll go to the prairie where my colleague Hubert Duncan will take you to your first rest stop."

"Rest stop?" Anna said, intrigued.

Noah nodded. "Yes, throughout your journey there will be safe houses or 'stations' for fugitive slaves. All of them will be marked by a burning candle in a window. Within the Underground Railroad network, we use code words and phrases. Whenever you reach one of these safe houses, greet the homeowners or 'station masters' with the password, 'A friend with friends.'"

He pointed on the map and traced the trail with his forefinger. "After Asheville, you'll cross into a place called

Kingsport, Tennessee where a housewife will take you in. Her husband is supposed to be out of town, but he's pro-slavery, so you must be careful at this stop. If it isn't safe to be in their house, she'll wave to signal you all a warning to hide into their barn. From there, you'll go to Scott County, Virginia, which is about fifteen miles from Kingsport. An immigrant farmer will give you food and refuge in his home. Afterward, my colleague Arthur Wagner will ride you into Harlan County, Kentucky."

He licked his lips and surveyed the group of eager slaves. "In Harlan County, you'll take another rest stop before being driven by an old farmer to Lexington. He'll also take you to the Louisville and Nashville Depot. Now, I'll help you through the wilderness and later meet you all in Louisville where you'll go aboard the train and cross the Ohio River into Cincinnati. Some of you will ride along with me and the others of you will hide in coffins for your protection."

"Coffins?" Joseph wrinkled his face.

"Yes," Noah answered, "if all four of you at once board the train with me, the conductor will probably get suspicious. It would be too risky without certified papers for each of you. It's safer if some of you stay hidden; at least, until after we reach the Michigan state line. The rider, who's an undertaker, will have coffins in his wagon. These he'll transfer into a boxcar of the train." He sighed and continued. "After another rest top, from Cincinnati, you'll take on a lengthy journey into Toledo,

Ohio. From there, you'll go from Toledo to Detroit, Michigan. Then you'll sail in a businessman's ship across the Detroit River into a place called Windsor in Canada."

He folded the map and placed it back in his case, looking at Pearl and the others. "I'll do my absolute best to assist you, but there's a chance I could get caught before we reach the destination. If this happens, you all must help one another and stick together. Many slaves made it themselves to freedom. It simply takes wise choices, strength, and courage to survive the rest of the journey."

"Is that everything?" I asked.

Noah nodded again. "Yes, that's the whole journey." He closed his case and turned his attention back to the others again. "We should leave now." He stood from the table. "I've carried some cayenne pepper with me in my jacket. It'll throw off our body scents in case we have to outrun some dogs."

"I'm coming too," I spoke up.

Noah paused, stunned. "What? It's too dangerous. You should stay with your father."

"No, I want to go," I said.

Noah stood in front of me and gripped my shoulders. "I can't let you do that, Millie. You're . . . not strong enough for this."

"Who do you think I am?" I looked up and studied him. "I'm not a child or little girl, Mr. Shepherd. I'm a young woman."

He frowned and released out a weary sigh. "Do you understand the risk you're taking, Millie? You could get prosecuted and thrown in jail."

"I don't care." Unshed tears filled my eyes. "I cannot bear to stay on my father's plantation anymore, waiting to relive the miserable life of my late mother. My father's arranged for me to marry Chauncey McMillan for partnership in his plantation. You didn't know that, did you? I want to be a children's author and a woman with more opportunities. And you said, 'Never let anyone crumple my dreams.' That there's a whole world outside the South."

"And so, I did." Noah smiled slowly. "All right, fine, but don't say I didn't warn you. The journey won't be an easy one."

My spirits buoyed. "Thank you. I have my father's compass and his pistol in my bag in case we need it."

"Good thinking," Noah said, "we might need it for bounty hunters." He grabbed his violin case and walked to the door as everyone gave farewell hugs and said their goodbyes to Ozzie and Randall.

"Goodbye, little sis. Make it to Canaan for Mama and Papa. Take care now, ya hear?" Ozzie kissed his sister's forehead.

"I will, Ozzie. I love you." Anna embraced her older brother.

"Let's go," Noah ordered.

The others and I trailed in single file behind Noah out of the cabin, keeping a lookout for my Papa and the overseer. Seeing no one, we ran across the front lawn into the forest aside from the white-pillared house. First entering, it was so dark by the canopy of leafy trees I couldn't see my hand in front of my face.

I hadn't realized how big the forest was until we ran and ran down a long trail for what seemed like forever. Having a lantern would've helped, but we couldn't risk getting caught by the light. Owls hooted, frogs croaked, and locusts droned. I couldn't see these wild animals in my whereabouts, but I was more concerned about not tripping on a rock or tree root; or worse, getting bitten by a snake.

"Maybe we should try in the morning," Jed said, walking and leading his horse by the reins.

"I reckon you're right," Papa agreed and growled. "But if we can't find her, I'll send for a bounty hunter or two. She's my most expensive slave, and I've suffered enough financial loss as it is."

"Quick, behind the trees!" Noah whispered, looking back at me and the others.

We dodged behind two huge oak trees and ducked down while Papa and Jed walked by us with their horses and lantern toward the mansion.

It grew quiet and Noah checked if we were all alone. Once we saw we were safe, we continued our journey a few extra miles through the forest.

I took a deep inhale of the smell of wet earth and already sensed my liberty. It felt wonderful leaving behind the tainted, Southern customs of my family. A couple of times, I snapped twigs and my long dress got snagged on sharp, overgrown bushes and branches of the trees. But thankfully, my socks hadn't gotten soaked from the water puddles I splashed in with my boots.

At last, in the middle of the forest, we stopped to rest for the night. Like a sickle, the silver crescent moon in the black velvet sky beamed above our heads, a sign an angel of God was surely watching over us.

"All right, we'll sleep here." Noah exhaled loudly and plopped on a pile of dead leaves. "In the morning, we'll cross the creek."

Pearl and I sat on a tree log covered with thick moss on Noah's left side. We shared her brown shawl around our shoulders from the chill of the summer night. I reckon I should've brought one for myself, but I was so in the rush to run away I hadn't thought of it.

"Phew, good Lord." Margaret panted, exhausted. "Thank you, Mr. Shepherd, I needed a rest. Anybody hungry?"

"Not me," Anna said and shook her head.

Joseph narrowed his eyes. "Whatcha got in dat bundle?"

"Just apples and biscuits," Margaret answered.

"Gimme an apple," Joseph said.

Margaret untied the cloth bundle. She threw Joseph an apple, which he caught in his hands.

"How much longer until we reach the end of the forest?" I asked.

Noah took off his fedora and wiped his forehead. "Not too long. We're a couple of miles away from your father's place now." He dug his elbows into the ground, reclined back on the leaves for a bed, and placed his hat over his tired face.

I folded my arms on my knees and bowed my head as everyone else likewise adjusted as comfortably as they could get and fell asleep. Tomorrow would be a rough and frightening day for us all.

11 *Escaping the Hunters*

T HE BARKS OF ANGRY dogs in the forest awoke me from my sleep and dread plunged into my gut. I raised my head from resting on my crossed arms and gasped, feeling a strong sense of alarm throughout my body. *Bounty Hunters*. It was time to move again. The others were still asleep shoulder-to-shoulder against the hard trunks of oak trees. Noah yawned and awakened, adjusting his hat.

"We have to run," I said, jumping to my feet. "Bounty hunters are coming."

"I know." Noah rubbed the tiredness from his face. "Everyone, wake up."

Turning toward Pearl, I nudged her shoulder. "Wake up, Pearl. We're running again."

"Huh?" Pearl fluttered her hazel eyes at the dappled sunlight.

"We have to run. Come on." Grabbing her arm, I helped her from the ground to her feet. Margaret, Anna, and Joseph likewise awoke. We ran farther into the forest as the hunters with their bloodhounds trailed behind our path. Mumbling voices of men drew closer as they and the dogs rattled through the underbrush.

"Follow me, son. We're gonna catch us some stray negroes," one of them said.

Noah stayed last in line and allowed everyone else to run ahead of him.

Leaning against a tree trunk, I glanced back out of concern and paused a second, catching my breath. Using his clever wisdom, Noah took a small jar of cayenne pepper from his jacket pocket and sprinkled some in different spots, mixing it with the dirt and dried leaves so the dogs would lose our scents.

"Don't wait for me! Keep running!" he urged in a whisper.

I continued following the others as Noah trotted behind me. We ran until we reached the end of the forest and came to the rocky creek. Large, brown and black rocks formed a path to the other side of dry grassland, but getting across them would be a challenge. As Noah warned in the cabin, the water was deep and reached our waists. I took off my shoes and socks so not to get them wet—as did the other women—and put them in my carpetbag. But Joseph was the only one who kept his shoes on. Caring more about his freedom, he leaped like a toad from one stone to another, leaving the women to fend for themselves. But I didn't blame him. Our lives were threatened and we couldn't afford to lag behind.

Along the way, I slipped and missed a step. Splashing in the gurgling flow of water, a shock from its coldness injected through my system.

Pearl looked wide-eyed at me from a short distance. "Millie! Are you all right?"

"Yes," I answered and climbed to the surface of a rock. "Just keep running!"

She did as I asked and jumped from the last stone, joining the others on the grassland.

I checked behind and saw Noah not far away, gaining up on me.

"Everything fine, Miss Millie?" he asked.

I nodded and continued going across the rocks, holding my wet bag. Apparently, I should've done the same as Joseph, but I was a young lady of a wealthy family and accustomed to what seemed proper in my eyes.

After I made it to the grassland with the others, I squeezed the excess water from the skirt of my dress. Looking down, I discovered I had skinned my left knee. I wrung out one of my soaked stockings and tied it over my knee to stop the bleeding. Then I slipped my boots back on again.

"I think we're safe now," Noah said, when he reached the grass with us. "The bounty hunters must've been looking for someone else who ran off."

A gunshot fired in the distance behind us. For a long moment, there was dead silence. Nobody spoke as we listened to the babbling creek. Maybe we survived, but that fast; somehow, we knew someone—possibly a runaway slave—had died.

Noah wore a pensive face and bowed and shook his head, loss of words. He inhaled a slow, long breath and squared his shoulders, looking straight ahead. "We must keep moving." His words were forceful, knowing there was nothing he could do to help a dead slave.

Everyone else followed him, but I was stuck in a speechless daze. After running from the hunters and the vicious hounds, a flood of emotions washed over me as I realized an alarming epiphany, the fear and despair my fellow friends experienced every day of their lives.

How it felt to be a slave.

Slavery was a plight difficult to handle for anyone, and despite their hard labor to prosper the economy, slaves' lives held little value compared to the rest of society to be taken so ruthlessly.

Noah walked through the tall blades of grass toward me. With compassion in his brown, moist eyes, he spoke in a gentle voice of heartfelt concern. "You don't have to continue if you don't want to, Millie. I'll understand."

I wiped my runny nose with my trembling hand. "No . . . I-I wanna go on. I have to keep moving."

"All right," Noah said. "We're going to the meadow. Everyone be careful and look out for rattlesnakes."

Rattlesnakes? I wasn't prepared for those long critters, but I willed back my tears and drew a brave inhale, following him and the others.

For several minutes, we traveled uphill as the dirt trail between the forest grassland became steeper to walk on. Then we passed a rocky waterfall in the forest and stepped across a meadow of grassy undergrowth flowing with a long, leafy stream. The cool breeze was refreshing and relieved some of the humidity from the heat and the sun flickering in my face.

Thankfully, we saw no rattlesnakes, but we came upon a few purple, flower plants that I thought were beautiful. I started to pick one off, but after Noah said they were poisonous, I backed away. For two days, we stopped and traveled through the steep grassland and the meadow until we finally reached the prairie fields, seeking refuge two nights in a row in the woods. I didn't expect it to take so long, but as Noah said, the journey North was long and tiresome.

Once we reached the prairie, for hours on end, we journeyed through a field of dried, straw-like grass like golden hay. The rough, bristly texture brushing against my raw, damp skin and the invisible sting of buzzing mosquitos made me itch. I stopped from time to time and slapped and scratched my legs. For several acres, we saw nothing, except a couple of pine trees. At first, I thought we were going in the wrong direction, but Noah was the leader, so I reckoned he knew better than me.

He paused and scanned the open field, blocking the sunlight from his face. "We'll wait here."

"Oh, thank the Lord," Anna exclaimed.

I chuckled and plopped on the ground with the others, all of us hiding in the middle of the wild, yellow field. Taking a rest stop, I took advantage of the time and slipped on a new pair of socks and replaced my shoes.

Margaret opened her bundle she carried with her and offered everyone food.

"Have something?" she said, smiling and holding open the checkered cloth.

Two biscuits and three apples were left.

"Thanks, Marge." I smiled and grabbed an apple. Biting into the crisp, sweet fruit, my stomach rumbled and growled. It was the first, decent thing I'd eaten this morning. Seeing everyone eating one or the other, the apples and biscuits Margaret brought along wouldn't last us much longer.

I hoped we'd make it to Canada without dying of starvation. Some minutes later, hoofbeats and squeaky wheels of a wagon came toward us up the dusty trail. I crawled over and peeked from behind the straw weeds, squinting at the sun and clouds of dust kicked up by the wagon. A fat man wearing a wide-brimmed hat and farmer's clothes held the reins. Something about him seemed familiar, and the closer he got, I recalled where I'd seen him.

"Whoa, boy!" he said in a deep and mellow voice, coming to a halt.

"Everyone, this is Hubert Duncan. You can trust him," Noah said, gesturing a hand. "He's come to take you to the first safe house over the hill."

"You're?" I blinked in disbelief and hung open my mouth.

"Yes," Noah said, "the cellist from your birthday party. We were all undercover, Millie."

The fat man's plump, rosy cheeks rose, grinning at the group of us. "Everyone, hurry under the sheet before someone sees you. Hurry now!"

Pearl and the others scrambled into the wagon filled with sackcloth bags of potatoes. They hid under the cream-colored sheet, while I joined the driver on the front seat.

"Aren't you coming?" I asked Noah, concerned.

He shook his head. "No. I'll meet you at the train station in Louisville, Kentucky. You're the guardian for now, Millie, but the station masters will assist you. Be careful and look out for your friends."

"I promise I'll do my best," I said.

"Godspeed," Noah told Hubert.

Hubert tipped his hat. "Same to you, Shepherd." He struck his reins and drove off, taking us to the nearest safe house for the night.

Looking back at Noah as he waved and faded in the summer haze, I felt a great sense of responsibility for the task laid out before me.

Being a conductor.

12 *The First Safe House*

LIGHTNING FLASHED AND THUNDER rolled across the night sky. I shivered from the chill of the air in my seat as the whistling wind blew and crackled the surrounding branchy trees. By the time we stopped, I was ready for some proper rest before continuing our journey. My eyes barely stayed open, as the toss and rock of the wagon on the bumpy dirt road kept me awake. When I was almost asleep, we arrived at the first safe house and the wagon came to a forward halt.

"We're here," Hubert said. "Y'all can hop out. Stay safe. Make sure you give the password. Miss Perkins will provide you all with a meal and rest for early tomorrow."

My eyelids fluttered, coming wide awake. "Oh, all right. Thank you, sir." After climbing down from the high back seat with my carpetbag, I pulled the sheet off the back of the wagon. All of the others were asleep in a huddle, but gradually awoke from their rest.

Pearl and the others climbed out, and then Hubert turned around his wagon and rode back from whence he came.

More thunder rumbled as we glanced up at the North Star, shining and peeking out of the monstrous clouds.

"Oh, lord, it's gonna rain. What we do now?" Anna asked, rubbing the chill from her arms.

"Over yonder!" Joseph pointed at a little, gray house entangled with pink rose vines and guarded by a white picket fence. "A candle burns in the window."

"Yes," I said, "a lady named Miss Perkins lives here. I'll give her the password." I unlatched the picket fence and walked up the brick, paved pathway to the entrance. Taking a deep breath, I knocked on the front door.

"Who is it?" The woman's voice was weak and shaky.

"A friend with friends, ma'am," I answered.

The door whined open and there stood a thin, elderly woman in a black dress and white apron tied around her small waist. She wore circle, wire-framed eyeglasses on the tip of her pug nose, and a sheer white bonnet worn over her silver curls, tied under her chin. Her smile was warm and wholesome, and she supported herself with a wooden cane in one hand. She glanced behind me at the group of others.

"Welcome, child, and tell thine friends to come in likewise," the old woman said.

"Thank you, ma'am." I signaled to the others, and they followed me inside the lady's home.

Miss Perkins closed the door after Margaret entered. "I've got chicken and dumplings cooking in the kitchen. I also took out a tray of corn muffins too. Have a seat anywhere in the sitting room. Aside from passengers, I don't get too many visitors anyway." She gave a little, teasing laugh and walked with her cane into the kitchen.

Joseph and Anna sat on the floor by the unkindled fireplace, while Margaret, Pearl, and I sat in a row on a long settee draped with a multicolored knitted throw.

The lady served each of us a steamy bowl of her chicken and dumplings and a muffin. We ate and listened to her speak while she reclined in her rocking chair, talking about herself in the Society of Friends. She said most Quakers had moved to Ohio due to harassment from anti-abolitionist mobs. Afterward, she spoke about a list of other "passengers" who she housed that made it to freedom.

"One might think at my old age I shouldn't remember them," she said, rocking away, "but I do. My frail body is slowly failing me, but my memory is as sharp as a tack. The first ones were Johnny and Pam. They were brother and sister. Their slave master sold their parents long before they knew who they were. Johnny liked to go fishing, and Pam said her favorite season was spring." She stopped rocking and looked at us with a gentle smile. "You all knowst I'm Miss Winifred Perkins. I'd like it if you all introduced yourselves to me."

Joseph ate a spoonful and wiped his mouth with the long-sleeve of his olive-green, tattered shirt. "Name's Joe, ma'am, but dere ain't much to no about me. I ain't seen my mama since I was four. I reckon I'm the same as most other slaves, tryin to keep my head above water. I ain't got no family aside from those I lived with on Massa Crabtree's plantation."

Miss Perkins eyed the young woman in a blue shawl, sitting beside Joseph on the floor. "And thou, miss?"

"I be Anna," she said and bowed her head. "My big brother Ozzie. He . . . he still left on the plantation. I and the others had to run cause Massa Crabtree waz gonna sell us. I caint read, but I like to learn after gittin my freedom in the Promised Land."

"Greetings, Miss Anna," Miss Perkins said, "I'm pleased to meet thee."

Anna wore a shy smile and nodded. "Likewise."

"I'm Marge," Margaret said, "I been a house slave since I was a young girl, but I can make a good pot of hot stew; beans, chicken, beef, any kind you can think of."

"That's nice. How dost thou like my chicken and dumplings? I hope I did them justice," Miss Perkins said and started rocking again.

Margaret grinned. "Oh, it's fine, ma'am. Best meal I had for hours."

"And who art thou?" Miss Perkins asked, looking at my best friend.

"I'm Pearl, ma'am," she said, "I worked in the cotton fields as a child, but later became a house slave. I came to Crabtree Plantation when I was nine. My pappy was Massa Addison from Fayetteville. He sold my mama after she . . . after she had me. He took what he wanted and gave her away like she was nothing. Never saw her again."

Dreadful silence filled the room.

I studied Pearl's dull expression and sobbed for her. Her old emotions from childhood were still there, her hurt of losing her beloved mother, and a white, selfish father who disowned her. I could only imagine the scars of her pain caused by him, my Papa's advances, and the insufferable curse of slavery. When it was my turn to speak, I could hardly say anything. For my story couldn't compare to what the others went through, but I spoke up anyway.

"And thou, ma'am? What has thou traveling with the others?" Miss Perkins asked.

I opened my mouth and hesitated. "My . . . my name's Mildred, but folks call me Millie. My dream is to be a published author someday. I'm the daughter of Master Crabtree, but he and I don't see eye to eye, especially over slavery. I ran away from my father's plantation to escape an arranged, unhappy marriage. My mother was sickly and suffered several miscarriages. She died on my eighteenth birthday some time ago."

Miss Perkins knitted her sparse brows. "Oh, I'm sorry to hear that." Her wrinkled, saggy face lifted. "But it's wonderful thou want to be an author. There are many women authors in the North. Back in March, Mrs. Harriet Beecher Stowe recently published *Uncle Tom's Cabin.* It's caused quite a stir in the public eye about slavery and said to have advanced and influenced the anti-slavery movement. Have thou read that one?"

"No, ma'am," I answered, "but I've read about its publication in the *Carolina Watchman* newspaper."

"What dost thou like writing?" Miss Perkins asked, raising her eyebrows.

I smiled, flattered by her interest in my creative endeavor. "Children's fiction, ma'am."

"She's pretty good," Pearl said, smiling. "I read some of her work."

Miss Perkins stood slowly. "Lovely. I'll be looking forward to reading thy debut story. I'm an avid reader and like reading all kinds of books, but my favorite is romance. I suppose because I haven't had one myself." She cackled her little laugh again. "But thee knowst, some men are kind of like books too. Hardback and full of words."

Flickers of lightning shined outside the windows and rolls of thunder rumbled over the house.

The old woman glanced up in wonder. "Oh, dear, a storm's fixin' to come."

"Good thing we got shelter," Anna said. "Thank you kindly, ma'am."

Miss Perkins beamed. "Thou art welcome, dear." She sighed and balanced herself. "If you all are through, you can place the dishes in the sink and hit the sack in here for the night."

"I can help clean up," Margaret offered and stood. She took Pearl's bowl from her and stacked everyone else's together, taking them to the kitchen.

"Thank you," Miss Perkins said. "I appreciate it."

"It's no bother at all, ma'am. It's the least I could do for your kindness," Margaret said, walking off.

Steady rain showered, tapped the roof, and slapped against the windows. That was when I remembered about my skinned knee and figured I should treat it properly while I still could.

"Miss Perkins?" I asked.

The old woman wore a warm smile. "Yes, dear?"

"We've come a long way, and I've personally skinned my knee on the way here. Do you have ointment and dressing we could use before we go tomorrow?"

"Certainly. I'll be right back, dear." Miss Perkins waddled into her bedroom for a moment and returned to me with a white rag, a small brown bottle of alcohol, and a roll of bandage. She placed them on the center table in the room.

"Thank you, ma'am," I said, smiling. As I raised the skirt of my plaid dress to tend to my knee, Joseph—the only man in the room—turned his head and looked away from me.

"Thou art welcome, dear." Miss Perkins pointed her crooked forefinger. "There's scissors to cut the bandage in my sewing kit on the side table. Can thou get them, Pearl?"

"Yes, ma'am." Pearl opened the basket kit on the table beside her and took out the scissors. She handed them to me. "Here you go, Millie."

"Thank you." I took the rag and dabbed it with the alcohol from the bottle. Gently applying the alcohol to my knee, I bit my lip to withstand the burning sting as Miss Perkins went on talking about her first train ride.

"I suppose you all are looking forward to catching the train in Louisville. I remember my first ride. It was to visit my niece and her family in Portsmouth, Ohio," she said.

Anna gasped with enthusiasm. "Dat's wonderful! I ain't never been on a train before."

"Oh, it's marvelous," Miss Perkins said, smiling, "hearing the whistle and seeing the thick smoke rise up from the blast pipe . . . it's the greatest invention of the century." She sighed and took her head out of the clouds, returning to the present moment. "You all are some nice, kindhearted people."

"You too, ma'am." Pearl glanced at me. "How's your knee coming, Millie?"

I cut some bandage and wrapped it over my knee, applying more alcohol to help it stick. "It's all right. I'm sure it'll heal." I tied my stocking back on it for extra support. "I'm done. Much obliged, Miss Perkins."

"My pleasure, dear. I'm called to help others," Miss Perkins said. "The good Lord tells us, 'Love thy neighbor as thyself.' That's what my godly duty is, and why I've taken part in the railroad network. We're all special in the eyes of God, sacred gifts to the world." She picked up the candlestick from the sill on one of her front windows. "Sleep well, everyone." She blew out the flame.

"Night, Miss Perkins," we said in a cacophony of overlapped voices.

Everyone shut their eyes and rested in the sitting room on the floor or on the sofa as the old woman walked away, finally enjoying a peaceful night's rest. In the morning, we could finally begin leaving out of North Carolina and moving toward Tennessee.

I couldn't wait until we got to the train station and saw Noah again. As I fell into sleep, a smile spread on my lips and a little dance tickled my heart, recalling his smooth-sounding voice, his charming smile, and his vibrant, curly red hair. We barely knew each other, but for some odd reason, I missed him.

13 *Bounty Hunters*

WARM SUNLIGHT CARESSED MY face, waking me to a brand-new day. I was the first to awake in the room. Looking out the window at the sunrise, the sky was the most beautiful and amazing thing I had seen in a long time. It was a portrait of autumn during mid-summer, arrayed with brush strokes of golden yellow, orange pumpkin spice, fiery flames of red, and inky blue. The radiant sun was peeking behind a blanket of rolling grass hills in the distance, not yet risen above the horizon.

I smiled and admired the morning view, listening to the chirping of the early birds in the treetops. Today was going to be a long day, but a good one. I was sure of it.

Pearl stirred and yawned. "Good morning, Millie."

"Good morning, Pearl," I said. "Sleep well?"

Pearl shrugged and chuckled. "Well, it was better than the woods. How's your knee feel?"

I checked it under my dress. "It still stings some, but it's all right."

Pearl yawned again. "It's good you cleaned it. You don't want it to get infected. We still have a long way to go."

"Yes, that's true," I said with a wry smile. "I hope my bandage stays in place."

Miss Perkins came into the sitting room, tapping her cane on the hardwood floor as she took each one of her slow steps. "Rise and shine, everyone! Breakfast awaits."

"Breakfast?" Joseph yawned and stretched his arms.

"Yes, indeedy! Pork sausage, boiled eggs, and toast with jam," Miss Perkins said joyfully. "Help yourselves."

"I'll help serve." Margaret entered the kitchen and returned with a dish of breakfast in each of her hands. She handed one to Joseph and another to Anna and went to get three more for the rest of us and herself. She served me a plate of toast, a boiled egg and sausage like the others.

"Thank you, Marge," I said.

Miss Perkins sighed. "I'll miss you all. It gets quiet around here. My niece Tabitha thinks I should move up North with her and her family, but I'm an independent woman and I suppose I don't want to be a burden to them with my old age."

I bit my piece of toast as galloping horses' hooves sounded outside.

"That must be the driver," Miss Perkins said.

Pearl peeked out of the curtain of a front window behind the sofa and shook her head. "There's two men out there, but there's no wagon."

I panicked and looked out of the window too. Each of the men climbed from their saddled horse in front of the house. Fear skittered through my heart, looking at the others in the sitting room. "Pearl's right. I think they're bounty hunters. Papa talked about hiring one or two back in the forest."

A disturbing knock came from the front door. "Open up!"

"Quick! Hide into my bedroom and be silent," Miss Perkins whispered, shooing us out of the sitting room.

Another loud knock came.

The others and I left our plates of food and hurried into her bedroom aside from the sitting room.

I spied on the commotion through a crack in the bedroom door as she walked over to answer the visitors. "Who art thou?"

Watching her with uneasiness, she placed her ear to the door and waited for the password.

"We're two kind gentlemen passing through and looking for some folks. We're wondering if you've seen them, ma'am," the same man who spoke to the door said.

Miss Perkins opened the door.

My eyes grew wide at the two men standing in the doorway as the others and I eavesdropped on their conversation.

"My name's Jack Crenshaw, ma'am," one of the men said, holding a black cowboy hat. He was a tall, red-skinned man with slick, jet black hair who looked like an Injun. He wore an all-black outfit of a long-sleeve shirt, a leather vest, pants, boots, and gloves.

On his hip, he also wore a holster loaded with a gun. "My partner Sal and I wanted to know if you've seen four negro slaves; one man and three women. They may be with a young, white teenage girl named Millie. She's eighteen, of average height, and has brown hair with blue eyes. Mr. Crabtree hired us to catch the negroes and his daughter. Have you seen them?"

"No, sir," Miss Perkins said, shaking her head. "I haven't seen them. I don't get many visitors here in these parts, aside from family."

"Can we take a look around?" the other man asked, holding a tan bowler hat. He was a stout, negro man. He wore a white dress shirt, a brown-and-cream gingham vest, dark brown trousers fastened with braces, and light brown leather boots. Like the other, he carried a revolver in a holster.

"They're bounty hunters," I whispered to the others.

They gasped and flinched at my remark. Margaret and Anna bit their nails and huddled together, and Pearl stood closer to Joseph.

"Oh, no. What're we gonna do?" Pearl whispered.

Joseph grimaced and glanced at me and the other women. "I say we run for it. We ain't got no time waitin for a wagon."

"Where're we gonna go?" I said. "There's only a closet and no windows. They might see us and start shooting." Taking the pistol out of my carpetbag, my hands sweat and shook as I clicked down the hammer. Mama never thought it proper for women to use guns, but I knew what I might have to do for my sake and the others.

Kill somebody.

With frightened faces, we listened in on the men and Miss Perkins' conversation again.

"Well," Miss Perkins answered, "I uh . . . I was in the middle of cleaning. It's not a good time right now. I hate others seeing my house messy."

"Oh, we won't be here long, ma'am," Jack said.

"But I—"

Pushing Miss Perkins aside, Jack and Sal barged into the house. They put on their hats and surveyed the small sitting room, noticing the five plates of barely touched food.

Jack growled. He grabbed a plate on the table, tossed the food on the floor, and shattered the plate to pieces, terrifying the old, feeble woman. "Is somebody else here with you?"

Miss Perkins whimpered and fought to keep her composure. "They were, but they've left. My sons and grandsons. You know how men are. Please, I don't want any trouble."

"What's in there?" Sal looked directly at me and approached the bedroom, holding up his revolver.

My heart pounded as I closed my eyes and pointed the gun.

The door moved back against me and creaked open slowly—then, like a cannon during warfare, the gun fired and I smelt smoke.

"Aaaah!" Sal screeched.

"Hurry! It ain't a closet. It's a washroom through the door," Joseph said.

Opening my eyes, I found Sal on the floor, rocking and holding a hand over his charred and bleeding shin. Staring in shock, I couldn't move a muscle, as my feet were planted on the floor.

"Millie, come on!" Pearl yanked me from my steady gaze, leading me by my arm to follow the others as Sal fired with his other hand at the wall.

"Hey, girls! Get back here!" Jack's pounding footsteps followed after us as we sought refuge with the others into the washroom. Pearl and I locked the door, buying us some time before Jack could reach us.

The bounty hunter banged his fists on the door and twisted and rattled the knob. "Open up! I know you're in there!" He banged again.

"Joe! Open the window, Joe!" Margaret urged. She and Anna whimpered and cried, clinging to each other.

Joseph growled and struggled to lift the mildewed window. "I'm tryin but it stuck!"

The women and I looked around nervously from Joseph to the closed door. Jack continued bumping his body against it and fidgeting with the knob. The bangs became louder as the odds of escape stacked against us.

At last, Joseph wrestled open the window, and each one of the women climbed outside, including me. As I ran with the other women toward the wagon, two gunshots fired intermittently.

Joseph yelped after each shot, and I knew he'd been hit.

I gasped and my heart sank. Looking behind me, Joseph held a hand on his bleeding shoulder, following the rest of us.

A bald driver came riding in a covered wagon.

"Quickly! We haven't got much time!" the bald man with a wild, curled mustache said.

I never forgot his silly mustache. Although I didn't know his name yet, he was the same pianist from my birthday party. I presumed he was another undercover friend in the railroad network. Screaming and dodging sporadic gunshots, we ran over and gathered into the wagon. The driver struck his reins and rode up the paved road behind the small house.

Jack growled and shoved his gun in his holster.

As our wagon rode farther away from Miss Perkins' place, he raced back to the front of the house. It was a close one; but as for now, by the grace of God, we were safe and sound.

Now it was time to go to Asheville.

14 *In the Wilderness*

COMING FACE-TO-FACE with bounty hunters at Miss Perkins' house, we were aware of how much our lives were in danger, especially Pearl and the others. Gratitude filled my heart that we got away from the men, but it wouldn't be the last we'd see them. The driver, whose name I learned while riding was Arthur Wagner, drove for miles toward Kingsport, Tennessee. Like the others, I worried about Joseph. His arm and shoulder were bleeding badly from the shots, but Dr. Grayson was a long way from the road on which we traveled.

There wasn't a house or living soul anywhere, only green-leafed oak trees on both sides of the long, country road. The sun shone from a faded blue, cloudless sky, but the humidity was still clammy. Sweat beaded on my forehead and over my upper lip. Being wet and sticky from the climate and scorching weather, my dress and undergarments stuck against my moist skin, making me uncomfortable. Hours passed since this morning. I wondered if we had left North Carolina yet.

"How much farther before we arrive to Kingsport?" I wiped my forehead.

Arthur twitched his mustache. "Not much longer. Do you see them?"

I glanced at the dirt road behind us. "Not anymore. I think we've out ridden them. Can we take a rest? Joseph can't last much longer without tending to his wounds."

"Of course," Arthur said, "but it can't be too long. We've got to keep moving to stay ahead." He pulled over into a forest filled with a field of twigs and dried leaves. "Whoa, boy."

The horse came to a halt.

I hopped from the wagon and checked on Joseph and the others. "Is everyone all right back here?"

Joseph lay motionless on his back, comforted in the arms of Margaret. Anna sat on one side of the two of them, while Pearl sat on the other side, all of the women looking at the poor injured man.

"We ladies fine," Anna said, "but I think Joe's thirsty."

I looked at Joseph as he moaned, tossing and turning his head. His face was slick with sweat and the right shoulder and sleeve of his green shirt were stained with his blood.

"He probably is," I said. "I'll get the canteen."

I walked back to the front of the wagon. "Can we use your canteen?"

"Certainly, here." Arthur handed me his canteen.

I returned to the back of the wagon. "Sit him up."

Margaret and Anna helped Joseph sit upright.

"Is there a doctor nearby?" Pearl asked, desperately.

I shook my head. "Not for miles, I afraid. I can wash his wounds, but it's about all I can do. First, he needs water. Here, Joseph. Drink, but not too much." I handed him the canteen in his strong hand.

"Thank you, Miss Millie." He drank a few gulps and gave the canteen back to me, wiping his mouth on his clean sleeve.

My eyes welled from the hopeless looks on their faces. If I had taken some of the bandage from Miss Winifred, I could've wrapped Joseph's arm. But even with that on, if the bullets ruptured vessels, he would get worse from too much blood loss.

I unbuttoned and rolled up the left sleeve of Joseph's green shirt to his shoulder. Abrasion rings had seared his shoulder and the back of his arm from the close range shot of Jack's revolver. The bullets could hardly be seen, lodged in the inner muscles of his shoulder and triceps, surrounded by circular tattoos of gunpowder.

Pouring water over his wounds, I washed off the soot and some of the dried blood. "Marge, do you have the cloth from the bundle of food you brought?"

"Yessum," she said, "it's in my apron pocket." She took it out and gave it to me.

I bound it over Joseph's arm and shoulder as a sling to apply pressure. "I know it's tight, but maybe it'll stop the bleeding."

Joseph wore a half-smile. "Thanks, Miss Millie. God bless you."

I pleaded with him, feeling responsible for the others' lives. "Please, don't leave us. Hold on, Joseph, I beg you."

"I'll try," Joseph replied with a nod, "but regardless of what happens to me, I thank you for your help . . . for not letting me die on your Papa's plantation. You an angel, Miss Millie."

"Let him rest and make sure he drinks water. I'll leave the water back here for you and the others." I handed the canteen over to Pearl. "If he bleeds more, one of you rip some cloth off your dress to bind him."

"All right. Thank you," Anna said, helping Margaret lie Joseph back down.

I climbed back on the front of the wagon and sat in the high-raised seat beside Arthur. Then the journey continued until nightfall.

ARTHUR PULLED OVER IN the neighboring woods, and we stayed there for another short rest stop. Thankfully, Arthur had a couple of packages of homemade bread and a crate of fruit preserves in the wagon, which he shared with us. He said he'd gotten them from his aunt on the way over to Miss Perkins' house. While the others ate, I took a light face and hand wash in a slow-flowing stream. After I returned, I checked on Joseph in the wagon and discovered he was getting worse.

"Joe's got chills," Margaret said, terrified.

Dumbfounded, I stared at Joseph. His breaths were rapid, his body shivering with trembles. He mumbled for his mama and spoke words Margaret informed me was a Gullah dialect I couldn't understand, tossing and turning his head. Being in the wilderness, I didn't know what to do, but Joseph needed immediate help.

One side of the checkered cloth tied on his upper arm was completely stained red from his blood. It was clear the shots had broken a couple of veins. I hoped his physical reactions weren't the onset of lead poisoning, but fever from a mild infection.

I rushed to Arthur who'd returned after me from refilling his canteen at the stream. "We have to find help. Joseph needs a doctor."

"I know," Arthur said. "We'll be making another rest stop in town soon. After a few more miles, we'll reach the second safe house at my Aunt Ethel's place. We've got a few days before we reach Kingsport, Tennessee." He handed the canteen to Pearl. "Make him drink and keep him calm."

"Where're we now?" Anna asked.

"Most likely somewhere in the outskirts of Charlotte, still in North Carolina. We should reach my aunt's house by early morning." Arthur climbed back on the wagon.

I gripped the smooth, wooden edge of the back of the wagon, eyeing Joseph. *Hold on, Joseph. Please, hold on.*

Margaret sobbed and stroked Joseph's short, woolly, receding hair. "We'll be praying while we travel."

"Good," I said, "I will too." I joined Arthur up front, and he struck his reins and continued riding along the way again.

We journeyed down the road until it turned from a dirt trail to a paved highway. Whispering prayers for Joseph, I dozed in and out of sleep, pleading and hoping to God he'll survive the next few miles. After sunrise, I blocked the bright sun from my vision and looked over a barbed-wire fence at the open cotton fields, reminded of my former life. Should I have come? Was running away worth risking my life for?

These were easy questions to answer for the others; but as a naive and spoiled young lady; for me, it was different. We still had a way to go and there was no telling what was coming next. So many slaves died for the sake of their freedom. Was I willing to do the same for mine? Despite my differences, life for me in my family's mansion was safe and comfortable, and I didn't need to worry about anything other than my future.

I glanced back at the others in the wagon.

Anna and Pearl fell asleep, but Margaret was the only one still awake. I don't believe she ever went to sleep during the entire ride from the woods, watching Joseph like a mother hawk guarding her chick. Tears trickled from her eyes as she held Joseph's hand to one of her cheeks. She had torn a piece from the skirt of her tan dress and tied it to Joseph's arm to seep up more of his blood. Hoping help wasn't too late for him, I sighed and hung my head in prayer again. *God, we're getting there—closer to the Promised Land. Please, help Joseph and spare him to see it. Amen.*

15 *The Second Safe House*

ARTHUR STOPPED IN FRONT of a small brick house and pulled back the brake of the wagon. He let out a whistling exhale and swiped his forehead. "All right, everyone wake up." He hopped from the wagon as the others awoke from their sleep. Then he approached the front door of the low porch. Before he got there, an older, slender woman in a white nightgown and wrapped in a gingham robe came out on the porch. She wore a white nightcap and had a long, braided ponytail down her shoulder.

"Why, Arthur, back so soon? Couldn't get enough of my— "she paused in mid-sentence and stared at the rest of us— "who do we have here?"

Arthur sighed. "They're fugitives. I was wondering, if we could rest here a while?"

"Oh, no, not again," his aunt said, raising her hands, "I don't want no trouble."

Arthur stood on the porch. "Please, Aunt Ethel. We've got a hurt man in the back of the wagon. He needs help badly."

"I'm a Christian woman who believes in helping needy souls, but I'm putting my life on the line, Arthur." Aunt Ethel sighed and thought a second, hesitating to grant her nephew's wish. She smacked her lips and waved her hands. "Oh, all right, but make sure they're gone by tonight."

"Thanks, auntie," Arthur said, smiling.

"Thank you, ma'am," Margaret said from the back of the wagon.

I climbed from the front of the wagon and followed Arthur to the back.

Arthur unfastened the back of the canopy. "I'm not a doctor, but my aunt taught me to sew, so I'm good with a needle."

Margaret glanced at Arthur. "I'll help you get him out."

Anna, Pearl, and I moved out of the way. Then Arthur and Margaret helped Joseph out from the wagon and led him into the house, Joseph's good arm around Arthur's neck.

"You other ladies can come in for some rest," Aunt Ethel said.

I smiled. "Thank you, ma'am."

Anna, Pearl, and I followed the others into the house.

While Arthur worked on and stitched Joseph's gun wounds, Aunt Ethel served us women lemon ginger tea in the small kitchen. The women and I sat at a square table and listened to Aunt Ethel talking about old stories of Mr. Arthur Wagner and his childhood.

"He was a stubborn and messy little rascal, but I loved him so dearly. So, where are y'all from?" she asked and sipped from her teacup.

Pearl looked up. "Charlotte, North Carolina, ma'am. We're on our way to Kingsport, Tennessee."

Aunt Ethel placed her cup on her saucer, startled. "Oh, my, that's a little way from here. I give my prayers for safe travels."

"Thank you, ma'am," we all said in unison.

I narrowed my eyes and cocked my head, suspicious. "What's your family relation to Mr. Wagner?"

Aunt Ethel put her cup and saucer in the sink. She grinned over her shoulder. "I'm his mother's youngest sister. Arthur's mother died in a boating accident when he was six, and she asked me to help raise him in her death will if something should ever happen to her. Sometimes, he calls me his mama."

I finished my tea and pushed up the cup and saucer on the table.

"I'll go see about Joe. Excuse me, everyone." Margaret stood from the small center table.

I rose up. "I'll come with you." Margaret and I walked through the entryway and up the narrow hallway to the right of the kitchen. We peeked around the corner in the guest bedroom.

Joseph was lying on the bed while Arthur wrapped his shoulder and arm with a clean bandage. The dressing on Joseph's shoulder covered and led down to his right arm.

"Did you get the bullets out?" I asked, glancing from Arthur to Joseph.

Arthur turned on the stool on which he sat and faced me. "Yes, but it wasn't easy. They were stubborn little suckers, but I pulled them out. Your friend Joe lost a lot of blood. Any more and I wouldn't have been able to save him."

"So . . . he'll be all right?" Margaret asked meekly.

Arthur grinned and nodded. "Yes, ma'am. He'll be fine. He just needs sleep and to keep drinking water."

"Oh, thank God," Margaret said with relief, a hand over her heart. She knelt beside the bedside. "I wouldn't let you go, Joe. I knew you'd be all right."

Joseph fluttered open his weary eyes. He smiled at Margaret and then looked at Arthur. "Thank you, sir. I appreciate your help. God bless you and your aunt."

"Thanks." Arthur sighed. "Well, I reckon' we'd better get some shuteye for a few hours. Joseph needs it to regain strength after his injury. Where are the others?"

"They're in the kitchen," I said.

Pearl and Anna came through the doorway.

"Is Joseph doin better?" Anna asked.

Arthur nodded and cleaned off his hands with a rag. "Yes. He's doing well and only needs rest at the moment, which we all should get right now."

Aunt Ethel entered with two folded blankets. She glanced from her nephew to the rest of us. "I brought some blankets for you ladies. Rest well, everyone."

"Thank you, ma'am," I said, taking the blankets. Pearl and I shared one blanket, and Anna and Margaret took the other one. Arthur sat and slept in a cushioned wood chair by a chest closet, while Joseph continued resting on the bed.

Even though it was already morning, we took the chance and opportunity to rest our tired bodies. There were many more miles to go to get to Canada, and we had to make sure we rose to leave for Tennessee before the bounty hunters came.

As I closed my eyes and lay beside Pearl on the floor, I spoke a brief prayer for our sakes and a successful rest of our journey to the North. *Dear God, protect us and give us safe travels to Canada. Amen.*

16 *The Third Safe House*

IT TOOK US ABOUT four and a half days to reach the next destination. On the second day to Kingsport, we were caught in a cold rainstorm and sought shelter and refuge in a young couple's outside barn. When we finally reached Kingsport, we arrived at a little cabin house.

A middle-aged housewife was in her backyard garden, hoeing weeds in the ground as we rode up. She had ash brown hair tied away from her slightly grubby face and wore a plain black day dress, a gray, ruffled apron, and black laced shoes for her hard labor. She paused with her instrument, looked at us from afar a second, and then continued working.

"Mrs. Talbot didn't wave. Their house is safe," Arthur said to me while stirring the reins.

I released an exhale and smiled. *Thank you, God.*

Arthur brought the wagon to a halt.

"Hello, Mr. Wagner." Mrs. Talbot shook his hand. "I almost thought y'all weren't coming. I was getting some yard work done before my boy wakes up for breakfast." Her countenance had a raw beauty and innocence, despite her less-than-perfect appearance, a smear of dirt on her forehead. Her olive-green eyes sparkled as she grinned at all of us sitting in the wagon. "Hello, everybody. I'm Penelope Talbot. Y'all can call me Penny. Welcome to Eastern Tennessee. Please, come inside. I've already got a meal for y'all."

"Thank you, ma'am," Anna said.

Mrs. Talbot laid her gardening tool on the ground and led the way to her log cabin home.

We all climbed out of the wagon, and Arthur and Margaret helped Joseph walk into the house again.

Inside, it was wooden and very plain-looking. By the door, there was a rectangular wood table, and below the loft above was a stone-built fireplace. The kitchen and logwood stove were off in a little room beside the eating area.

"Y'all can have a seat at the table." Mrs. Talbot walked to a small bed on one side of the bottom floor of the house. "Precious, wake up."

"Mama?" a little boy said, sitting up under the quilted blanket. He resembled his mother, having the same brown hair, olive-green eyes, and button nose.

"Henry, tell our guests, hello," Mrs. Talbot said, smiling and helping him out of bed.

"Hello." The little boy rubbed his tired eyes and stood barefoot in a long white gown before us.

Joseph inched up a smile. "How old you be, sonny?"

Henry held open his hand. "Five, sir."

"Henry's my son," Mrs. Talbot said. "He's smart and loves books—said he wants to be a doctor someday. Isn't that right, honey?"

"Yes, mama." Henry walked over to the table and sat in a chair beside Joseph. He frowned and curiously looked at the man wearing a sling. "What happened to your arm, mister?"

"Oh, I got shot on the way here," Joseph said, "but it don't hurt too much no more."

Mrs. Talbot rubbed her hands on her apron and looked sheepishly at everyone at the table. "We've got porridge and bacon, but that's 'bout it."

"That'll do fine, ma'am," Arthur said. "We appreciate it."

Margaret arose from the table. "Let me help serve." She followed Mrs. Talbot into the side kitchen.

The women returned with bowls, plates, and spoons and spread them on the table for each person.

"Mrs. Talbot, where's your husband?" I asked.

She placed a bowl in front of me and wore a timid look. "Walter's gone to Lexington, Kentucky for a pro-slavery rally. Because we don't own slaves, I find it ridiculous, but he's convinced slavery is what's best for our nation. He and I have had many squabbles about the matter."

She spooned porridge from a kettle pot into my bowl and the others and took a seat in a rocking chair with her little boy in her lap.

"I'll say grace," Arthur said, volunteering. "Everyone bow and hold hands."

He and everyone else bowed their heads. "Dear God, we thank you for this food. Bless us and keep us in your holy name, we pray. Amen."

"Amen," echoed the rest of us after him.

As we ate together, Henry read one of his storybooks to us. Seeing his enthusiasm while telling the story inspired me and my pursuit of becoming a children's fiction author. It was what I wanted to do with the stories I wrote—get children excited about reading and using their imagination.

About an hour later, Mrs. Talbot managed to rock her son back to sleep and tucked him in bed. Shortly after, we departed and headed toward Virginia.

Mrs. Talbot stood outside their small cabin home and waved as we rode away.

"Goodbye. Y'all have a safe trip," she said.

Arthur and the rest of us waved and returned our goodbyes.

Staying ahead of the bounty hunters, it seemed we were making good time, but it was too good to be true. Trouble was on the horizon and in a couple of more miles, we'd soon have a worrisome experience none of us saw coming.

Getting lost in the woods.

17 *The Fourth Safe House*

SOME HOURS LATER, WE arrived at the fourth safe house in Scott County, Virginia. Coming up to it before dawn, another candle burned in one of the small front windows of the home. As Arthur stopped the wagon, the front door swung open from the strong, whistling wind and the shadow of a man wearing a wide-brimmed hat startled me.

Had Jack and Sal reached the next place before us? The man stepped off from the doorway for a second and returned, holding up a lit lantern to his face.

A calmness settled within me, drawing a breath.

It was a yeoman farmer. He was a rugged-looking man in a black, raggedy, wide-brimmed hat, flapping in the breeze.

"Greetings, ye all," the man said in an Irish accent. "I'm Paul Kilgore. A pleasure to meet ye, friends."

A smile of relief spread across my lips. "Nice to meet you, sir."

"Come for some grub and rest," Mr. Kilgore said. "Dere's potato soup warmin' on de stove."

"Thank you," Arthur said, "we haven't had too much to eat and are starving from our journey."

Carrying his lantern, Mr. Kilgore thumped into his house in his blue, white-striped dress shirt and black, patent leather boots.

Arthur and the rest of us climbed out of the wagon and entered the home. First coming in, it seemed there was a woman that touched up the place. From the furniture to the delicate, China dishes in the tall cabinet, everything was clean and organized. It surprised me after seeing Mr. Kilgore's sloppy presence.

The aromas of potato soup and freshly baked bread wafted in the home as we gathered in the sitting room, and I couldn't wait until I got a bite. I don't believe I've ever been so hungry in my life. But because of the shorter distance from Kingsport to Scott County, Arthur made some stops before we reached Virginia overnight. The bounty hunters were nearby, and he said he had an inkling they were gaining on us.

"I'm starvin. I can eat a cow right bout now," Anna said, tugging her blue shawl around her.

Pearl nodded. "Me too, two cows."

Mr. Kilgore thudded into the sitting room. His brownish-blonde hair was in a short-cut style, with long sideburns connected to his whiskery beard. Not wearing his black hat accentuated his appearance more than before. "Food's ready. It's my late wife's specialty. She always made it for visitin' guests."

I looked at a side round table and picked up a black-and-white photograph of a young woman smiling over her shoulder and hanging up clothes on a line. "Is this her in the photo?"

Sadness clouded Mr. Kilgore's features. "Yes, that's my Greta. She was sweet, playful, and loved to laugh. We're immigrants from Ireland. We moved and left home because of a terrible drought. I started a potato and livestock farm. The soil's good 'ere."

"She was pretty. I'm sorry you lost her," I said. "What . . . what happened to her?"

Mr. Kilgore sighed, shook his head, and smacked his lips. "She had influenza—terrible fever. I miss her every day but never mind that. Let me bring ye all de food." He rose to his feet.

"We can help you, sir." Margaret and Pearl stood and entered the little kitchen.

The soup was creamy and delicious. Within it were chunks of soft potatoes, diced onion, and vegetables. For a garnish, it was sprinkled with fresh chives. The bread was golden brown and buttered right after it was taken from the oven. Everyone got a bowl of soup with a slice of bread on the side.

Mr. Kilgore handed me a bowl. "Enjoy, ma'am."

"Thank you, sir," I said, taking it from him.

Margaret licked her lips. "Mmm, this the best soup I ever had."

Mr. Kilgore blushed and stroked his thin, whiskery beard. "Glad ye like it, ma'am. I can never make it as well as Greta, but I try. Where are ye all headed next?"

"Harlon County, Kentucky," Arthur said and ate a spoonful. "We ran into trouble with bounty hunters. I suppose we'll be gone in a few hours to stay ahead of them."

Mr. Kilgore drank from his tin mug. "Ahh, be very careful, especially in Lexington. Bounty hunters are prowlin' all over the city like bloodsuckin' leeches."

"I know," Arthur answered, "that's why another rider will be taking them into Lexington after we enter Kentucky. It's to sneak them in town without bounty hunters suspecting anything."

"Sandbags are hangin' beneath your glasses, Arthur. Get some sleep before ye go, eh?"

Arthur chuckled. "I will, Mr. Kilgore."

Mr. Kilgore glanced from inside his mug to us. "I give prayers to ye all for a safe rest of the journey to Canada."

"Thank you. It's much appreciated," Arthur said, smiling.

After we ate, Mr. Kilgore started a soothing fire in the fireplace and told us goodnight before going to bed himself. Afterward, we rested a little while in the sitting room. Forty-minutes after nine at night, we left Virginia and continued our journey. Riding to Kentucky was one of the scariest places for us all. As Mr. Kilgore said, slave catchers were everywhere and we needed to keep watch for them. These men were merciless and didn't care who they got their hands on as long as they made a profit at auctions and earned money to fatten their pockets.

I glanced at the others in the back of the wagon as we rode. Amid their silence, I saw the worry plastered on their faces, their fearful eyes shifting and looking at one another.

Bowing my head, I whispered another prayer on their behalf. *Please, God, don't let my friends be sold back into slavery. Amen.*

After sunrise, I blocked the sun from my vision and looked over a wooden fence at the lush, healthy-green, open fields. Smelling the strong aroma of manure wafting in the thin air, I smiled as we passed a small farm of horses, sheep, and cows. Their animal calls of neighs, baas, and moos were a morning melody of welcome to the otherwise quiet Kentucky town.

Arthur rode past a wooden sign on our way toward a two-story farmhouse, which I didn't get to read, but I didn't have to. Based on the driver's course of action, we arrived at the next place.

The fifth safe house.

MONDAY, AUGUST 9, 9:40 A.M.
THE FELDMANS' FARMHOUSE
Harlon County, Kentucky

"GOOD MORNING, MR. WAGNER! I see you've brought us some new passengers," a short, pudgy woman said, grinning and drying her hands with a dishcloth. Based on the crow's feet etched around her brown eyes and her worn presence, she was a hardworking housewife.

She stood on the porch of the farmhouse, adorned in a lace-collared, baby-blue dress with a white ruffled apron and black booties. Honey-brown ringlets dangled along her rounded face, the rest of her hair tucked back in a neat bun.

"Nice to meet, y'all. I'm Mrs. Feldman," she greeted, looking at the covered wagon. She peered at me on the front seat. "Now, Arthur and his musical friends I know, but I wasn't expecting you. What's your name, miss?"

"Millie, ma'am," I said. "I'm a fellow conductor in place of Mr. Shepherd, helping friends of mine away from my father's plantation."

The farm wife beamed and marveled at me. "Well, ain't that something? God bless you, child."

Arthur climbed from the wagon. He tilted his bald head and squinted from the glare of the sun. "Where's Matthew?"

Mrs. Feldman glanced from me to Arthur. "He's out back, cleaning the horse stables. I was preparing lunch." She called over her shoulder. "Matt-heeew!"

Mr. Feldman, a lanky, hunchbacked man with a long, gray beard and thin, salt-and-pepper hair strode out of the beaten-up barn from alongside the house, taking slow, wide steps. He was holding a pitchfork tangled with a few strings of hay. He looked a couple of years older than his wife in a short-sleeve, button-down shirt, olive-green work pants with braces, and leather boots. His bushy-browed frown raised and changed to a wide grin when he saw us. "Well, goodness me! Welcome to our farm, everyone!"

"We've got an injured man in the back," Arthur said. "He's been tended to, but he needs some new bandages."

"Sure, I'll help you get him out." Mr. Feldman walked over as Arthur came around to the back of the wagon.

The two men helped the women climb down and then helped Joseph out of the wagon and led him into the farmhouse.

"The rest of y'all can come in and have a bite," Mrs. Feldman said. "With all the traveling you've been doing the past days, you need to build your strength up before your train ride."

"Yes, ma'am. We'd like that very much." I stepped from the wagon.

The other women and I followed Mrs. Feldman into the house. We washed our hands and faces and ate lunch in the kitchen. Everything was pleasant-tasting, and the best we'd eaten in a long time. Fresh fruits and vegetables from their garden beautified the wooden table. Ham slices and Swiss cheese, a jar of mayonnaise, and fresh loaves of bread were put beside the wooden bowls of colorful produce for us to make sandwiches.

Terribly hungry, I ate my sandwich so fast I bit my tongue. Nonetheless, it went down well. The others and I were so thankful to rest, be refreshed, and have our stomachs filled again.

"Well, it was nice talking with y'all. I wish you ladies a wonderful train ride." Mrs. Feldman poured a glass of milk from a pitcher and handed it to Anna.

"Thank you, ma'am," Pearl said. "I can hardly wait to get to Cincinnati. I've heard many negro people have gone to Ohio."

Mrs. Feldman nodded. "Yes, our friend Mr. Waldo Finley lives there."

"Well, I should go," Arthur said, entering the kitchen. After a several days trip, the Feldmans had allowed him to freshen up a bit too. With a smile on his clean face, he looked at Mrs. Feldman and tilted his head, holding her hand in both of his. "Thank you for your hospitality, Mrs. Feldman."

"You're welcome, Mr. Wagner," Mrs. Feldman said. "Tell Noah and the others I said hello."

"Certainly, I will." Arthur picked up a small basket of food Mrs. Feldman made for his journey to Lexington and turned to the rest of us with a pensive expression. "I hate to be leaving you all like this, but it's merely for your safety. Don't worry, you'll be in good hands. Mr. Feldman will ride you to the next stop after fixing Joseph's dressing. I bid you Godspeed and hope to see you all later in Cincinnati. Goodbye for now."

"Goodbye, Mr. Wagner," Pearl and I said in unison.

Arthur left out the back door of the kitchen.

Mrs. Feldman placed the milk pitcher in a small cupboard. "Louisville is a hundred and fifty or so miles from Harlan County. I reckon y'all will take a rest stop in Lexington before getting to the train station."

She smiled and continued. "Mr. Shepherd sent a telegram informing me he's in Louisville. You should meet him there in a few days. All the rotations will lessen speculations. The more y'all move around, the greater the chances of y'all safely entering Canada." She opened a picnic basket on the counter. "I'll pack some food for your friend, Joseph. He was taken upstairs, first room on the left."

"Thank you, Mrs. Feldman." I stood from the table. "Let's go check on him."

Pearl, Margaret, and Anna followed me through the entryway and up the hardwood staircase beside the front door.

The bedroom door was half-open.

I glanced at the other women and knocked lightly. "Everything all right?"

"Yes, come right in," Mr. Feldman said, "I just finished putting new dressing on Joseph's wounds."

I opened the door, and we all entered the room.

Joseph was sitting on the bed in front of Mr. Feldman. He chuckled and gave a smile. "Any food left for me or it all gone?"

Margaret giggled and playfully waved her apron at him. "Of course, Joe. Mrs. Feldman packed your lunch in a basket. We're carrying it with us in the wagon."

Anna smiled. "You look better, Joe. There's a glow bout your face."

"Thanks, Anna. I feel better," Joseph replied.

Mr. Feldman cut the end of the bandage on Joseph's arm with a pair of scissors and helped him bend his arm back into his sling. "There you are. This dressing should last you at least until you reach Detroit."

"Thank you, sir," Joseph said.

Mr. Feldman and Margaret helped Joseph to his feet. Hoofbeats sounded outside, and I peeked out of the window behind the bed. My eyes went round and my heart pounded as I stared at Jack and Sal riding toward the farmhouse on their saddled horses.

I swiftly looked at the others. "The bounty hunters my Papa hired are out front. We have to get outta here!"

"Oh, Lord, no!" Margaret said, placing a hand to her mouth.

I took out the pistol from my carpetbag and followed Mr. Feldman and the others downstairs.

A loud knock at the front door startled us.

"Hurry to the kitchen!" Mr. Feldman whispered, leading the way.

As the knocks continued and Crenshaw shouted at the closed door, we followed the old man to the kitchen.

Worry cast on Mrs. Feldman's face. "Matthew, who's at the door?" She started leaving the kitchen.

"Don't answer it," Mr. Feldman whispered, stopping her. "It's bounty hunters."

Mrs. Feldman widened her eyes. "Bounty hunters? Oh, no, please, be careful, love."

"I will, Beatrice." Her husband placed a finger to his lips. "Stay calm and be quiet, dearest."

Mrs. Feldman nodded and watched as we escaped outside through the back door. We loaded up one by one into Mr. Feldman's covered evergreen wagon behind the house, but trouble still came.

Sal exited the wooden barn and spotted us before we left. "Aye, Jack! They're around back! I see'em! I see'em!"

He fired a few long-range shots that tore holes in the canopy of the wagon, making us scream and duck.

I peeked up and fired back at Sal, but he took cover by the swing door of the barn.

Jack joined his partner in the shootout as the men hopped on their horses and chased us.

Mr. Feldman struck the reins and rode off as the bounty hunters trailed behind and fired their revolvers. Before I knew it, he groaned and got shot by one of the flying bullets in his back. The old man fell aside on the ground to his death, the wagon careening down a steep road without a driver.

"Millie! Grab the reins!" Pearl screeched. She and Anna panicked and held on to each other.

I gasped, dropped the gun below in the front part of the wagon, and gripped the reins, steering the wagon as best as I could. The horse was charging at a fast pace down the hilly road. I didn't know where we were going from here, but I had to take charge. We had come too far and were too close to give up, and the others were counting on me for their freedom.

"They're gainin on us!" Anna said. "What we gonna do?"

Energy surged through my veins. I growled and clenched my teeth as I struck the horse with the reins and stirred the wagon. Everywhere I went the bounty hunters followed us. So, I did the only thing I could do—take a detour. I turned a corner near tall cornfields.

Approaching a two-way fork road, I detoured into the forest on the left behind a crowd of bushes and pulled the reins, bringing the horse to a safe, jerking halt. Then I pulled the brake and sat silently. Losing our trace, the bounty hunters zoomed past us on their horses and continued ahead up the two-way road. Brushing back my loose, brown bangs from my face, I exhaled a deep breath and looked above at the leafy branches of the trees swaying in the light breeze.

Pearl swallowed and paced her breathing. "Thank heavens! I thought we were dead."

"Poor Mr. Feldman. He was a nice man." Margaret hung and shook her head. "His death will break his wife's heart." She stifled a sob.

"It feels like a bad dream," I said, trying to process everything that happened in a quick flash. My eyes watered, rummaging through my thoughts the reality of life. Mr. Feldman's death made our situation more real to me. Our journey wasn't like one of my children's fairytale stories. This was *real*—and what happened to him could happen to any of us.

Margaret looked up, hopeless and frightened. "How we gonna get to Lexington now?"

Catching my breath, I thought of my best option and glanced over my shoulder at the others. "I'll have to ask somebody in town. From here, I'll use the compass along the way." I took Papa's gold compass out of my carpetbag and jumped from the front seat. Holding the compass before me, I read the turning needle as I faced the sun from whence we came. "The sun is northwest of us and we're diagonal of it, which means we must be southeast." I walked to the back opening of the wagon.

A gentleman in a neat, black dress suit and top hat approached us, riding in a black carriage. I figured it was the right time to ask for help, but would it make matters better or worse? Trusting strangers was risky with the others' freedom at stake. How could I be sure it was a wise decision?

"A man is coming," I whispered to them, gripping the cart.

"Well, he can't see us under the canopy," Pearl said. "Maybe he can help."

Anna nodded. "Pearl's right. Ask him, Millie."

"Are you all sure?" I asked, concerned. "He could be dangerous."

Their intrigued faces hinted at me to take a chance and speak to the man.

"All right. I'll do it." I gulped and spoke up. "Excuse me, sir!"

The man pulled his reins and stopped beside our wagon, facing the opposite direction. "Yes, madam?" He spoke with an unexpected English accent, an immigrant from Great Britain.

"Could you direct me to Lexington?" I asked.

The gentleman glanced behind me at the covered wagon and looked at me again. "You look young, lady. Carrying a load, are you?"

"Yes, sir," I answered, "just trying to drop off some goods."

"Very well," the man said. "Lexington is northwest. Follow the sun and listen for fiddles and a plucking banjo." He beamed and chuckled.

I grinned. "Thank you, sir. Have a wonderful day."

"My pleasure, dear. Sir William Benedict at your service." The man tipped his hat. "Cheerio!" He hit his reins and continued through the forest, humming the English folk song "Greensleeves" to himself.

After he left, I ran to the others in the back of the wagon again. "He said to follow the sun. We're far away, but I'll keep a watch for a safe house. Maybe I'll find one along the way." I climbed up and sat back in the front seat of the wagon.

"Giddy-up," I said, striking the reins.

The horse snorted and trotted toward the bright sun. Golden rays streamed through the branches of the oak trees and warmed my inner being. Our lives were still in danger, but somehow, as Margaret felt about Joseph, everything had to work out for us.

Faith was our only hope.

19 *Alone in the Dark*

MOONLIGHT WASHED THE EARTH as we traveled for miles, and my eyes grew wearier by the minute. We needed to take a rest stop, but doing so at night in the outdoors was unsafe and too dangerous now. Where could we find refuge? I couldn't drive all the way to the Louisville and Nashville Railroad by myself. Feeling drowsy, I nodded my head off and on, trying to stay awake. It was too hard—I couldn't help but stop.

As Arthur had back in Asheville, I pulled over and took a rest. Still, the bounty hunters weren't far behind. Between Lexington and Cincinnati, I was sure we'd find them lurking on our trail again. Going to Ohio sounded exciting with the many men and women abolitionists flowing in and out of Cincinnati.

Of course, every passing minute was precious to our lives. We wouldn't be there long enough to attend public events or hear speeches from any abolitionists, such as William Garrison or Frederick Douglass. Even so, I wondered if I'd encounter any well-known writers like Ralph Waldo Emerson or Harriet Beecher Stowe who Miss Perkins talked about. As an aspiring author, there were so many adventures I wanted to embark on and people I wanted to meet. Whether good or bad, life had a way of showing you things you never expect, and that's what I learned about myself along our journey to Canada.

The closer the others and I came to the Promised Land, the more I realized I was braver and stronger than I thought I was. And, riding along through the sinister, mysterious woods, how important my dreams were to me. Young white women from the South rarely struck out on their own—and certainly not at my age—so the thought of going to the busy city felt intimidating. It was safer under Papa's roof, but things were different now. I had to make my own decisions and choose what path I wanted in my life, and if failures arose, I would be the one to blame.

I pulled the brake and looked at the others through the opening of the canopy of the wagon.

All of them were sleeping again.

Noah wasn't jesting when he said it would be a rough journey. We all were tired and worn, ready to keep our feet still on solid ground without having to dodge a bullet or run for our lives. I knew I was, and I couldn't wait to take a deep breath of Canada's crisp, cool air. I also was looking forward to seeing Noah and getting on the train. Because we opposed slavery, I thought maybe we could hold a conversation while seated in one place and get to know each other better. From when we left North Carolina to now, we never talked too much. But I wanted to know more about Noah personally and how he got involved in the railroad network.

I couldn't find anyone the same as myself back at home. I always felt like a stranger in my house. *Curse of the family.* How could a father say that about his own daughter? Maybe I was a curse, or perhaps Dula's kindness changed me. How could I mistreat the woman who helped raise me? I couldn't. I didn't know if I'd ever return to North Carolina, but if I wanted to, it would only be to visit Dula, a woman with a heart of gold. What happened to Randall and the others? We were still a long way from town, but something told me some of them would meet us later in Ohio.

If Randall were with us, Pearl would've been thrilled. And Anna would've loved to see Ozzie, her big brother too. Since they were kids, they stayed together like salt and pepper. They always looked out for each other as they strove to survive the sorrows of slavery in the absence of their sold parents. The night we left the cabin was a sad occasion as they said their goodbyes. Ozzie was Papa's best slave on the plantation, a big, strong man, who barely said a word, but I had never seen him cry until his little sister left him. I was sad for Randall and Pearl too.

If only they had gotten away together the first time, things would've been different. Maybe Pearl wouldn't have suffered from my father's advances. The thought of what my father had done to her worried me. So far, Pearl seemed fine and healthy enough, but there was no telling what would develop after we reached Canada. If anything, it would be the most awkward situation I'd ever had to deal with in my life.

How would it all be, Pearl bearing my half-sibling? Would it ruin our friendship? Could she no longer stand to look at me, seeing her abuser in my eyes? I took my journal and pencil out of my carpetbag and wrote about everything that recently happened during our journey. I had enough information to write a book:

1852, Aug. 10 – Tuesday

It's a beautiful, moonlit night and we've finally reached Kentucky. We are all hungry and live every moment in fear. I can't wait until we finally get on the train. We'll breathe freely for the first time in many days. I hope Noah will be on guard like he promised, and that the bounty hunters won't find us. Everywhere we go it seems like they're there. We should keep moving. The hunters are lurking in the woods. With every breath I take . . . I feel like I can sense them close. But I'm as tired as an aged woman. Though, I have yet to reach twenty years of age. My body aches from my head to my feet, and I smell like a bag of rotten potatoes. None of us have had a proper bath since we left North Carolina. I'm filthy, sweaty, and exhausted. I miss Noah something fierce and feel safer having him with us. I pray he's all right and nothing terrible happened to him. Why did he have to go away? Why couldn't he stay with us on our journey? Every passing day, I worry about him. But why should I care? And why should I love him? We hardly know each other, and he's a gentleman who sees me as nothing more than a scared, innocent child—not a young woman.

I feel so silly and ashamed. What am I to do with my affection? Am I to cut out my heart and cast it in the sea? And how are we supposed to make it to Lexington without a rest stop while having so many miles to go? We need a miracle, a guiding light to show us a place of refuge.

God have mercy on our weary souls,

Mildred Crabtree

I sighed and closed my notebook, blinking back tears as I studied the silver-dollar moon glowing in the inky sky. *Please, help us make it safely. Please . . .* Thankfully, we at least had our dirty clothes on our backs, food, and a rifle with a little ammunition, but no shelter to hide us. Aside from a compass and wagon, to find safety and refuge all we had left was our unyielding hope.

"Millie?" Pearl called, peeking out the canopy of the wagon. "Are you well?"

I sniffled and looked at her over my shoulder. "Pearl, I can't make it and I don't know where to find a safe house. We've got to be at least a hundred more miles away from Lexington, but I'm all tuckered out."

Pearl climbed out to the front of the wagon. Like a caring mother, she joined me on the front seat and wrapped an arm around me, attempting to pull me into her lap. "Rest, then. I can keep a lookout while you take a quick nap. God will protect us."

With dilated eyes, I shook my head, looking downward. "No. We have to keep moving. We've sat in one place long enough already. The longer we sit still, the closer the hunters can gain on us. I don't want to fail you all." I drew a long breath and raised my face to hers. "You go on back with the others. I'll be all right."

"No," Pearl answered, "you rest up. I'll take over for now. We can take turns the rest of the way."

I smiled and hugged her. "Thanks, Pearl. Be careful."

We switched places on the front seat, and then Pearl took the reins.

"Giddy-up! Come on, boy." Pearl struck the horse and continued stirring the wagon down the highway as I sat beside her. In her high soprano voice, she broke out with the first verse of *Abide With Me*: "*Abide with me: fast falls the eventide; the darkness deepens; Lord, with me abide. When other helpers fail and comforts flee, help of the helpless; O abide with me. . .*"

While riding along, I joined her with my mellow tone in the second verse. We harmonized and sang the song from our last church service: "*Swift to its close, ebbs out life's little day; earth's joys grow dim, it's glories pass away. Change and decay in all around I see. O thou who changest not, abide with me. . .*"

From the rocking of the wagon, I fell asleep on Pearl's shoulder. The song was like a lullaby and comfort to my soul during our strenuous journey and this challenging time.

Then a miracle happened. As I fluttered open my weary eyes, things were looking up again. Like a snow-white angel, it was the most beautiful sight I had seen in the past few days, flickering in a smudged-up, four-square window.

A burning candle.

20 *The Sixth Safe House*

SEVEN DAYS—SEVEN LONG days and a hundred and fifty miles between rest stops and hopeful prayers, we rode from Harlan County through to Lexington. So far, it was the longest distance we had traveled. For food, Joseph found berries and Margaret fetched us a few squirrels. Swallowing my pride, I ate with the others so not to die from starvation, but my stomach felt terribly nauseous afterward.

Nonetheless, I was thankful to have Pearl and the other women with me who took turns and lent a hand because I couldn't have made it without them by my side.

Pearl nudged me out of my sleep. "Millie . . . Millie, I found a safe house."

I fluttered open my eyes and stared at the candle burning in the window of a tiny white house surrounded by tall pine trees. I smiled with tears and sighed with relief. "Praise God."

Pearl grinned and then laughed. "I reckon we should wake the others."

"Yes," I said, "I'll go first to the door, just to be safe."

Pearl nodded and tugged her brown shawl around her from the chill in the air. "All right."

I climbed from the wagon and walked on tired legs that felt as stiff as tree trunks. Before I said the secret password, the door opened to an old, slender Quaker man in a white dress shirt and black trousers fastened with braces over his thin shoulders. Upon raising my head to his towering stature, his long white beard was the first thing I noticed about his aged, wrinkled face.

"Hello, sir. My friends and I could use some help. We've been on the road for many days and—"

He smiled. "I have prayed much for thee. Bring thine friends into my home. Shepherd told me thou and thine passengers might be arriving."

"Oh, thank you," I said.

The others and I came into the old gentleman's home and he closed the door after us as we sat in his sitting room.

"Who you be, sir?" Margaret asked.

The old man turned and faced us in his black, wide-brimmed hat. "I'm Mr. Ezra Hadley, but others around call me Pastor Hadley. I'm a pastoral minister of the Lexington Circle of Friends Church and have been so for many years." He scanned our faces and our exhausted presence.

"You all must be hungry. I'll find something for you all to eat." He walked into the kitchen. After a couple of minutes, he returned to the sitting room. "I have some leftover sliced ham and lima bean soup."

"That will be fine, sir. Thank you," Joseph said.

As always, Margaret offered a hand with the food, but why wouldn't she? Being a cook and serving others a good meal was one thing she knew and loved to do. But it made a difference to do so without getting thrown harsh orders or the fear of someone dissatisfied and picking over her food.

"Father God, bless this food and let it nourish my dear friends. Bless everyone here in your holy name. Amen," Mr. Hadley said.

"Amen," everyone echoed after him.

On the center table of the sitting room was a small pot of soup and a wide plate spread with sliced ham.

Mr. Hadley grabbed a bowl and filled it with soup from a ladle. He handed it to Joseph and continued doing the same for the rest of us. Margaret took a fork and knife and placed some ham on small plates, giving each of us a slice.

The food was bland and simple, but something about it made it taste better. Maybe it was because of not having a decent meal the past few days. Or maybe it was the genuine kindness and humility in Mr. Hadley's blue-gray eyes. The minute I took the first bite of my lima bean soup, a sense of peace came over me. It was a feeling that regardless of whatever happened to us when we reached the busy town, everything was going to work out and be fine.

"How's the food?" Mr. Hadley asked and chuckled. "It's all right. You can be honest. I'm not the best cook in the world."

Margaret giggled. "Your soup could've used salt and pepper, but it's still doing its job, sir."

"Do you all know the song, *Abide With Me?*" Mr. Hadley asked.

I raised my head and smiled. "Yes, sir. Pearl and I were singing it on the way over here."

Mr. Hadley stood and sat at the wood piano in his sitting room. He lifted the cover of it, revealing the row of ivory and ebony keys. Sitting up straight, he flipped a page in his music book on the stand. "It's my absolute favorite hymn. During hard times, we may feel like we're alone, but the Lord is with us. For in John fourteen verse sixteen, He promised to abide with us forever. Dost thou mine if I sing and play a little?"

"No, sir," we answered in overlapped voices.

Mr. Hadley cleared his throat and played his piano, singing the lyrics. After we ate, Pearl, the others, and I stood and surrounded him, singing other hymns with him, including *"My Faith Looks Up to Thee"* and *"Rock of Ages."* The old man beautifully played the instrument, which gave the lyrics of the hymns more life. This was true fellowship, God's children singing together as one in love and wholeness, giving Him praise.

When we finished the last song, Mr. Hadley rolled his fingers across the keys to the higher octave of the piano for a nice finish. Afterward, the old man smiled and laughed. "How lovely! Well, I enjoyed you all singing with me, but it's time we go. I know you all are tired, so I'll take you into Louisville myself."

"What time it is?" Anna asked.

Mr. Hadley glanced at the ticking wall clock above his sofa. "It's two o'clock. You all should reach Louisville in eighty more miles or so. We'll be there when we see lots of dark smoke and hear a train whistle."

"Thank you for taking us, sir. We greatly appreciate your compassion and generosity," I said.

Mr. Hadley stood from his piano and lowered the wood cover over the row of keys. "My pleasure. May God bless you all."

As the others exited his house, I started leaving but came back to him. "You remind me of my grandfather, my mother's father. When I was five, he died from a heart attack in his sleep. I never realized how much I missed him until I met you. Thank you."

"You're welcome, child. Now off we must go." He shooed me away.

I smiled and wiped a few tears from my eye. "Yes, Mr. Hadley."

The old man was the last to exit. Then he closed the front door to his house. After the others climbed in the back of the wagon, I pulled down the sheet over the opening of the covered wagon and sat on the front seat. Then Mr. Hadley joined me at the front and took the reins.

He bowed his head. "Dear Lord, guard and protect us from harm of the enemy. Amen."

"Amen," I echoed after him.

Mr. Hadley struck the reins and drove us on our way.

Kentucky was a slave state where traders and hunters bought and sold slaves like ranchers do cattle. Lexington was a slave trade center where auctions were common in the bluegrass city. The thought of Pearl or my other friends getting taken into a slave concentration camp made going into town more nerve-wracking for me.

As we rode down the long, country highway past Mr. Hadley's house, I tried to keep Pearl's comforting words settled in my mind. *God will protect us.* Although she was a runaway slave in a slave state, she sounded so assured. I admired her faith and confidence and wished for the best outcome. God would certainly have to watch over us through the darkness of such a perilous time.

ON THE THIRD DAY toward Louisville, we stopped by another safe house of a Quaker family. Joseph, with his one useful arm, helped the young father of the family fix one of the back wheels of our wagon. All the miles we traveled through the terrain had caused some damage along the way. Afterward, we gave our thanks and continued our journey.

"You all have a safe trip," the father said.

His blonde wife stood aside from our wagon, rocking their swaddled baby in her arms. "We send our prayers, Pastor Hadley. God be with you all."

"Thank you, ma'am," Pastor Hadley said, sitting in front of the wagon.

"Goodbye now." The father slapped the backside of the horse, sending us off.

Pastor Hadley held the reins and continued riding to the train station. As another early morning arrived, I almost fell asleep, but then I smelt smoke and a strange, low blow shocked me to full consciousness. Fluttering open my drowsy eyes, I saw nothing but thick fog, an amber light piercing through the cloudiness around us.

A whistle blew and someone sang a bluegrass tune and plucked a banjo in the distance.

Then my heart leaped, hearing a ringing bell.

I exhaled and brushed my damp bangs from my face, overwhelmed we finally reached an area of civilization again.

The women awoke in the wagon.

"Are we at the train station?" Anna poked her gray-turban-wrapped head out of the front of the canopy and surveyed our surroundings.

"Yep. We've just arrived into town," Pastor Hadley said.

I wrinkled my nose, peering at the misty fog. Perhaps it was the weather, but it didn't seem to be too much around. Then before any of us knew it, a little man in a bowler hat and another tall gentleman walked across the crunchy gravel toward us through the fog. Was it Noah and another friend, or bounty hunters?

"Who's dat?" Anna's voice trembled as she pointed at the two men.

Pastor Hadley frowned. "Perhaps Mr. Shepherd? He's supposed to meet us in Louisville."

"But there's two of them!" Pearl shrieked.

My breaths quickened, and my forehead perspired. I snatched the rifle in the wagon and cocked the hammer, pointing the gun straight ahead at them. "Stop right there or I'll shoot!"

"It's all right! It's just us," a young man said.

Noah and an older man with tousled, brown hair and a brown, feathery mustache came forth from the fog with their hands raised.

I let out a relieved breath and slumped my shoulders, lowering the shotgun. "Noah?"

"Yes, Millie. It's me." Noah whispered, dropping his hands. "Everything will be fine. We're here to take you and the others into safety. This is Mr. Hughes, a fellow friend of mine."

"Thank heavens! You had us a little worried there for a minute," Pastor Hadley said and chuckled.

"Hurry! You all must come to my place," Mr. Hughes whispered.

We climbed out of the wagon.

"Noah, I'm so glad it's you." I sobbed and embraced him, wrapping my arms around his waist.

Noah cleared his throat and pulled me away from him. He blushed and wore a wry smile, holding me at arm's length. "You should go now. Follow me and the others in Mr. Hughes' home. You'll board the train later today."

"All right." Looking into his brown, luminous eyes, I smiled and slowly left his side.

While Pastor Hadley took care of the covered wagon, I followed the others and Mr. Hughes across the railroad tracks to his two-story home. Past the cloudy mist, there were a few other neighboring houses, spread out in the parched, low-cut grassland.

As I had hoped, we finally made it, and I was ever so grateful.

We were in Louisville, Kentucky.

21 *The Seventh Safe House*

A BLONDE LITTLE GIRL who was about eleven or twelve was playing Beethoven's "Moonlight Sonata" on the piano in the sitting room when we entered the Hughes' home. She stopped and glanced over her shoulder at us with freckled cheeks and an adorable heart-shaped face. Her large eyes were like blue gems from a jewel box, staring at us.

"This is my daughter, Savannah," Mr. Hughes said, closing the door behind me. "She's a little shy but friendly." He looked at the girl. "Savannah, dear, help your grandma get the ladies ready in the back rooms for their train ride. I'll help with Mr. Joseph."

"Yes, Papa," Savannah said in a soft-spoken voice. She stood from the piano in her plaid, pink dress and black leather boots and looked at us women. "We have two bedrooms in the back of the house. I'll show you."

The women and I followed Savannah, while Joseph went with Mr. Hughes in the opposite direction.

"Here's the guest room," Savannah said, gesturing a hand. She turned to Pearl and the others. "Grandma can help y'all in here. She has clean dresses and other clothes y'all can change into for your trip."

"Thank you," Pearl said. "We appreciate this." She and the others entered the room and closed the door.

"You can come to my room," she said to me. "Papa said you could wear one of my Mama's old dresses."

I followed the little girl to her bedroom.

In the center of the room was a large round basin, and near a gray-curtained window was a changing screen and full-body mirror. I observed the basin as relief rested on my shoulders. I almost felt like I was in heaven. Having a nice, warm bath was the thing I needed at the moment.

"You can go behind the changing screen while I fill the basin." Savannah picked up a wooden bucket and started to the door. She paused, holding the knob. "By the way, what's your name?"

"Mildred," I said, "but Millie will do fine. Where's your Ma?"

Savannah glanced down. "She died when I was born. Papa said it was scarlet fever, but I think he says this, so I don't blame myself." She tilted her head. "Where's yours?"

"My mother died too. She was a sickly woman," I said.

Savannah turned down her mouth. "I'm sorry." She sighed sadly. "I never met my mother, but somehow, I feel like I knew her. I'm sure you miss your mother too."

"Yes," I said. "She was a little like me. She didn't like Papa's dealings with the slaves on our family plantation, but many times, she still did what he told her to do. I refused to live that kind of life and ran away North with the others. I want to be a children's author."

Savannah beamed, raising her brows. "An author? How wonderful! I love to read, especially adventure books." She opened the door. "Let me get you some water. I'll be right back." She left.

I scanned the bedroom and sat on a stool behind the changing screen, untying and slipping off my dirty shoes. Since leaving my family's mansion, they had gone from pure white to muddy brown in the past weeks. I lifted the skirt of my dress and checked on my skinned knee. After all the chaos, thankfully my bandage stayed on with the support from my stocking. I untied the stocking and unraveled the dressing.

A pink, dark scab formed over my knee as it started healing. My other stocking was still a little damp from when I fell into the rocky creek, so my right foot was raw and peeling skin. I tied my stockings together in a knot and tossed them on the changing screen. My blue-and-white plaid dress was also smeared with dirt, grass, and dried leaves. I unbuttoned it from the back, looking over my shoulder in the full-body mirror.

Savannah returned to her room with the bucket. She poured steamy water into the basin. "It'll take about seven more to fill it up."

I tossed my dress on the changing screen and peeked over at her. "Thank you. I appreciate this a lot. Could you also bring me dressing and scissors? I want to make sure I keep my knee from getting infected."

"Of course," Savannah said. "I'm going to get more water." She left again.

When she filled the basin, Savannah came a final time with a towel, a sponge, a bar of soap, and some clean undergarments. She placed them on the clothing trunk. A purple gingham day dress with white stockings was draped over her bed for me beside the bandage and scissors.

"If you need anything, just holler," Savannah said, giggling.

I smiled, peeking from behind the screen. "All right, thanks."

Savannah exited and closed the door.

I came out from hiding and lowered myself into the basin. It felt so good. I hardly wanted to get back out. The hot, steamy water soothed my aching muscles and comforted my inner being. After everything I and the others had gone through, I'd take nothing for granted again. I washed and rinsed my messy hair and scrubbed my dirty face and body with soap and the sponge. When I dried off, I put on the clean undergarments, which fit me perfectly. Once I wrapped my knee and put on the linen undershirt, Savannah knocked on the door.

"Grandma said to check on you. Do you need help?" Savannah said, peeking inside.

I slipped on the stockings and pulled the shift blouse over my head. "Yes, please, with my corset and dress. I'm about to put them on now. You can come in."

Savannah entered and shut the door. For a second, she stood there and stared at me, as if overcome by emotion.

"What's wrong?" I asked.

Savannah sniffled and wiped her cheek with her long sleeve. "Nothing, I just imagined you as my Mama sitting there."

"I'm sorry," I said. "Maybe I shouldn't wear your mother's dress."

Savannah shook her head and smiled. "No, it's all right. I'm sure you'll look lovely in it. Let me help you finish getting dressed." She tightened the laces of the corset for me, tying them behind my back. Then she adjusted the petticoat around my waist and draped the dress over my head. It was a little big on me, but layered my stocky figure fairly well.

"Thanks for everything," I said. "I feel so much better. Where are the others?"

Savannah buttoned the back of the dress. "Some of them are eating in the kitchen. Papa cooked grits and biscuits while Grandma helped the other ladies get ready. It's the only thing he knows how to make for breakfast."

She fastened the last button. "There, you're all done. Have a look."

I turned and viewed my reflection, profiling in the full-body mirror and spreading the wrinkles from the dress. "Well, it's kind of baggy, but it should do fine."

"What's going to happen to the others?" I asked, tying my hair in a bun. "Mr. Shepherd mentioned something about coffins before we got here."

"Oh, yes, my father's an undertaker. He's got three wooden coffins the women will hide in during the train ride."

"Will they be fine in them?" I asked, concerned.

Savannah nodded. "I reckon so. Riding on the train it's a short trip to Cincinnati. It'll only be about two hours."

"How will he get them on board?"

"Papa said he's got a good story to tell the conductor." Savannah cocked her head and wrinkled her freckled nose, thinking. "Something about a wagon accident with a family. He'll be riding on the train to Cincinnati too after loading up the coffins. Follow me to the kitchen for breakfast."

I folded and tucked my blue-and-white plaid dress into my carpetbag and followed Savannah out of her bedroom to the kitchen.

Everyone was eating at the table. Like myself, Pearl and the other women were well-groomed and wore clean dresses and head wraps. Now Joseph looked more like an elegant house slave, arrayed in a white dress shirt and trousers with a gray suit jacket and bowler hat. Unlike the women, he was boarding the train with Noah and me as our slave, but I hoped his sling wouldn't cause suspicion.

Savannah and I arrived among the others as Noah practiced being the ruthless owner of a slave.

"Now, get over here, boy!" he yelled at Joseph.

Joseph shook his head and made a snorting laugh, tapping his spoon on his bowl. "It ain't in how loud your voice is, Mr. Shepherd."

"Oh," Noah said calmly, becoming himself again. He exhaled slowly. "I thought I did pretty well that time. But I'm most worried about the papers I brought with me. They belong to another slave man. I'm hoping the conductor won't make a big deal about Joseph's slight height difference."

"Let me see them," I said.

Noah wore a dopey grin. He blushed, took them out of his suit jacket, and handed them to me.

I examined the document and gave Noah a confused look. "Five-foot-nine? Joseph isn't five-foot-nine."

"I know, I know. It was a careless mistake." Noah sighed and gripped the edges of his ruby suit jacket. He tittered. "I didn't look at them too good before I left to get you all, but they'll have to do."

"What time is it?" Pearl asked.

Grandma Hughes, an elderly woman with dark-gray hair wrapped in a net, looked at the wall clock over her head. "A quarter to four."

"The train will go to Cincinnati at seven o'clock this morning," Noah said.

I chuckled. "I suppose you'd better come up with a good impression by then."

"Let me show you how it's done, Mr. Shepherd." Joseph stood from the table and acted the role with negligent eyes and a proud stance. Despite his injured arm, I felt as if I was watching my father, reminded by Papa's pompous character and expectations in front of the slaves. With a few words from my father, no one spoke against him.

"Carry my case, boy," Joseph said. It was so simple, so precise, yet convincing to every soul sitting in the room.

Joseph flared his nostrils and studied Noah. "You don't have to yell your words, Mr. Shepherd. Just believe in them. You're a wealthy slave owner who answers to no one. You can do whatever you want with me. I'm your slave . . . your *property*."

Pearl and the other women shamefully looked down, knowing from dire experience what Joseph was talking about as slaves.

Noah gulped and licked his lips. "I understand what you mean, but you must excuse me. I've never gone on the train before. Let's go over it again." He and Joseph went over their parts until they had everything down pat.

Then Savannah and Noah played different duets of Bluegrass songs in the living room until it was time to get aboard the train.

Grandma Hughes and I clapped and laughed as Joseph danced around with the women, switching from one of them to another during a square dance.

When the clock struck fifteen minutes before seven, Noah stopped playing his violin. "We'd best get ready to go now."

"Yes. I guess you're right," I said.

Mr. Hughes and Joseph carried the last coffin from outside into the sitting room.

Pearl nervously glanced from the coffins to me and gave a half-smile. "Well, I reckon this is it."

"Yes," I said, "but don't worry. I'm sure everything will work out fine. I read in the paper a slave man from Virginia named Henry Box who was mailed a few years ago in a wooden crate to Philadelphia."

"Really?" Pearl's hazel-brown eyes went round.

I giggled. "Uh-huh, and if he could make it, you and the others should be fine too. I'm sure you'll be in Cincinnati before you know it."

Pearl smiled. "Thanks, Millie." She and I hugged, and then she laid inside an open coffin.

Mr. Hughes covered her with the lid, and likewise did the same for Margaret and Anna of the other two coffins after they gave hugs and said their goodbyes.

"All right, let's get going," Mr. Hughes said.

Joseph held an end of a coffin and helped Mr. Hughes carry it outside into his wagon.

I turned toward Savannah and Grandma Hughes. "I'm much obliged to you both."

"You're welcome, dear," Grandma Hughes said. "Y'all and the others have a safe trip to Ohio."

"Yes, ma'am." I gave her and her granddaughter each a hug.

"It's time to go, Millie," Noah said.

After Joseph and Mr. Hughes took the last coffin out of the back of the house, I followed Noah outside the front door. As Noah, Joseph, and I walked across the railroad tracks to the train depot to get our tickets, I glanced heavenward at the sunrise sky, quoting Psalm 23 to myself: *Yea, though I walk through the valley of the shadow of death, I will fear no evil; for thou art with me; thy rod and thy staff they comfort me.* My heart raced as I observed people yapping and milling about the station with their trunks and travel bags.

We walked past a heavyset, fast-talking auctioneer and competitive bidders at a slave auction. Two slave women and one slave man stood chained in a row on the platform before a crowd of white, wealthy men. While looking at their sad, solemn faces, I wondered about the several terrifying thoughts flooding their minds.

Mumbling commotion from a grocery shop farther down from the train station startled me and caught my attention, causing me to lag behind. I couldn't believe my eyes. Two white men in dark wide-brimmed hats and dark-colored clothes wrestled a negro teenage boy into custody from the store, dragging him out of the door.

"Mama! No! I'm free! I'm free! I'm free!" the young negro boy in a white full-body apron hollered in the distance, fighting to keep hold of his mother.

"Jimmy! No! Please, don't do this," the negro mother said, whimpering and kneeling by the entrance of the store. "Please, don't take my son." Her voice trembled with heartbreaking despair.

One of the white men pulled the negro boy and his mother apart, cuffing the boy's wrists with chains, and I couldn't bear to watch the disturbing scene anymore. In an instant, a free man had become a slave without a word he said mattering to anyone. How could this be allowed in a nation of justice and freedom? The hypocrisy was surreal in our country of America.

Fear grew within me for Joseph's sake. Would the same thing happen to him or the others too?

I shivered and turned my attention to the depot entrance as a chill climbed up my spine. Somewhere the bounty hunters who trailed us were in the middle of the crowd—I sensed it in the light cool breeze.

SATURDAY, AUGUST 21, 7:00 A. M.
LOUISVILLE & NASHVILLE RAILROAD
Louisville, Kentucky

"THREE TICKETS TO CINCINNATI, ma'am, please?" Noah said to the saleswoman behind the counter, imitating a Southern accent.

The skinny brunette woman skimmed a wooden cabinet and grabbed three tickets off one of the small lower shelves. She placed them on the counter and peered from Joseph to us, pursing her lips. "That'll be $3.75," she said with a raspy, low-toned voice, arching her brow.

Noah dug in his suit jacket and pulled out his wallet. He tossed three silver dollars and three liberty-seated quarters on the counter.

The woman brushed the coins into her hand and slid the tickets to Noah under the glass screen.

"Thank you, ma'am," he said, taking them off the counter.

A loud whistle of the steam locomotive blew twice outside.

"The train leaves at seven," the woman said. "I reckon y'all had better hurry before ya get left. The next ride for Cincinnati won't be until eight in the morning."

Noah nodded. "Yes, ma'am. Thank you." He turned to Joseph. "Carry my case, boy."

Joseph took the violin case from Noah in his free hand.

"Come on, let's go board the train before we miss it," Noah said.

We exited the train depot, all of us keeping a lookout for the bounty hunters. None of us saw a sign of them. But as we walked along the platform of the train station, an old gentleman called for attention, hindering us from getting on the steam engine.

"Excuse me, sir! Could I detain you?" the uniformed conductor said.

In our huddle, we stopped and turned around to the old man as other passengers walked past us, put their luggage in a baggage car, and boarded the train.

"Yes, sir. Is there a problem?" Noah said, raising his head.

"Yes," the conductor said and glanced over his sepia-tinted glasses at Joseph. "You got papers for this negro?"

"Do I have papers for this negro?" Noah mocked a laugh. He smirked and pulled them out of his ruby suit jacket. "As a matter of fact, I do. I keep Josiah's papers with me in case annoying *sleuths* like yourself become overly suspicious."

The conductor took the document and scanned it over. "It says here he's five-foot-nine. Did he shrink?"

"No," Noah said, "he was wearing his work boots. That added a few inches to his height, you understand?"

The conductor folded the document and handed it over. He peered at Noah suspiciously. "Where you from, mister?"

"That's none of your business," Noah said smugly. "Now, do you have any more questions, or can we board this train?"

The whistle blew twice again.

"Of course not, sorry, sir. Y'all can proceed directly," the conductor said, tipping his dress cap.

"Thank you, sir." Noah took a courteous bow and continued leading the way to the train. We climbed onto a passenger car connected to the coal car. Over twenty white faces turned and stared at us in unison with irritated expressions, all of the passengers sitting in their designated seats.

Noah cleared his throat. "Excuse us, everyone. Sorry for the wait."

We walked down the narrow aisle and sat in our designated seats, Joseph sitting alone behind us.

A grouchy, tight-eyed ticket checker with a scarred cheek stepped up the thin aisle, punching holes in each passenger's ticket. He stopped near our seats. "Tickets!"

Noah and I gave our tickets to him, which the man handed back afterward.

The ticket checker man glared at Joseph, grounding his jaw. "Whatcha doing here? Negroes ain't allowed with passengers."

"He's our house slave," Noah answered.

The man scowled and inclined his bearded face to Noah. His single, thick eyebrow wrinkled over his tight eyes like a dark, long worm. "I don't care if he's Old King Cole. He goes in the back!"

"But his ticket says—" I said.

"It's all right, missus," Joseph interrupted. "I'll be fine." He stood and held out his ticket. "My ticket, sir?"

The ticket collector snatched it from Joseph, punched a hole, and shoved it against his chest.

Joseph studied the group of white passengers staring at and surrounding him. He shook his head and walked through the blue velvet curtain to the rear negro section of the passenger car.

I peeked of out the window as Mr. Hughes spoke to the same conductor that stopped us. He rolled a coffin on a hand truck. I couldn't make out their conversation from the loud noises of the train, but the conductor pointed toward the back of the locomotive.

Mr. Hughes tipped his cap and moved as directed, so I assumed everything was going as planned. Then Mr. Hughes spotted me from the window and gave a wink as he pushed the hand truck to the boxcar behind our passenger car. He got the other two coffins off his wagon with help from another negro man I'd never met. As he pushed the last one, I saw the bounty hunters looking around for us. They were frantically arguing with the conductor.

Being delayed from our departure, some of the passengers whispered and grumbled under their breath.

"For heaven's sake, what's holding up the train? I'm expected in Cincinnati by nine-thirty," an old woman sitting across from us said. She huffed and puffed, impatiently flapping her hand fan.

Worry pricked my heart and a cold sweat broke out on my forehead as I turned away. I took a few breaths to calm my pounding heart and reclined in my seat next to Noah, who stared forward and sat as still as a statue in his seat.

"The bounty hunters are outside," I whispered.

Noah licked his lips and gulped. "Don't look at them. Just act natural."

"All right, they're all good—finally," the ticket collector said.

The engineer blew the whistle, and the train moved down the tracks.

In my peripheral vision, the bounty hunters and conductor were yelling, running, and waving their arms for the train to stop. Looking straight ahead, I pulled the curtain across the window and relaxed my tensed shoulders.

"What are they saying?" one man asked with a frown.

"They're trying to catch the train," an old man answered. He tried to get the attention of the grumpy ticket collector, but the man walked by and ignored him.

More commotion stirred in the passenger car as others noticed the two bounty hunters. Some people laughed at them and others whispered behind their hands. In the end, the train continued chugging on the tracks, leaving them behind.

I closed my eyes and let out a sigh of relief as the men's little yelling voices outside faded away. Laughter tickled me within, forming a smile on my face. Some obstacles had gotten in our path, but by God's grace, we had slipped away from the hunters' clutches again. The men would have to ride their horses, or catch the next train to arrive in Ohio, and that wouldn't be until tomorrow.

Noah exhaled and chuckled. "Phew, that was a close one."

"It was," I agreed, glancing down, "but too bad for the young salesman."

"Salesman?"

I nodded and then looked at Noah gravely. "Yes. Something happened outside the train depot." On the verge of tears, I bit my lip and whispered. "I . . . I'd rather not discuss it here."

"Oh, that's okay," Noah whispered back. He glimpsed over at the other white passengers. "I understand."

We sat in silence as the train chugged, neither of us knowing what else to say. Then, after a short moment, I asked Noah about his family background. Aside from his participation in the railroad network and his musical profession, I knew nothing else about him.

"Mr. Shepherd, are your parents still alive?"

Noah laid his head back and sighed, closing his eyes. "I don't know. My mother abandoned me when I was young, and I never knew my father. I grew up in an orphanage until I ran away when I was sixteen."

My tired eyes ached, glancing at him. "I'm sorry. I didn't know. Maybe I shouldn't have asked that."

"No," Noah said and smiled at me. "It's quite all right."

I fiddled with the buckle of my carpetbag. "Noah, I . . . I'd like to ask you something, but I don't know how to say it."

Noah looked at me. "What is it? I'm all ears, literally."

I giggled and glanced over at him again. "Well, it's kind of a personal question. It's . . . you're doing all this traveling and well . . . do you have a lady?" I looked up and studied him, noticing his sudden apprehension.

"A lady?" Noah squirmed and laughed it off. "Uh, no, why do you ask?"

"Just wondering." I adjusted myself in my seat and closed my eyes to rest, smiling a little. With no other woman in his life, could I win his heart? Since my eighteenth birthday, I greatly admired him, but I hadn't realized it until after we separated for some time.

From his curly, red locks and endearing stature, to his eloquent speech and passionate violin music; except for my dear mother, I hadn't missed anyone before as much as I had Noah. Perhaps there was hope, but with so little time, we were practically strangers. After our journey ended and we reached Canada, there was a chance we'd never trace each other's path again.

I sighed and fell asleep. Moving toward Cincinnati, we still had a long way to go, and seeing the bounty hunters nearly everywhere we'd gone, the men weren't going away anytime soon.

They would likely follow us to Canada.

23 *Harboring Fugitives*

"MILLIE, WE'RE HERE. IT'S time to get off the train," Noah said, nudging me out of my sleep. "We have to hurry and get to the others."

The ear-splitting whistle droned, followed by the ringing of the steam engine's bell. It seemed we arrived faster than I thought we would. I opened my eyes as passengers walked off the train. Besides a few other passengers, it was nearly empty in the seating area. Noah and I were the last ones to step off the front passenger car of the train.

The grouchy ticket collector knitted his single thick eyebrow, chewing a mouthful of tobacco, if I could tell from the stench of his breath.

"Welcome to Cincinnati," he said in his low, scratchy voice.

Noah jerked back his head and fluttered his eyelids, getting a dense waft of his breath. He cleared his throat.

"Uh, thank you, sir. Have a nice night." He tipped his derby as we walked down the stairs of the passenger car.

Noah held his forefinger under his nose, mumbling to me. "Good grief, what's he eating horseradish?"

I giggled. "It's tobacco, Noah. Haven't you ever seen anyone chew it before?"

"No," Noah said, "chewing tobacco isn't too common among men in Canada. Come now, we must find Mr. Hughes."

I inhaled and smelt the scent of burning coal as I surveyed the bustling station. On one side of the middle railroad tracks was another small train depot and on the other side were a few scattered farmhouses on the flat, muddy ground. We weren't in the center of the city, but somewhere in an outer nearby area.

Joseph walked through from the negro passenger car and followed us. "What do we do now?"

"We need to find Mr. Hughes. He must be around here somewhere," Noah said. "Let's walk a little farther down."

Together, the three of us searched for him in the crowd of bobbing heads passing by under a row of streetlight poles. As passengers received their luggage from the baggage car, we found Mr. Hughes and another kind gentleman placing the coffins into the back of a wagon and having a conversation.

"It's a shame the family died," the gentleman said. "How did it happen?"

Mr. Hughes shook his head and sucked his teeth. "I'm afraid they had an accident. The husband was riding down a steep hill in Kentucky, some bystanders said, and he lost control of the wagon." He grunted as he and the other man pushed the second coffin into the wagon.

"What a terrible tragedy!" the gentleman said.

Mr. Hughes spotted us standing by, waiting to get Noah's case from the baggage car. "There's the witness and their butler now."

"Witnesses?" Noah frowned, but got Mr. Hughes' cue when he winked at him behind the other gentleman.

"Oh, yes, of course," Noah said, joining the make-believe story. "My wife and I saw the whole thing. Isn't that right, Mildred, dear?" He nudged his violin case into my side.

I kept their cover and nodded. "Yes, that's right."

Mr. Hughes and the other man placed the last coffin in the wagon.

"Well, that'll do it," Mr. Hughes said. "Thanks for your help with loading them."

"You're welcome, sir," the other man said. "Give the remaining family my condolences. I've got to go. There are passengers I've got to pick up over on Fourth Street. Be careful with my wagon and be sure you return it back when you've transported the bodies to the undertaker."

"Of course," Mr. Hughes said. "I'll take good care of it."

The gentleman walked off to his livery yard.

Joseph inhaled a deep breath and looked around with a bright smile on his face. "It sure feels good."

"What feels good?" I asked him.

Joseph tightened his mouth, blinking back tears. "My first time . . . standing on *free* soil."

Of course, how could I have forgotten? Ohio was a free state, a place that for a time was the gateway to freedom for fugitive slaves. Now, it was a refuge for blacks who didn't want to leave the country, but there were also special terms, which I learned when we reached the next location in Toledo, Ohio.

"Phew, thanks for the cover," Mr. Hughes said.

Noah chuckled. "You're welcome. Now, I suppose we should ride into town." He kept a lookout and lowered his voice. "Take the coffins to the bookstore. I'll meet you all there shortly after I pick up a telegram from Hubert."

"Right. Take care," Mr. Hughes said.

Noah tipped his derby. "You too." He walked off to the small post office.

Mr. Hughes climbed and sat on the front seat with the reins. Then I joined him while Joseph sat in the back with the coffins. After fifteen more miles, we arrived at the soul of Cincinnati.

Rows of street gas lamps were on each side of the paved road. I couldn't wait to see what they looked like glowing at night time. We rode by brick apartments and small business shops. Amazement blossomed within me, sightseeing the surroundings of the city. One brick building with green shades covering the second-floor windows stood out to me. The sign above the door said, 'Wendell Books Inc.

From the distance, it looked as though it was out of business. A pang hit my chest. Was there still a chance for me to make it as an author in the city? Reading books was a simple leisure someone either did or didn't like during their spare time. I hoped to God my journey to the North wasn't in vain. While riding, I inhaled the breeze. A cool wind carried the scent of brewing apple cider from somewhere.

I sniffed and looked around to find where it might've been coming from. Horses pulling black buggies and wooden wagons pranced on the cobblestone streets as drivers carried wooden barrels of cargo or passengers in and out of town. A few people dressed in elegant and country wear walked to and from the stores.

Fishermen and vendors at fruit and vegetable stands called out to the city people walking by, trying to make as many sales as possible. One man drove a wagon past us painted with "Cincinnati Ice Company" on the side. I marveled at how ice was hauled in this way during the summer.

"Land sakes! Dis da biggest city I ever saw," Joseph said, surveying his whereabouts.

I chuckled and smiled. "Me too. I've never been to the city before."

Mr. Hughes pulled the wagon behind the bookstore in a narrow alley below a clothesline pinned with clothes swinging in the wind. A brick apartment building of boarding rooms was next to the Wendell Bookstore.

"This bookstore is magnificent. I was expecting us to seek refuge in another house," I whispered.

Mr. Hughes stepped down from his seat, walked around, and helped me from the wagon. He glanced both ways and looked into my eyes, whispering. "This is our secret hideout. Here the women can finally get out of the coffins safely and rest until the next trip toward Toledo."

"Can you please hurry?" Pearl mumbled from her coffin. "I'm fixin' to be sick."

It was good to hear Pearl's voice, but concern clouded my face.

"We better hurry," Mr. Hughes said. "Joseph, help me take the coffins in." He faced me. "Miss Millie, you can enter the store from the front to avoid suspicion. Just tap the knocker on the door."

"All right. Thank you." As I turned the street corner with my carpetbag, a black carriage with a gray horse clacked up the road. Noah was sitting in the front seat with a well-dressed middle-aged man in a top hat.

The carriage came to a halt.

Noah stepped out with his violin case. "Thank you, sir.

Have a good day." He waved as the man stirred around his wagon and rode away.

We walked to the door of the bookstore together.

"And so, we meet again," Noah joked.

I smiled and shrugged. "Looks that way."

Noah tapped the knocker and we quietly waited for a response on the front concrete steps.

Mr. Arthur Wagner answered the door.

Without his ridiculous, curled mustache, I almost didn't recognize him. He was dressed in an elegant, evergreen vest and white dress shirt with tan trousers and brown, leather dress shoes. The chain of his golden pocket watch was clipped to his vest, the watch tucked snugly in his side pocket. He grinned. "Well, I see you've finally made it over the shore. Come in, both of you."

When we entered, the first room facing the busy street had two bookcases filled with loads of books. The floorboards were dusty and arrayed with spiderwebs, but the store had an old and cozy feeling I loved. On the front counter was a small handbell and a few stacks of other books, and mousetraps were in two corners of the room.

Arthur pulled down the shades on the first-floor windows. He walked to one of the bookcases against the wall and pulled back the whole shelf, revealing a secret passageway behind the bookcase. It was the most ingenious thing I'd seen and the safest place to harbor fugitives. I doubted the bounty hunters would search for us here come tomorrow morning.

"I hope the women made it with you," Arthur said.

Noah took off his gray derby and threaded his hand through his red curls. "They did, thankfully."

"Yes," I added, "Mr. Hughes and Joseph went around back with the coffins."

Arthur led the way through the opening behind the five-shelf bookcase. "Excellent! Come upstairs. We have many fugitives and Mrs. Simmons needs help serving her stew."

Noah and I followed Arthur to the second floor. On the left after entering the bookcase opening was a narrow pathway to another door that went to outside or another room.

"Who's Mrs. Simmons?" I asked, carefully taking my steps beside Noah.

Noah glanced over, stepping beside me up the dusty staircase. "She's the lady cook who feeds the fugitives. You'll meet her soon. I hope you don't mind helping us. More fugitives are coming tomorrow."

"Oh, it's my pleasure," I said. "I'd be glad to help them."

We reached the top of the hardwood staircase.

Murmuring voices bumbled from behind a half-open brown door in front of us.

Noah and I walked inside to check things out. As we entered the medium-sized room, I couldn't believe my eyes. Bunk and spring beds were lined in rows like in a town hospital. Some of the slaves were sitting around or lying on the beds. Others were eating bowls of chow. All of them had escaped their masters' plantations from all over the Deep South. Some of them were scarred from brandings or beatings on their arms and legs, and some were barefoot and bandaged from foot injuries.

A short, dark-haired woman wearing a colorful paisley shawl and a gray apron hanging with chatelaine trinkets and keys walked over to us.

"How are you, Mr. Shepherd?" She shook Noah's hand in both of hers.

Noah grinned. "I'm fine, Mrs. Simmons." He gestured to me. "This is Millie Crabtree, a fellow friend of mine."

Mrs. Simmons shook my hand vigorously, my arm jiggling from her manly handshake. "A pleasure to meet you, ma'am. I'm Caroline . . . Mrs. Caroline Simmons, but thanks to Noah, I reckon you already knew my last name." She chuckled a goofy, hearty laugh that made me smile.

Mr. Hughes and Joseph placed the last wood casket on the middle of the hardwood floor beside the other two coffins.

"Well, sir. You got somethin to open dem with?" Joseph took off his bowler hat and wiped his sweaty forehead.

"You can use the crowbar above the fireplace," Mrs. Simmons said.

Mr. Hughes grabbed the tool and stuck the curved end of it in a slot of one in the coffins. He applied pressure and loosened the wood lid until it popped off. Everyone surrounded the coffin and looked in, hoping whoever was inside was alive and well. Slave men and women folded their hands and mumbled prayers during the first reveal.

Anna's hands were over her face, peeking through her fingers. "Is it safe?"

Warmhearted grins and smiles were on everyone's faces in the room. Some of the slaves laughed, clapped, and praised GOD another smuggled one survived and made it over "River Jordan," otherwise known as the Ohio River.

"Yes, it's safe, Anna," Noah said, smiling. "Welcome to Ohio."

She stepped out of the box.

"Oh, Anna, I'm glad you're all right." I hugged her.

"Me too," Anna replied and giggled.

Mr. Hughes opened another coffin, which turned out to be Pearl this time. Her arm was covering her eyes, panicking.

"It's all right, Pearl. You're in a safe place now," Noah said.

I knelt beside the coffin. "We're in a bookstore for fugitives. Everything's all right, Pearl."

She lowered her arm and fluttered her eyes open. "Millie?"

I smiled and nodded.

"Oh, Millie, I'm so glad." Pearl sat up in the coffin and clung to me, sniffling and sobbing.

Mr. Hughes popped the lid off the last coffin.

With a still face, Margaret remained motionless, her arms crossed over her chest.

"Marge?" Noah said.

She stayed motionless in the coffin, and my heart felt like it stopped.

"Marge, wake up. You're in Ohio," Noah said.

Apprehension spread on many of the others' faces and settled in the room as we looked at one another and observed her still not moving again.

Dread fell in my stomach, glancing from Noah to Margaret. "What's wrong with her? Is she . . .?"

Noah squatted in a crouch and checked her pulse. He turned his head and looked up at us with a relieved smile. "No, she's sleeping."

A sigh of relief and light laughter filled the room.

Noah nudged her. "Wake up, dear friend. You'll need some food to continue your journey."

"What?" Margaret awoke and looked startled from everyone standing around her. "Are we in Canada?"

"Not yet, ma'am," Noah said, "but we're almost there. You gave us a little scare."

"I'm sorry," Margaret answered. "I reckon the train ride made me sleepy along the way." She got out of the coffin and brushed off her clothes.

Noah turned and shook Mr. Hughes' hand. "Thank you for your assistance, sir."

"Of course," Mr. Hughes said with a smile, "now I must hurry and return the wagon to the livery. Let's hope no one saw us." He winked and left the room.

"There's plenty of chicken stew for everyone," Mrs. Simmons said, stirring a big, black kettle pot. She filled wooden bowls for us and the other slaves with an iron ladle. Noah, Margaret, and I helped pass out the bowls to everyone else as she made them.

I handed a bowl to a middle-aged slave woman and her little girl.

"Thank you, ma'am. God bless you," the woman said.

As we ate, Noah talked about our trip to Michigan, and the next steps we needed to take to safely cross the Canadian border.

"Bright tomorrow, you'll all need to leave Ohio as quickly as you can." He studied the group of slaves encircled around him. "All of you will need to be out of here to avoid getting auctioned back down South again. I'm aware bounty hunters do that. If they can't get who they were after, they can take advantage of any runaway slaves without documentation for a dollar. That's how desperate these sick men are."

"Who gonna take us to Michigan?" Anna asked.

"I will," Arthur answered, "as well as Hubert when he arrives tomorrow, but first we have to get to Toledo."

I looked at Noah with wonder. "What about you?"

"I'll ride in the front of the wagon with Arthur or Hubert to make sure you all get to Canada safely," Noah said.

"And after that?" I asked.

There was long hesitation as I sensed the unpleasant coming of disappointing news.

Noah ate a spoonful of his stew. He hung his head and stirred his spoon in his bowl. "Then I'll be going back down South to North Carolina." He looked up and studied me. "There are still many more slaves trapped in bondage to set free, Millie. Helping them is what I do."

I drew a deep breath and touched his shoulder. "I know. Just please . . . be careful."

"There's always a risk, Millie," Noah said, "but I promise I'll try."

I knew he meant what he said, but fear was in his eyes and made me a little nervous and afraid.

Pearl dropped her spoon into her bowl. She grimaced and rubbed a trembling hand over her forehead.

I frowned. "What's wrong? You don't like the stew?"

"No, it's fine. It's just . . . I have to tell you something." Pearl took a slow breath and looked at me. Moisture welled up in her hazel-brown eyes and she spoke in almost a whisper, her chin quivering. "Your Papa . . . he . . . he snuck in my room and forced me to be with him. The encounters . . . they went on for many years since I was a little girl, even before I entered the big house." A tear slipped down her right cheek. "The first time . . . he walked me by the hand far into the forest, claimed he had a special gift for me. After it was over, he . . . he told me not to say anything . . . gave me a cornhusk doll. I'd never had a doll or a toy before. I'm sorry this happened, Millie. I'm so sorry." Ashamed, she buried her face in her shaking hand and wept.

I stared speechless at Pearl. "Why didn't you tell me about this sooner?"

Pearl lifted her head and bit her lower lip. She hesitated and blinked her teary eyes, reflecting on the past. "I-I was terrified of hell . . . I wanted *so badly* to go to heaven and I knew how you *loved* your father. I was scared you wouldn't believe me or want to be friends anymore."

Noah, Arthur, and the other slaves remained silent and wore solemn looks on their faces.

Sobbing, I hugged my best friend. "Oh, I'm so sorry, Pearl. It wasn't your fault. You never deserved this."

She leaned her head against me and sniveled. "I don't feel well." She squirmed away from my embrace and whimpered with her hand over her mouth. "I'm sorry. I need to go outside for a moment. Excuse me, everyone." She left.

Mrs. Simmons face fell. "I'll look after her." She exited the room to console Pearl and closed the door.

At that instant, I was trapped in shock as humiliation stung me. I felt as though an arrow pierced my side or a knife had sliced my heart. I closed my eyes to dissipate the onset of more tears, thankful my best friend had at least gotten away from my Papa's evil deeds.

I didn't know what was the matter with her, but under her circumstances, a disturbing thought traced my mind. Somehow, I sensed a premonition of Pearl's condition. Because of this, it essentially appeared the outcome of my father's vile sin had begun the gestation of fate I had hoped wouldn't come true.

Pearl was with child.

24 *Departing Cincinnati*

BEFORE DAWN, THE SOUND of a wagon outside the bookstore awoke me out of my sleep. While the others continued resting, I arose from the hardwood floor and peeked out the green shade of one window. My heart smiled when I saw Hubert hop down from the front high-backed seat. He had changed his disguise because he was wearing the same yellow suit jacket he wore when he played his cello at my birthday party. He glanced both ways down the street and pulled a tan blanket off the back of the wagon.

Joy filled me when Ozzie and two other slave girls came out from hiding.

It would please Anna to reunite with her big brother.

I didn't want to spoil the big surprise, so I resisted the urge to wake her before the others entered inside the bookstore.

From below, Hubert and the others came in through the back door of the brick building.

I rushed over to the door as footsteps approached the staircase to the second floor of the bookstore.

"Anybody up?" Hubert asked in his deep voice.

I opened the door and gestured a hand. "In here!"

Hubert and the other slaves entered the room.

"Hi, Miss Millie," Ozzie said.

I smiled and nodded. "Ozzie, I'm glad you're here. Anna's asleep on a cot."

Ozzie walked over to his sister's cot as Noah and some of the other slaves stirred. He knelt by her bedside and nudged her a little. "Anna . . . sis, it's me, Ozzie."

Anna opened and widened her eyes. She blinked in disbelief. "Ozzie?" She jolted up and flung her arms around his neck, embracing him. "Ozzie! Praise God! I can't believe it's you. What are—how'd you git here?"

"Well," Ozzie began, "what'd you think, little sis? Dat I'd let you make it to Canaan without me? I had to run, and not just for you and myself, but for Mama and Papa too." He held his sister at arm's length. "Mr. Hubert came back and got a few more of us the next night after he dropped y'all off at Miss Winifred's place."

"Good to see you, Ozzie." Joseph grinned.

"You too, Joe," Ozzie said, "Massa Crabtree's real mad. Since y'all left, he bought more field slaves on the cotton plantation and became harsher cauze of his debt. He's real mad about us leavin. Massa McMillan too."

"We be the Murphy sisters," the older of the slave girls that arrived with Ozzie said. "Massa McMillan waz gonna separate my little sister and me and sell me farther south to Mississippi, but I couldn't let dat happen. We ran into Mr. Donovan and the others in da forest and joined dem da rest of the way here."

Pearl stood from a bottom cot. "Where's Randy?" She breathed with panic and kneaded her white apron.

A dead silence filled the room, others looking at one another.

Ozzie bit his lip and hesitated to answer, glancing back at Hubert.

"I'm afraid he didn't make it, ma'am," Hubert said. "He tried to keep up, but his ankle injury slowed him down. A bounty hunter shot him while we were running to Willow Creek."

Pearl buried her face in her hands and whimpered, walking off toward a window. The other slaves moaned, grumbled, and sobbed, and one of the negro women got up and tried to console Pearl.

My heart shattered in pieces. It wasn't fair seeing her go through so much. After being born from a violent act, she was rejected by her father and separated from her mother and grandmother. Against her will, she was forced to relive the curse that caused her birth, all in the name of God. Now she'd lost the love of her life. How much more would she suffer? How much more would Pearl have to endure?

I walked over and wrapped an arm around her shoulders. "I'm so sorry. I wish there was something I could do to ease your pain."

Pearl wore a wistful smile and faced me with her tear-stained cheeks. "You already are . . . being my friend." She drew a shaking breath and sighed. "Randy had so many plans for us. He was gonna build our own house, he said. I can't believe he's gone. I can feel him. He's still alive . . . in my heart. . ." Her words trailed off as she broke down again. She dropped her head and wrapped an arm around my and another slave woman's waists, hugging us at the same time.

The slave woman standing with us in our group of three recited Numbers chapter six verses twenty-four to twenty-six as we cried in our huddle. *"The LORD bless thee and keep thee; the LORD make his face shine upon thee, and be gracious unto thee: The LORD lift up his countenance upon thee, and give thee peace."*

Pearl sniffled and gave a weak smile to her. "Thank you."

"What time is it?" a fellow male slave said.

Arthur checked his pocket watch. "It's a quarter to six."

"We better get an early start and take everyone out of here now," Noah suggested. "The bounty hunters will likely catch up to us soon in Michigan." He switched hats and put on his fedora again.

"I'll get one of the wagons ready." Arthur grabbed a pear from a fruit bowl and took a bite, marching out of the door to the stairs.

"If anyone's hungry, I can cook some oatmeal," Mrs. Simmons said.

"Sounds good, ma'am," Ozzie said.

Everyone gathered their belongings. Some took turns washing their hands, arms, and faces with basins and pitchers of water behind a folding screen, the women with one and the men with the other.

After breakfast and the wagons were prepared, it was time to go. The slaves and I followed Noah, Arthur, and Hubert downstairs through a narrow passageway beside the hardwood staircase and walked outside through the door.

Several slaves climbed into the back of Arthur's new covered wagon, and others hid under a load of potato bags in Hubert's freight wagon under the tan blanket. I chose to ride in the covered wagon, though it was densely packed and muggy inside. Some of us sat on the siding of the interior of the covered wagon, while the rest sat Indian-style in the center of the floor.

Standing outside the wagon, Noah smiled and whispered at us. "After we finally reach Toledo, we'll travel to Detroit, Michigan. There's a businessman's ship will transport you all across the Detroit River when we reach the shoreline. Keep quiet and don't move around too much."

"Yes, sir," an older, gray-headed slave man said. He looked around at the other younger slaves and chuckled. "I'll make sure everyone keeps still."

Noah nodded, winked, and shut the canopy of the wagon.

As soon as he did, it was very dark inside. Only a stream of light shone through the opening of the canopy. While we journeyed along, the sun rose more and the light became brighter, shining through the tan fabric of the covered wagon. None of us had a clue where we were, but we trusted Noah and the others would take us where we needed to go.

Because of the bumpy ride, I figured we were riding over cobblestone roads. Other horse-drawn wagons past us and people outside talked on the streets. Some of the slaves fell asleep from the rock and sway of the wagon, but for a while, I stayed awake during the trip.

The voyage to Canada from the South had been a long one, but I thanked God we were almost to the Promised Land. After reaching Detroit, all we had to do was sail into the safety zone. Some hours later, I felt the wagon stop and overheard Noah and Arthur talking to another gentleman who'd told them to halt. It didn't sound too good as we had run into a little hindrance.

"Drop your weapons—and slowly," one man said.

"We have none, sir," Noah answered. "Please, j-j-just don't shoot us."

"Step down from the wagon," the man said.

"What for?" Arthur asked, confused.

"I said step down!" the man demanded.

There was silence, and then the wagon shifted as the men climbed from their front seats. Footsteps moved toward the back of the covered wagon and someone fiddled with the canopy, unraveling it.

"What are you doing?" Noah said, startled.

"Please, sir! Stop! You can't go in there!" Arthur said. "It's an invasion of privacy!"

Some of the fugitive slaves awoke and gasped with stretched-wide mouths, startled from their peaceful sleep. Others huddled closer to one another, some of the women hiding behind the men.

Oh, God. It's a bounty hunter. My heart banged inside my chest as I covered my eyes, anticipating the presence of the intruder.

The sun shone in our faces, and I peeked between my fingers at the dark shadowy figure in a wide-brimmed hat standing before us.

Looking into the man's fiery eyes showed he was anguished and ready to take revenge. After this, nothing else entered my mind, except one scary thought.

This was the end of our journey.

25 *Sold into Slavery*

THE MAN STOOD WITH a shotgun in one hand and studied us wild-eyed with his nostrils flared, huffing and puffing like a wild, mean ox. Behind him, Noah, and Arthur, the road was vacant, except for Hubert's wagon. I reckon we were in a smaller town, almost completely outside of Cincinnati.

"Please, sir," one of the slave women said, holding her little girl in her arms. "We don't want no trouble. We's just tryin' to make it North."

"Who are you? What do you want with them?" Arthur asked.

The man pursed his lips and glanced back at the two white men. "My name's Joel—Joel Peterson. I'm a free man looking for my only son Jimmy. Greedy, good-for-nothing slave catchers kidnapped him while I was sending a telegram for some more supplies. I won't rest 'til I find him. I'll kill those dirty, rotten thieves—I'll kill'em all!" He desperately looked around inside the wagon. "Jimmy . . . Jimmy!"

"I'm sorry, sir," Noah said, "but we have no Jimmy here. We're on our way to Toledo. I don't know what else we can do, but I promise we'll keep a lookout for your son."

Arthur placed his hand on the negro man's shoulder. "That's right. You can trust us to do our best to help find him."

The man sighed and dropped his head. He nodded and shook Noah's and Arthur's hands. "Thank you. I'm sorry if I scared y'all." His chin trembled. "I'm just so angry and distressed. He. . . he could be anywhere. I may never see him again."

"I think I saw when they took him," I confessed.

The negro man raised his head. "You did?"

"Yes, sir," I said, "it was two white bounty hunters in dark hats and dark clothes. One of them cuffed a boy named Jimmy. Do you have a grocery shop in Louisville?"

"Yes, ma'am, I do. It's near the Louisville Railroad."

I nodded. "That was probably them, sir."

"Thank you for telling me, miss." The negro man observed the others in the covered wagon and stuck out his broad chest, taking a deep breath. "I give y'all my blessing and bid you Godspeed."

"Thank you, sir," the mother slave woman said.

The man tipped his hat and went on his way. He

climbed on his horse and rode down the long highway, continuing his tiring, endless search for his son.

Noah turned to us. "Is everyone all right?"

"Yes, sir." The old man grinned. "We're fine. Just fine."

"Where are we, sir?" a young boy asked.

"We're still in Cincinnati. We'll have to seek refuge in another nearby town before we reach Toledo," Arthur said. "This is the longest stretch of our journey."

Hoofbeats pounded up the road in the distance. "Everyone remain quiet," Noah whispered. "We've got a long way to go." He pulled down the back sheet and fastened the fabric of the canopy before the rider coming could see us in the wagon.

There was another moment of silence as we waited for what would happen next, and then we moved again.

Leaning my head against the inside of the wagon, I listened to the others talk about their tragic experiences with their masters. They also discussed all the things they wanted to do after getting free.

"My girl's gonna have a better life dan I ever had," the slave mother with the little girl said. "She's gonna learn to read in school and make her mark on dis world. I'll see to dat."

"What about you, missy?" the old man asked me.

"Oh, sir, I plan to publish my first children's book," I said. "Perhaps I'll also participate in the increasing abolitionist movement. Maybe I'll write my own anti-slavery, weekly newspaper like William Garrison's *The Liberator*. You know, I think I will."

"That would be wonderful," Pearl said, smiling.

A sea of disturbing thoughts tossed inside my mind. I took out my journal and pencil from my carpetbag. As the sun streamed dappled light through the canopy onto my pages, a flow of words came to me, inspiring me to write another entry:

1852, Aug. 22 — Sunday

We're on our way to Toledo, Ohio, but we have to stop in another town before getting there. Afterward, we'll be going to Detroit, Michigan. I can hardly believe it. After much running, traveling, and hiding out, we're almost to the Promised Land, as the others call it. I'm riding with friends whose faces I may never see again beyond this journey, but whose desire and heart-wrenching stories I'll never forget. My father and the townspeople at home probably think I'm a fool to have gone on this perilous journey, but I have learned a lot. For it showed me the hypocrisy of our country, which is portrayed as the land of the free. The scarred backs and shackled lives of my fellow friends are evidence of the lies woven into the corrupted republic of our nation.

America is a leech, sucking the blood of hardworking citizens, regarded as nothing better than horses and mules. It's a disgrace to God and the religious faith. If our country is truly a steeple of justice, equality, and love for our fellow man, we must practice what we preach. I don't know what my white neighbors will do, but I cannot remain a bystander in the comfort of superiority. They shall hear my plea and the voices of sufferers.

A while ago, a free negro man stopped our wagon, looking for his beloved son that was sold into slavery. I believe I witnessed when bounty hunters took his son away. I saw the bitterness and tears in the negro man's eyes. He had every right to want revenge. Slavery is an inhumane nightmare. It's time for our political leaders to wake up from their negligent slumber, pull off the blanket, and act accordingly.

Freedom shouldn't be a privilege for some. It should be a must for all!

May God resurrect the soul of our country,
Mildred Crabtree

I closed my journal with my pencil in the loop holder and put it into my bag. As minutes turned into hours and the mother hummed her little girl to sleep, I fell asleep into a blurry dream of chaos, smoke, and explosions:

Young and old uniformed soldiers hollered, running through muddy puddles and over grassy hills. Some fired rifles and threw grenades, others laid dead or injured. Corpses of men from countless bloody deaths covered countryside landscapes and open wide fields. Wives, sisters, and mothers mourned the losses of husbands, brothers, and sons, both black and white. There

*was a war of differences, and no one knew when the wretched
battle would end. . . .*

"Millie . . . Millie, wake up, we've stopped again," Pearl
said, shaking me out of my sleep.

"Huh? What's wrong?" I opened my eyes and came
back to reality, my heart racing in my chest.

Crickets chirped and the night had fallen again.

"The wagon stopped," the old man said. "I reckon'
we're taking a rest stop."

The back sheet of the wagon opened.

Arthur held up a lit lantern, looking at us sitting
inside. "Well, dear friends, we're here in Kettering
tonight, a small farmland city about five miles from
Dayton. We're taking an unplanned stop to be safe. We'll
rest here for the night, but we'll leave bright and early
tomorrow morning."

"When will we reach Toledo?" I asked.

Arthur sighed wearily. "If we travel by wagon, not
until another eight or nine days, but we're hoping to
board another train. Some negro families have offered to
let y'all stay in their homes. Noah, Hubert, and I will keep
a watch for you all and we've got weapons in case we need
them. Pray for a safe night's rest and journey to Toledo."
He left with his lantern.

With worried eyes, we looked at one another in the
wagon. How could we sleep in peace knowing bounty
hunters could come and find us any minute? We still had
a long way before we exited the state of Ohio. And with

the government on the side of white slave owners, there was always the risk of recapture no matter where fugitive slaves went in the country. Being a free, white woman, I could only imagine what Mr. Peterson's son and other slaves felt like to be recaptured into slavery. Would this happen to my fellow friends too?

"Precious Lord, please, keep us from harm. Amen," the mother said, looking at the full moon and holding her little girl in her lap.

We stepped out of the wagon one by one and surveyed our surroundings. From the outside, we saw our wagons were in a fenced-in dry grassland, hidden behind tall trees. A couple of cabin homes were also surrounding the area. At one of them, a negro man came outside and picked up an axe from a tree stump. He placed a small log on the stump and chopped it in half, afterward chopping more logs for firewood.

While he worked, the door of the same cabin house opened again and a young, negro woman in a blue dress and a white shawl stood out in front of the home. She smiled and waved. "Greetings to y'all. I'm Nina and the man chopping wood is Gerald, my husband. Come inside for a warm meal and rest." She pushed back the wooden door and held it open for some of the members from the covered wagon.

"Thank . . . thank you so much, ma'am," the mother of the little girl said, entering with her sleeping, little daughter in her arms.

As the others walked into the little cabin house, I looked a few houses down and saw those from Hubert's wagon were going to rest in another family's cabin.

"You coming, miss?" Nina said.

Turning my attention to her, I smiled. "Oh, yes, ma'am. Thank you." I stepped in and she closed the door.

Although there wasn't much space for everyone, I was thankful the others and I were safe indoors. Two lanterns were lit, one on the table and another on the fireplace mantel.

"Gerald will be back in shortly to start a fire. It gets chilly in our home at night," Nina said, tugging her knitted shawl closer around her shoulders. "Have a seat anywhere."

Some of us sat on the hardwood floor and some on the chairs at the table.

"Gerald went fishing. I was scaling the fish he caught for supper." Nina picked up her knife and continued scaling and slicing pieces on her cutting board on the table.

Her husband entered through the door with an armful of logs and knelt by the fireplace, ordering and placing logs in the furnace.

I cocked my head, inquisitive. "I've never been this way before. How's it like in Kettering, ma'am?"

Nina glanced at me with a smile. "It's nice here. Lots of colored folks moved this way for farmland."

"How long y'all been here?" The mother rocked her little girl in her lap.

Nina tossed a piece of raw fish in a bowl of flour. "It's been about two years now. Ain't that right, Gerry?"

"Yep." Gerald lit a match and tossed it in the furnace. The fire danced and spread over the logs, crackling the wood. It was pleasant to watch and hear it during the calm evening.

Nina chuckled and glanced at her husband with a teasing smile. "Y'all will have to *excuse* my husband. He ain't much for talking to folks."

"You got that right—" Gerald looked at us— "but with Nina, I don't need to. She does all of it for me." With a witty look, he nodded sharply.

Pearl and Margaret giggled.

Nina sucked her teeth, glaring at her husband. "Go on away from here, Gerald. I am *not* a gabby woman."

The mother observed the cabin house. "Having your freedom and your own home here must be nice."

"Mostly," Nina said, "but black folks still have it rough in these parts. Sure, we have a home and land, but to ensure our liberty, we have to carry our freedom papers everywhere. We strive to stay out of white folks' way, but that doesn't change the justice system. If we ever get assaulted or robbed by a white person, the law prohibits us from testifying against them in the court of law."

I blinked in shock. Her words were unbelievable and only proved how runaway slaves weren't *entirely* free in the "free states" of America. Restrictions limited and hindered them from the same treatment as their white neighbors.

Nina scaled another fish, getting feisty. "Why, just to live in Ohio alone, we had to pay a five-hundred-dollar bond! Ain't that right, Gerry?"

"Uh-huh," Gerald answered.

Pearl frowned and shook her head. "We'd think blacks would be treated equally in a free state."

"That ain't the case, honey," Nina said, shaking her head, "but hardly anybody talks about it. Most folks talk about slaves being free in the free states. But the truth is, negroes won't *truly* be free until they're no longer discriminated against and the law gives them the same equal rights as white people."

This was true, and I hoped for everyone to have a better life when they crossed the Canadian border. After Nina cleaned and floured the fish, she fried some pieces and served us all plates with a side of baked beans. The food was tasty, and I wanted to ask for seconds, but the old man had before me and there wasn't enough food to go around. At last, Nina closed out the night by reading Psalm 121 from her holy bible in her rocking chair as everyone drifted asleep.

She finished the last few verses. *"The LORD shall preserve thee from all evil: he shall preserve thy soul. The LORD shall preserve thy going out and thy coming in from this time forth, even for evermore. Amen.*" She smiled and closed her bible. "Good night, everyone."

"Good night, Nina," Pearl and I whispered in unison.

Nina left her bible in her rocking chair. Then she stood and blew out the lantern on the table and the one on the mantel. "Sweet dreams, girls."

I curled up in a ball and used my carpetbag for a pillow, trying to get comfortable on the hard floor. Sleep was what I needed more than anything—it was what we all needed at the time. A long journey was still ahead before we reached Toledo. Closing my eyes, I prayed other kindhearted people would provide us with safe houses in the next coming days. Having bounty hunters on our trail, I wasn't sure we'd survive without them.

26 *Back to the Train*

THE SUNRISE BEGAN, AND it was time to leave and continue on our journey. Someone nudged my shoulder, waking me up. I opened my eyes and saw Pearl kneeling beside me. "Millie, it's time to go. We're going to the Springfield and Dayton Railroad." I sat up and refocused my eyes. "Railroad?" I didn't know we were all going on another train, but considering the long distance we still needed to travel, it was safer and made sense.

"Thank you, ma'am," Noah said, shaking Nina's hand and standing by the entrance.

"No, problem, sir," Nina said. "I'm glad to be of help to the railroad network."

Noah entered and stood before everybody as the rest of the others awoke from sleep. "All right, everyone. The horses are pretty tired and we have a long way to Toledo, so we're riding to Dayton to catch another train."

"Another train?" the mother said, frowning. "How will everyone git aboard dis time?"

Noah looked at the mother. "We're doing the same process as before, ma'am. Only we're smuggling some of you in wooden crates. However, because of the number of you, we cannot risk taking everyone on the same train in Dayton. Therefore, my colleagues and I have decided it would be best to use two different train rides."

He sighed and continued. "It means you all must decide among yourselves along with the others from Hubert's wagon who will take which train. The first train leaves at eight in the morning, and the second train ride is tomorrow at six. Both rides will be long and tiresome, as there will be several stops along the way before the engineer reaches to Toledo."

"I'll stay behind," the old man said, rubbing his knees.

His grandson wore a saddened face. "No, Gramps. Please, don't stay. You gotta come. You been waitin your whole life for the dawn of freedom."

"Naw, sonny," the old man said, holding the boy at arm's length. He inched up a smile. "It's all right. I'll let the younger and womenfolk go first. God be my helper, I'll still make it to the Promised Land."

"Well—" the boy bit his lower lip, pondering over the matter— "I ain't lettin you stay by yourself. If you stayin Gramps, then I will too."

"How many of us can go?" Margaret asked.

Noah kneaded his fedora. "Not including myself, Joseph, and Millie, I'm afraid only two of you can come on the first train ride. But Arthur has agreed to ride the second train, so he won't leave those who go aboard the next ride unattended."

"Is Ozzie goin?" Anna asked.

"No, and neither are the Murphy Sisters," Noah said.

"I'll catch the second train den," Anna said, wrapping tighter in her shawl. "If Ozzie's stayin, I'm stayin too. I caint leave my brother again."

I looked at Anna, concerned. "Are you sure? You don't have to do this if you don't want to."

Anna nodded. "I'm stayin, Millie. We separated once, and we ain't doin it again. Just please, say a prayer for us."

I walked over and hugged Anna. "I'll pray for y'all. I promise."

"What about you, ma'am?" Noah asked the mother.

The mother sighed and held her girl closer. "I reckon we'll stay with the old man and the boy. I doubt two people can fit in one crate."

"All right," Noah said, "I guess we should get moving." He put on his fedora, opened the door, and left.

Then Pearl, Joseph, Margaret, and I followed behind him, telling our goodbyes to the others and Miss Nina and Mr. Gerald. While Noah took the reins, the four of us climbed back into the covered wagon.

It was a short trip to Dayton, about fifteen or twenty minutes. The sheet of the covered wagon opened, and Noah and a dirty-faced man wearing a sea cap stood in back of the wagon.

"All right, we're in the livery," Noah said. "Pearl and Margaret, you two can step out. The crates are ready."

"Hello, everyone. I'm Willie Fisher," the man in the sea cap said. He glanced at Pearl and Margaret. "You ladies should hurry. The train will be leaving soon."

"Yes, sir. Thank you," Margaret said.

While riding over, Pearl was frightened by being trapped into a wooden crate, and I had to admit I was also concerned about her and her sensitive condition.

I looked at Pearl and read the fear etched on her face. "Don't worry. Just remember Henry Brown." I smiled a little, trying to help her feel better.

Pearl smiled timidly. "Thanks, Millie. I'll try."

We hugged, and then she and Margaret climbed out of the wagon.

"You two can follow me to the train depot," Noah said.

Joseph and I stepped from the wagon. Like our other train ride, Noah bought three tickets for us from a kind, old ticket salesman and we boarded the Springfield and Dayton train. Noah offered to show slave papers for Joseph, but surprisingly, the young conductor let us pass without evaluating his records. However, Joseph still had to sit in the back negro section.

I held my carpetbag in my lap. "Do you think they'll be fine?"

"I suppose," Noah said, "I certainly hope so."

I glanced at him. "How far is Dayton from Toledo?"

"It's a good hundred some miles," Noah said. "With all the stops, it'll be afternoon or evening by the time we reach Toledo. Mr. Fisher told the conductor the crates are filled with—"

Noah stopped talking as some other passengers passed us and took their designated seats. He glanced at them and back at me, mumbling. "He said they're filled with livestock animal feed."

A friendly, younger ticket collector walked up the narrow aisle and took our tickets, punching holes in them. "Thank you. Enjoy your ride."

"Thank you, sir," Noah said and nodded.

As the train puffed and smoked, I peeked out of the curtain at Mr. Fisher carrying a wooden crate with the conductor to the back of the train. As I exhaled a deep breath, my hands sweat, gripping the strap handle of my carpetbag. I couldn't shake off my nervousness over Pearl and Margaret's lives.

A hundred miles was a long trip to travel in confined boxes. I also hoped Anna and the others would be safe and later meet us in Toledo, Ohio tomorrow without the bounty hunters catching them.

The whistle blew, and the train started moving on the tracks, taking us onward to our journey to Canada.

I bowed my head and prayed for everyone's behalf. *God, watch over my friends and keep us all safe. Help us make it to the next safe house together. Amen.*

27 *Arriving in Toledo*

BETWEEN THE STOPS IN the surrounding cities of Springfield, Urbana, West Liberty, and other townships, to my discomfort, I fell in and out of sleep. When the whistle blew in Toledo, I nearly jumped out of my skin, waking up from peacefully resting on Noah's shoulder. I looked at his weary face.

A wry smile spread across Noah's lips. He fluttered his heavy eyelids. "Well, I suppose that's our signal to leave." He exhaled a breath, arose, and stepped into the line in the middle aisle. "Come on, Miss Millie."

I grabbed my carpetbag and slid out from the passenger seats after him, being the last one off the train car. The sounds of countless indistinct voices, horses' hoofbeats, and dinging train and ship bells welcomed us to the city of Toledo.

Peering through the thick smoke, I discovered the railroad we were at was near a shipyard of sail and rowboats gliding across a large body of water. "Is all that water part of the Ohio River?"

"Close," Noah said, "but it's actually Lake Erie."

Lake Erie. I should've known. With a bright smile, I inhaled the cool air and marveled at the gigantic ships, their big white sails fluttering in the breeze. Back in North Carolina, I hadn't ever been as close up to ships or sailboats before, and I was excited to ride in one when we reached the Michigan state line.

Joseph stepped down from the negro passenger car. He surveyed the environment and grouped with us. "My Lord, I feel like an ant at a backyard picnic. Everything's so big here."

I giggled. "Me too."

Standing in line, Noah got his bag from the baggage car, and then we proceeded into the neighborhood. We started to cross the flat wooden bridge near the railroad, but men riding buggies and wagons rode past us from another road beside the train. On the side of one wagon was painted "Toledo Shipyard & Dock." The bearded man in this wagon looked at me while stirring his reins and gave me a nod.

When the road was clear, Noah and I walked across and turned left up the middle toward another livery stable.

"What are we doin now?" Joseph asked.

Noah glanced around him and lowered his tone. "Hiding in the livery. Mr. Fisher will meet us there with the other women."

We entered the livery and Noah opened his violin case and took out some matches. He struck one of them and lit a lantern hanging on the gate of one of the horse stables. Then he shut the front doors and placed a plank between the slats to keep them closed. He opened the back doors. "Joseph, could you hand me two of those bricks by your feet?"

"Sure, here." Joseph picked up the bricks and handed them over as Noah placed one on the ground to prop open each door.

Shortly after, Mr. Fisher and another man rode freight wagons in the stable, each one of them hauling a wooden crate. As they climbed down from the wagons, Noah kicked the brick props out of place and shut the doors of the stable again, locking them with another plank.

Noah, Joseph, and I surrounded the two wagons as Mr. Fisher and the other horseman lifted and placed each of the crates on the ground.

I spoke to one of the wooden boxes. "Are you all right in there?"

There was no response.

Noah and I shared a startled look and faced the two men.

"Quickly! Open the lids. Hurry!" Noah said.

Mr. Fisher grabbed a crowbar from the top bales of hay and loosened the lid off from one of the wooden crates. We all looked inside and found Pearl with her eyes closed, breathing shallowly.

"Pearl?" Fear suffused my features. "Pearl, can you hear me?"

"Let's get her out of there." Noah glanced at me. "Draw her some water from the barrel."

"All right." While Mr. Fisher and Noah helped Pearl out and the other horseman opened the other wooden crate, I walked over to a wood barrel and scooped water in a tin cup.

Mr. Fisher and Noah sat Pearl on the ground as I brought over the cup of water for her. She was the worst I had seen her during the whole trip, sweaty, exhausted, and incapacitated from her lack of oxygen.

I knelt beside her. "Here, Pearl. Have some water, but drink slowly so you don't choke."

For a split second, Pearl looked at me as if she didn't recognize who I was. She hinted a weak smile. "Oh, thank you . . . thank you, Millie." She took the cup and sipped it.

I glanced over as Mr. Fisher and the other horseman helped Margaret out of the other crate. Being an older woman, she looked worse. Tired and almost breathless. My heart ached for their poor souls, going through these harsh conditions just to obtain their freedom. But the time of their misery was nearly over, and I was ever so grateful.

Joseph removed his bowler hat and wiped his sweaty forehead with the cuff of his sleeve. "What now, Mr. Shepherd?"

"We'll stay with Mr. Waldo—Miss Ophelia's cousin's house for the night. He'll provide you all with food and shelter before the journey to Detroit tomorrow."

"What about the others?" I asked.

Noah spoke on. "The others should hopefully meet us at the next safe house before we leave for Detroit."

"When we goin to Mr. Waldo's house?" Joseph said.

"Soon," Noah replied, watching Pearl and Margaret, "but for now, we'll let the women breathe and rest a little while."

"I was so scared," Pearl said, "I thought I was gonna die." She squeezed her eyes tightly and whimpered like a helpless, little child.

I rested Pearl's head on my shoulder, holding her close. "It's all right. You and Margaret are safe and will be just fine." While consoling Pearl, my mind slipped back to Anna, Ozzie, and the other slaves who were left behind, wondering what happened to them.

They needed a miracle to make it to Toledo together.

28 *Miss Ophelia's Cousin*

MONDAY, AUGUST 23, 1852, 6:10 P. M.

WALDO FINLEY'S HOUSE

Toledo, Ohio

NOAH KNOCKED ON THE back door of the white, two-story house resting on a steep hill and the three of us waited for a response. When the door opened, a tall, deep-brown-skinned negro man with an elongated face and receding hairline stood before us. He was dressed in a long-sleeve, brown-striped shirt rolled up to his elbows, brown trousers, and leather, patent boots. His facial features and wide forehead etched with wrinkles were as sharp as iron but seemed to soften when he smiled.

He searched the surroundings and then looked at our pleading faces. "Come inside, quickly." He brushed each one of us into his home and shut the door.

"We heard you're da cousin of Miss Ophelia," Joseph said. "What's your name, sir?"

The negro man turned around, facing us. "My name's Waldo . . . Waldo Finley. My master's surname was Finley. He fell ill and never had children, so I kept it after earning my freedom from him. Miss Ophelia, you'll meet soon in Canada. She's my younger cousin." He gestured to the sofa and chairs in his sitting room. "Please, have a seat while I warm some food. The other *bundles of wood* should be here tomorrow."

"Bundles of wood?" I said, frowning.

Noah chuckled and elaborated on Mr. Finley's remark. "Yes, that's a code phrase. He's talking about the slaves. Those who will take the second train. They'll hopefully meet us tomorrow afternoon."

Another knock came from the back door.

Mr. Finley walked over in his thumping boots and answered it after hearing the password. Standing before him in the doorway were Mr. Fisher with Pearl and Margaret, both of them draped in hooded cloaks. As he had with us, Mr. Finley welcomed Pearl and Margaret into his house and closed the door.

Pearl removed the hood of her cloak. "Thank you so much, sir."

"Yes, thank you," Margaret added, likewise pulling down her hood. "Both of us are tired and hungry from our trip to here in Toledo."

"I imagine y'all are," Mr. Finley said, "it's quite a way from Cincinnati to Toledo, but thank the good Lord for the railroad."

"Amen," Joseph said, smiling.

"I'll get y'all something to eat for supper." Mr. Finley strutted into the kitchen.

"Thank you, Mr. Finley," Noah said.

We sat in the sitting room and waited together. When the food was ready, the Cajun cuisine of Mr. Finley's shrimp gumbo and cornbread quite impressed me. While we ate, he told us about his family's secret recipes and working on a Louisiana sugar plantation. Then he reflected on his time as a slave and how he had gotten his freedom from his former master.

"Master Finley was an old, fair-haired, thin man and bought me and my Papa when I was a little boy. We worked on his small farm in Baton Rouge, Louisiana, but he wasn't cruel like other slave masters. He was a little rough on the edges, so ladies couldn't stand him. He yelled, but he never beat me. He also drank and couldn't afford much, so I reckon he thought to keep his *goods* in good condition. Simply put, he needed us."

Mr. Finley chuckled and continued. "Unfortunately, back in 1832, an outbreak of yellow fever spread and killed a lot of folks in Louisiana. Even Master Finley contracted the illness. I was twenty-eight then and took charge on working the land until he died. Before he passed away, he looked at me with his yellowed eyes and said, "Boy, you done good work for me all these years . . . but I got no more use for you. I grant you your freedom on one condition—carry my name. And so, I do to this day." Mr. Finley pointed his forefinger on his knee.

"Amazing story," Pearl said. "When did you get to Ohio?"

Mr. Finley sipped from his tin mug. "After Master Finley died, I buried him behind his house and left the same night, but it wasn't easy getting here. I was alone and deprived. I had to be wise, so I don't get caught by hunters looking for runaways. I'd heard of Quakers and knew they were kind, religious people, so I mostly relied on them. One lady who was a Quaker lived not far away from Finley Farm. She told me about the Underground Railroad and helped direct me on what route to go up North."

He sighed. "The hardest part of my journey was going through Mississippi and Kentucky, two states greatly involved and reliant on slavery. Bounty hunters on horseback chased me in Lexington. I could've gotten auctioned, but I narrowly escaped by going in hiding and holding my breath under a lake. I was sure I was gonna die, but the Lord and his mercy spared me. A good friend of mine let me know when they'd left and I could come out."

"Thank God, you got away," I said. "You must've been frightened."

Mr. Finley nodded. "Yes, I was. Well, I reckon y'all had better get some shuteye. It's a big day tomorrow."

"I suppose you're right. Thank you for everything," Noah said.

Mr. Finley smiled and stood. "God bless y'all while crossing over *midnight*. Word gets around fast. There might be some danger."

"Let's hope that's not the case," Noah said. "Good night, sir."

"Good night, Mr. Shepherd and everyone." Mr. Finley took a lantern on his windowsill and blew out the flame. The code words Mr. Finley and the others used were interesting to me. I wondered what *midnight* meant and what approaching danger was on the horizon.

Bounty hunters were desperate men and there was no telling whether they'd try to kill or auction runaway slaves after getting their hands on them. But no matter what, I would help Pearl, and I refused to let anyone stop me from keeping my word.

A promise to my friend.

29 *And So We Meet Again*

"A FRIEND WITH FRIENDS," HUBERT answered behind the closed door.

Mr. Finley arose from his chair in the sitting room and answered him.

Joy fluttered within me the moment I saw all the others in the doorway. It was like a big family reunion. All eight of the other slaves had safely made it into town along with Hubert and Arthur. Ozzie and Anna were more sophisticated in their apparel, wearing different clothes than we'd last seen them. Everyone hurried inside one by one and gathered together with the rest of us in the sitting room.

"Anna," Margaret rushed over and embraced her. "Praise God, y'all made it." She laughed joyously.

Anna giggled. "Yes, praise God indeed. Ozzie and I rode in the negro car together. We pretended to be a married couple. Mr. Arthur gave us freedom papers and everything."

I smiled and hugged Anna after Margaret. "I'm so glad you and the others are all right."

"Yes," Anna said, "we are too."

Ozzie took off and held his derby hat. "I never sat in a train with passengers before 'til we left Cincinnati. It waz nice seein the other cities we stopped in before Toledo."

"When will we leave to go to Detroit?" the mother of the little girl asked.

Arthur glanced at his pocket watch. "Soon. We have to get fresh horses from the livery and then we'll be on our way."

The front window of the house shattered as a brick flew inside the sitting room, startling everyone. Some screamed and others wailed from the sudden incident.

The mother held her crying little girl in her arms and hushed her, trying to quiet her down.

Horses galloped away outside in the distance.

"What's dat?" the young boy said, panicking.

Noah picked up the brick and unraveled the note tied on it. He skimmed the paper.

"What's it say, Shepherd?" Arthur arched his brow.

Noah frowned and scanned everyone surrounding him. "It's a threat. It says, *Death by the River.*"

"Death?" Anna shrieked and moved closer to her big brother.

Mr. Finley shook his head, his hands planted on his hips. "Y'all should leave. It sounds like serious trouble."

"You're right," Noah agreed, folding the note. "Arthur, Hubert, Mr. Fisher has some wagons prepared for our ride to Detroit. Get them, please." He tucked the note in the pocket of his ruby jacket.

Arthur and Hubert left to the livery yard together.

WHEN WE EXITED THE house, there were two covered wagons waiting for our departure. Arthur drove one of them, and Hubert drove the other one. Pearl, Margaret, Anna, Joseph, the others, and I climbed into the back of Arthur's wagon, while Ozzie and the Murphy sisters hid in Hubert's wagon.

"How much farther to Detroit?" I asked.

Noah adjusted his fedora. "We should reach it in another fifty miles. Keep your voices low and stay calm. We don't know what's ahead, but we're prepared to take action if needed."

"God bless you, Mr. Shepherd," the mother said.

Noah smiled and draped the sheet over the back opening of Arthur's covered wagon.

A few moments later, we were traveling on the road again.

"What happens when we git to Detroit?" the young boy said, sitting Indian style in the middle of the adults.

"We'll ride a sailboat across the Detroit River," I answered. "Noah mentioned about a businessman's ship back in North Carolina."

"I've never been on a boat," the young boy said.

"Me neither," I added, "I'm hoping I don't get seasick."

Some of us chuckled and giggled.

"I'm hoping we don't get killed." Margaret wore a solemn face, staring at the leafy shadows formed across the tan canopy shading us from the sun.

My smile slowly faded as a chill rose up my spine, looking away from her.

A dreadful silence grew while we rocked in the wagon. Being so close to the end of our journey, none of us wanted to think about it, but the possibility of death still lingered in the air. Whether we wanted to face the truth, the note from earlier was a sign someone threatened to attack us. And although we'd done good staying ahead of them, our enemies were lurking close behind, and closer than anyone of us thought.

We needed a shield of GOD's protection now more than ever.

FRIDAY, AUGUST 27, 1852, 4:00 P. M.
THE POINDEXTER INN
Detroit, Michigan

WE CLIMBED OUT OF Arthur's wagon, while the others came out from hiding in Hubert's wagon, all of us finding ourselves in a large wooden barn. Aside from the horses that brought us to the next safe house, there wasn't any other animals in sight. I looked around the empty stables with hay bedding in them, and thought to ask where we were, but Anna took the words out of my mouth.

"Where are we?" Anna wiped the sweat from her forehead with the long sleeve of her dress.

Arthur closed the sheet on the back of his covered wagon. "We're at the Poindexter Inn. We'll be resting a short while before you all aboard Mr. Poindexter's ship."

Noah entered, conversing with two people. The young man was a mulatto wearing a chocolate brown suit and bowtie. Standing beside him was a beautiful, slender white woman in an evergreen gingham dress. Her auburn hair was parted and wrapped in a braided bun with ringlets along both sides of her face. I assumed they were other abolitionists or the owners of the place.

"Everyone, this is Mr. and Mrs. Poindexter," Noah said, gesturing a hand to them.

I smiled, greeted the Poindexters like the others, and tried not to blatantly stare at them. I'd never seen an interracial couple before. If they'd ever lived in the South, I knew they must've suffered harassment and racial slurs from the segregated public, which was likely why they lived in a Northern state. Judging from Mr. Poindexter's elegant presence and confident stance, he was an educated, colored man coming from a past of harsh circumstances.

His redheaded wife—Mrs. Poindexter—wore a pleasant countenance, which spoke of her kind heart. Her delicacy and fun-loving wit showed she was a woman of poise, charm, and grace. I startled them a little as they glanced nervously at each other. Perhaps, worried I'd tell someone unapproving about their forbidden marriage.

Mrs. Poindexter laced her small hands and stepped forward. She smiled. "Good afternoon, everyone! My name's Clarissa. Welcome to the Poindexter Inn." She giggled and blushed, observing the surrounding people. "It looks like I'll have to make more sandwiches. Come and follow me. You all must be tired and hungry from your long trip." She held the wide skirt of her plaid dress and led the way as Pearl, Hubert, and the fugitives from Hubert's wagon followed her.

"Dr. Wilkins will arrive to examine the passengers," Mr. Poindexter added. He led me, Noah, Arthur, and the other slaves from Arthur's covered wagon toward their home. It was a two-story, maroon brick Victorian boarding house in a small, straggly yard.

When we walked inside, I felt like I was back home in the Crabtree mansion. A crystal chandelier dangled from the high ceiling above, sparkling in the afternoon sun. The parlor was the first room on the right. Inside was ornate Victorian furniture, and silk, laced draperies on the long windows reminded me of a bride's wedding gown. In front of the floral sofa was a wooden rifle cabinet, and in one corner stood a grandfather clock ticking in the silence.

"Please, make yourselves at home," Mr. Poindexter said. He let us enter and closed the door. "I hope you all like chicken salad. It's Clarissa's specialty."

Our footsteps echoed down the lengthy hardwood hallway to the dining room. Some of the other slaves were sitting at the table and eating when the rest of us came. But Pearl stared at her plate of food in front of her and fiddled with one of her brown twists of hair hanging from her tan turban. Her flat expression revealed her mind had drifted somewhere else again, and I worried about her. She stood and left the table.

I followed her in the mesh-screened sunroom. "Pearl, why aren't you eating? You haven't eaten since we left Toledo this morning."

She glanced at me over her shoulder and then looked out at the screen.

I gulped and conjured up a thought. "Are you scared to get checked by the doctor?"

Pearl said nothing and wrapped her arms around herself. She sniffled and shrugged, wiping her nose.

With concern etched on her face, Mrs. Poindexter walked into the sunroom to check on us. "Is everything all right?"

"My best friend needs help," I said and glanced apprehensively at Pearl. "I think she's . . . well . . . expecting."

Mrs. Poindexter twitched her mouth, thinking. She approached Pearl and wrapped an arm around her shoulder. "Don't worry yourself. There's no need to fear the doctor. I'll stay with you during the examination so you don't be alone. Everything's going to be fine."

"Dr. Wilkins is here!" Mr. Poindexter called from inside.

"Come, child. It's time you let a doctor check your condition." Mrs. Poindexter left with Pearl under her arm, consoling her like a loving mother as they walked past me.

I followed them back into the house and walked up the hallway while they went upstairs to the second floor.

As Mr. Poindexter greeted the doctor upon entering, I peeked in the parlor and eavesdropped on their conversation.

"You look disturbed, Doc? What is it, sir?" Mr. Poindexter said.

Dr. Wilkins, a stout, white gentleman with a gray, whiskery full beard and bushy sideburns, sighed and plopped on the sofa with his black valise beside him. "I've got news, Lewis."

"What's the matter, Doc?" Mr. Poindexter sighed and placed his hands on his hips.

"Some man gave me this on the way over here." Dr. Wilkins dug in his black vest pocket and pulled out a slip of paper. "He told me to give it to you." He handed it over. "I didn't think it was my business."

Mr. Poindexter unfolded it and skimmed the note. Then he crumpled it in his hand. "Nothing, but trash!" He grimaced and threw it aside on the floor.

"Oh, dear, I guess it wasn't good news," Dr. Wilkins said. "I'm sorry, Lewis. There are rumors going around too. I stopped by a mercantile to get some supplies and the storekeeper said a group of bounty hunters are planning an ambush at the river to keep the fugitive slaves from reaching the Canadian border."

The doctor leaned forward, nervously stroking his beard. "You and the others should take precautions. Bring rifles and plenty of ammunition on your journey over. Give the slave men guns too. It's better to be armed and safe than sorry later." He stood with his bag and patted Mr. Poindexter's shoulder. "I'd better treat and examine the fugitives and the others before you all leave."

I moved aside and greeted the doctor as he walked past me.

"Hello, ma'am." Dr. Wilkins smiled. "I don't believe we've met."

I smiled back. "I'm Mildred . . . Mildred Crabtree. I've been helping some friends of mine for their freedom through the Underground Railroad movement."

"Is that so? You seem so young and innocent," Dr. Wilkins said. "How old are you, dear?"

"Eighteen, sir," I answered.

Dr. Wilkins raised his eyebrows. "Eighteen . . . such a tender age."

I wanted to tell him all the things this young girl had survived and endured, but he strode off before I got the chance and left into the dining room. Cautiously, I entered the parlor as Mr. Poindexter took shotguns out of the cabinet and loaded them with paper cartridges from a box. If this ambush was true, I wanted to help in whatever way I could and thought of reloading my father's pistol.

I licked my lips. "I heard about the ambush. I'm sorry."

"What are you sorry for? You didn't do anything to me." Mr. Poindexter clicked the breech block of a rifle and blew off the excess gunpowder around the closed bullet site.

"I know," I said, "but I still feel awful about it. Do you have .36 calibers?" I pulled out Papa's Navy Colt pistol from my carpetbag.

Mr. Poindexter widened his eyes and paused, holding another rifle. He looked at me, holding open his mouth. "Uh, yes, I do. So, what's a lady like you doing with a gun?"

"Well, I had to carry something to stay alive, didn't I?" I said. "Bounty hunters followed us everywhere we went. They're probably in Michigan waiting for us by the river. Someone anonymous threw a brick with a threat tied on it through the window of Mr. Finley's home back in Toledo. They might be a part of the ambush."

"Maybe so." Mr. Poindexter smiled and chuckled. "I like you, Millie. You're a nice, young lady. The 36 cal. bullets are in the top cabinet drawer on the left. Gunpowder too, if you need it."

"Thank you, sir." I opened the drawer and took out the box of lead balls and a bronze tube of gunpowder. Having watched Papa do it many times, I reloaded my father's pistol.

Mrs. Poindexter's countenance turned pale as she came into the room, startled by all of the weaponry. "Why are you loading so many guns?"

"Dr. Wilkins," Mr. Poindexter said, loading a rifle. "Some man sent him a note directed at us. There could be a massive ambush at the Detroit River. We should be prepared."

Mrs. Poindexter walked over to her husband as he clicked the breech of the rifle in his hand and started loading the last few shotguns. "What did the note say?"

He ignored her and clicked the breech blocker of the next rifle he had loaded up, picking up another one.

"Lew, what did it say?" his wife urged, devastated, gripping the shotgun in his hands.

Mr. Poindexter stopped and stared at her panic-stricken face. "What does it matter? It was written because of me anyway!" Sadness and frustration were in Mr. Poindexter's tone of voice, and like his wife, I wanted to cry, my heart sinking in despair. It wasn't fair seeing a couple's love and marriage on edge all because of a racial divide and stubborn traditions.

"It's me," Lewis whispered sadly, "always because of me. . ." Although he was a mixed man, like Pearl, having a negro parent to the American white society noted him as a shameful human being.

The clock ticked in the silence, but it felt as if time had stopped in that instant.

Mrs. Poindexter embraced her husband and pressed her cheek to his. She kissed and held him. "It's both of us, Lew, not only you." She sighed hopelessly, fluttering her eyelids, alarmed. "What should I do?"

"Stay here," Mr. Poindexter said. "Lock all the doors, hide in the apple cellar, and don't come out until I come back."

"*If* . . . you come back," Mrs. Poindexter said dispiritedly, whimpering.

Mr. Poindexter pulled away and studied her face, wiping her wet cheek with the back of his hand. "Don't say if. I will come back again. I promise." He gazed lovingly at her for moment. Then he swallowed and forced his attention back to me. "It's time we go. The sooner we leave, the more likely we are to miss the ambush."

"Please, be careful," Mrs. Poindexter said to her husband. "I'll be praying for a safe crossover to Canada. Tell Ma and Pa I said hello and that I love and miss them."

"I will." Mr. Poindexter carried a rifle underarm as I followed him to the dining room with my carpetbag. He informed the slaves and others of the trouble facing us. Then everyone got to work, putting the rifles and boxes of ammunition into the wagons in the barn. When Dr. Wilkins finished examining and treating the different slaves' injuries, we left for the Detroit River.

Along the journey to the shoreline, I reflected on the dream I had, wondering if the grievance of slavery would come to a war. Some folks thought the free states of the Compromise would solve everything. But with a probable ambush on the rise, I got a feeling it wouldn't, and a dreadful fear settled in my stomach.

Someone was going to die.

31 *Crossing Over Midnight*

THE CREAM-COLORED SHEET OF Arthur's covered wagon was open so we could keep a lookout for bounty hunters and be ready for them. We drove down the long, paved road alongside rows of similar-designed homes fenced off at the coast of the river. It took us a total of six and a half days—longer than I expected it would to get to the river. I ripped off a side patch sewn on the canopy and peeked out of the hole, looking at the glorious sunset.

According to Noah, his musical comrades, and Mr. Poindexter, *Midnight* was the secret code word for the 'Detroit River' of the Underground Railroad. The river was wide and flowed with ripples and small currents as the summer breeze blew against the body of water. Along the road was a huge shipyard of big, fishing ships with off-white sails and riverboats lined in rows at the wooden harbor. Far, far away ship bells dinged and echoed. In the distance was the flat outline of the beautiful land of Canada and its neighboring ships and docks awaiting our arrival. A couple seagulls squawked and glided like flying white kites in the sky.

I smiled and inhaled the fishy and earthy scents wafting in the air. "I see it! I can see the Promised Land!"

"Let me see," Pearl said and crawled over to me.

I moved out of the way and let her peek out of the hole.

"Millie's right. It's right over yonder," Pearl said, smiling.

Margaret gasped and shrieked. "So are the hunters! Look!" She pointed out the back of the wagon.

I glanced over in the same direction. Blood drained from my face and fear plunged in my stomach, watching a gang of bounty hunters galloping on their horses, their four-legged, powerful stallions kicking up clouds of dust. A few more men came riding out from hiding behind bushes and joined the group behind our wagon. Some of them had pistols in their hands and others carried army rifles. Two of the hunters were Jack and Sal as I had expected of them, staring us down like two scavengers eyeing dead prey.

I pulled my father's pistol out of my bag and took a long-range shot at Jack in defense of us, hoping to spook his horse or slow him down. My gunshots ricocheted from the ground near his horse's hooves, spitting up a few stones and dirt. Holding the pistol, I saved my next gunshots and watched them until we stopped at the pier.

Mr. Poindexter's ship was tied to one of the wooden stakes. He had called his body ship *The Odyssey* like the ancient poem by the Greek poet Homer in honor of slaves' long, rough journeys for freedom.

The wagon turned around and halted. We studied one another as men hollered and guns and rifles shot off, wondering what our fates would be after going outside in the line of fire. The back of the covered wagon was facing away from the gang of bounty hunters, but our lives were still in danger.

"Heavenly Father, please, watch over us!" the mother cried, shielding her crying little girl.

Noah came to the opening of the back of the covered wagon. "Come on out! Hurry over to Mr. Poindexter and Arthur behind the bushes! Hurry! Take cover!"

We climbed and leaped out one by one screaming as gunshots blazed through the air and bore holes through the wood and canopy of the wagon. The horses neighed and snorted with a panic, wanting to run, but the hefty weight of the cargo and wagon stalled them.

Mr. Poindexter held a rifle, ducking behind a crowd of bushes. He gestured a hand for us to come to him and shot his rifle at our enemies as we scrambled in a group behind the bushes.

My nose tingled from the burnt scent of gunpowder. Will this be the end of us? Peering through misty clouds of smoke at Hubert, I saw he and the others were also taking cover behind other bushes a short distance beside us. The wagon they rode in was set behind Arthur's wagon in the wide field, their horses likewise stuck but frightened by the violent gunfire.

"We've got to sneak over to the ship somehow," Mr. Poindexter said, frustrated, keeping a lookout.

Anna caught her breath. "How we gonna do dat?"

"Maybe we should ride da wagon over," Joseph said.

"No," Noah said, "we have to keep cover. Besides, either way, you all have to be out in the open to get in Mr. Poindexter's ship." He fired and took down another bounty hunter. "Millie, can I count on you?"

"What do you want me to do?" I asked.

"The others will run over onto the pier while you, Joseph, and Mr. Poindexter do a shooting spree toward the hunters. I'll stay behind to help Arthur and Hubert protect the other three. More than likely, they won't shoot you. Can you do it?"

"I think I can," I said and gulped.

Mr. Poindexter smiled and put a hand on my shoulder. "Good. We'll do it on the count of three. One . . . two . . . three!" He, Joseph, and I ran out from hiding and fired our guns as we guarded the women and others, blasting shots at the hunters while making our way toward the pier.

Sal lifted his bald head and aimed his revolver behind a wagon. He shot one gunshot.

"Joe! He got Joe!" Pearl and Margaret screamed, crying and holding each other.

I gasped and saw Mr. Poindexter and everyone else had made it in the ship, except him. His injured body and rifle were lying on the ground, a short distance from the pier.

"No!" A burst of energy rushed through my veins, shooting in defense of Joseph. It went off quicker than I thought of where to aim, and before I knew it, I had killed a man.

Sal cried out and fell backward on the ground, shot in his chest.

For a second, I was in a daze about what happened and what I had done. I rushed over and checked if Joseph was still alive. He blinked faintly, his last breaths heavy and shallow.

My vision blurred. "Joseph? Joseph, it's Millie. Can you get up?"

A tear spilled from the corner of his left eye, but a smile played on his lips. "Miss Millie, tell Marge . . . tell her . . . I love her." He exhaled a wheezy breath and leaned his head over. His eyes remained open, as if he was looking at me or into the heavens above. Chills got hold of me as I struggled to bear the death of another loved one I had known in my life.

"Joseph? Joseph, please?" I said, crying and shaking him.

"Come on over! We've got no time to waste!" Mr. Poindexter yelled.

I glanced from my dead friend to the others in the ship. I didn't want to leave him behind. He was so close to freedom, but in a split moment after everything he's gone through, freedom was a treasure snatched from his grasp, or was it? I closed my eyes and whimpered, reflecting on his reaction when we reached Cincinnati, Ohio, his first time stepping on *free* soil. But time wasn't standing still during the ambush. As much as I hated it, there wasn't anything I could do to help him.

I scurried over to the pier and climbed into The Odyssey ship, but we couldn't leave just yet. Ozzie and those from the other wagon had to make it over too. We watched as Hubert, Ozzie, and the Murphy sisters took cover behind a closer middle crowd of bushes, gradually making their way over to Noah and Arthur. Gunshots flew faster through the air as the group of bounty hunters expressed their rage. Some of them took shots at us in the ship.

"Get down!" Mr. Poindexter shot his rifle again.

Everyone did as he advised and knelt on our knees.

"I caint watch." Anna turned her face and hugged the old slave man.

"They're outnumbered. They'll never make it," the mother said.

Noah and Arthur fired their revolvers together as Hubert and the others dodged over and joined them behind their bushes. Being a large and muscular man, Ozzie guarded the women and ran over with them while the three abolitionists fired their rifles against the hunters.

An old bounty hunter shot Ozzie in his shoulder and leg, but he placed a hand over his bloody shoulder and continued leaping toward us with the women. After making it over, he collapsed on his stomach on the floor of the ship. Thankfully, all of them made it into the boat, but the whole incident shook the two sisters up quite a bit.

"Ozzie!" Anna cried, rushing over to her brother.

I hugged each of the girls. "It's all right. You're safe now."

Mr. Poindexter untied the ship and it drifted away from the pier.

I gripped an edge of the ship and watched the trio of musicians shooting it out with the remaining bounty hunters, feeling a mixture of sadness and relief. Joseph, a serious, hardworking, and humorous man who had dreamed of living as a free man was gone forever, and as a conductor, I felt like a failure. As we left the shoreline and sailed away, the commotion calmed down.

Mr. Poindexter studied the rolling currents and steered the ship helm. "Once we reach the Canadian border, you all are no longer slaves."

"Haaa-llee-luujah!" the mother clapped her hands, grinning.

The others smiled with tears of joy and laughed at the mother's exuberant reaction.

Margaret walked up and stood beside me.

Seagulls and other birds squawked and glided across the fiery-orange sky.

"You all right?" Margaret asked.

I sobbed and hung my head. "I lost Joseph."

"Everyone did, Miss Millie," Margaret said. "We saw when it happened. Joseph shot Sal in his arm, and he shot him back."

I pulled out a loose strand of my brown hair that had blown into my mouth. "But I was a conductor. He was my friend—I failed him."

"Don't worry, missy," the old man said. "Joe's restin well. He's as free as us . . . maybe freer—he ain't got to suffer on Pharaoh's land no more." His chin trembled as his glassy eyes welled up.

I closed my eyes and felt a tear slip down my cheek. "Before he died, he told me to tell you he loved you." I looked at Margaret.

Margaret nodded and pressed her lips together. She sniffled and stifled a sob. "Yes, I know he did. He was just a rigid and timid man." She held me in a side hug and leaned her turbaned head on my shoulder.

"There's four of us left, not counting the others from Massa McMillan's plantation." Anna was sitting on the wooden beams of the floor with her legs propped to her chest. "I hope the hunters don't come back again. I'm so tired of running."

"Yes, me too." Ozzie sighed and observed as the oldest Murphy sister wrapped his shoulder with the blue kerchief she wore around her neck.

"Well, I got Sal, but Jack . . . he's still out there," I said, peering into the distance at the strip of Detroit's land. Seeing Joseph killed off, it occurred to me there were only two who Jack wanted to bring back into captivity now.

No longer did he care about the others' lives, and I doubted Papa did either while going into partnership with Chauncey and after buying more slaves to replace those who'd run away. Anna, Ozzie, and the others from different plantations were safe and sound while living their new, free lifestyles. But Jack would stop at nothing until he captured the young women who held his and my father's fortune.

My best friend and I.

FRIDAY, SEPTEMBER 3, 1852, 6:30 P. M.
THE DOCKS OF WINDSOR
Windsor - Ontario, Canada

AS THE SHIP STOPPED at the dock, I closed my eyes and inhaled a deep breath of the crisp, cool air. I shaded the sunlight from my eyes and beheld three greeters in the distance waving at us. Birds chirped and locusts droned in the forested trees of the land of Canada. Brass bells rang as other ships and riverboats of black and white passengers joined us on the borderline. It had been so long since we'd felt a part of a community, but after spending a lot of time in nature and moving from place to place, everything had changed.

As we reached the Canadian border, I had changed too, and like the others, a new chapter had begun in my life. Being faced with death and taking risks during our strenuous journey to Canada strengthened me. It taught me to be brave in my pursuit of not only becoming a published author but also being a woman. No longer was

I afraid, as I understood in primarily a man's world, I still had the wisdom and skills to be successful while pursuing and reaching my dreams.

On the dock stood a tall negro woman and a white couple, all of them dressed in the finest wear I had ever seen. The women wore elegant day dresses embellished with pearl buttons and straw bonnets tied with shiny ribbons. The older white gentleman wore a cream dress shirt, a satin burgundy necktie, tucked in a double-breasted vest, and brown kickers with leather boots.

"Welcome to freedom, friends!" the negro woman said, spreading her arms and bowing with courtesy. "Come onto the platform."

Mr. Poindexter tied the ship to a piling of the wooden pier, and then the rest of us stepped out of the ship.

"I'm Ophelia Vaughn." The negro woman gestured a hand to the older couple standing beside her. "This is Mr. and Mrs. Carlson, Clarissa's parents. GOD bless you all." She gave each of us a hug as we came onto the dock, as well as Mrs. Carlson.

"Hello, sonny!" Mr. Carlson said, greeting his son-in-law. "We heard about the ambush and saw it across the river, but we're glad you made it over again."

"Thank you, sir." Mr. Poindexter took hold of Mr. Carlson's hand, who helped him up onto the dock. He looked at the older couple. "Clarissa sends her hello and love. She told me to tell y'all she misses you. Before I left, I told her to hide in the apple cellar, just in case. She should be safe there, but I'll be heading back to the Poindexter Inn shortly after my visit here."

"Well, that's good to know. But, please consider the two of you staying here in Windsor." Mr. Carlson turned his attention and smiled at the group of us. "GOD bless you all. We should go to the church. There, you'll eat and be able to rest for the night."

We followed Miss Ophelia and the Carlsons to two wagons. Some of us went in one, and some of us in the other. Mr. Poindexter rode Miss Vaugh's wagon, and Pearl and I sat with the mother and her little girl in the back. When we arrived, we stopped in a neighborhood called Sandwich. We arrived at a maroon brick church with gothic stained-glass windows and a two-door entrance. Across the street was a mercantile, a post office, a couple of other small shops, and a few houses. Negro and white children were outside playing ball and running around on the front lawn.

Watching them for a second, I thought about when Pearl and I were little girls, giggling while playing hide and seek or trying to chase our shadows. Some weeks ago, Pearl and I had a pillow fight over a silly matter one time in the spring. White feathers were all over the place in my bedroom, but we laughed and had so much fun we forgot what we were arguing about. Of course, Papa wasn't too pleased by the big mess, but we had never let his callousness and resentment bring down our close friendship. Sorrow sank in my heart. Would we remain friends forever? With circumstances changing and Pearl having her freedom, I wasn't sure I could go on living my life without her.

I blinked to dissipate my tears. Even despite being in Canada, the brutal memories of slavery would never go away. Not for me, and certainly not for the others. They would forever be branded on our minds. As slaves, Papa and other masters gave them their needs. Now free, they had to find work and meet their everyday needs for themselves, as well as myself.

"Here we are," Miss Ophelia said, smiling.

An elderly, snowy-bearded negro clergyman exited from the church and shooed children out of his way. "Hello, everyone! I'm Pastor Samuel Combs, the leader of Savior Jesus Tabernacle Church." He walked to the wagons and shook our hands one by one, greeting the others to freedom. "Please, come inside all of you for some vittles and rest."

Everyone climbed out of the wagons and entered the church, following the preacher to a small kitchen. A steamy kettle pot was boiling something on a cast-iron stove. I didn't know what was in it, but the food sure smelled good.

"Your soup smells wonderful, pastor. Are my muffins done?" Miss Ophelia said, taking off and hanging up her cloak on a wall hook.

"The muffins! Lord, have mercy!" The elderly pastor snatched a potholder hanging on a hook above the stove and yanked open the oven door. "I was so distracted in my prayer session and plum forgot about them."

Pearl and I giggled as the preacher took out a tin pan of corn muffins and placed it on the stovetop.

Miss Ophelia and Mrs. Carlson laughed, bumping shoulders.

"I thought they were burnt, but they're saved," Pastor Combs joked, grinning. "Lunch is served, everybody!"

Everyone stood in line and got a bowl of homemade vegetable soup and a corn muffin as Ophelia and the preacher served us. Pastor Combs said the blessing and then we ate and talked about our hopes and dreams with our new Canadian friends. Miss Ophelia and the Carlsons discussed opportunities for the others, such as if a black man owned land, he could also gain the right to vote.

Miss Ophelia sipped from her mug. "Maybe someday the same will apply to women."

"Well," I began, "I think they should be able to vote. It's time they get the same treatment. After all, they're citizens of the country too."

Mrs. Carlson nodded, drawing her forefinger around the brim of her teacup. "You're right, Millie, but it'll take a lot of convincing for stubborn-minded men."

"Canada hasn't been perfect through the years," Mr. Carlson said. "I mean, we've had our share of slavery too. Thankfully, it was abolished back in 1833. But Canada's a charitable country and I'm sure will improve its women's rights in the future. Over time, you all will fit right in like native citizens."

"That's true. I've been here four years and feel right at home," Miss Ophelia said. "Honestly, I don't know why my cousin Waldo won't cross the border himself."

Mr. Poindexter frowned, thinking deeply. He put his mug on the table. "Bounty hunters might've gone to the Poindexter Inn to threaten Clarissa, but I'm not sure. I'd better go to check on her and the boarding inn."

Concern formed on Mrs. Carlson's pale, wrinkled face, fidgeting with her lace collar. "All right, but please, think about staying over here when you come back. You two are a part of the abolitionist movement, but perhaps it would be better for both of you to live in Windsor. I worry so much sometimes, and it would be safer in the end."

"I supposed you're right, Mother Carlson. I'll talk it over with Clarissa when I arrive home." Mr. Poindexter glanced at the preacher, biting his lower lip. "I'm going to need a prayer for a safe trip across the river, pastor."

"Certainly," Pastor Combs replied. "Everyone, hold hands and bow your heads, please."

We held hands in a circle and bowed our heads as the preacher said, waiting for him to share with us his words of comfort.

"Dear Lord, please watch over our friend Lewis Poindexter on his return home to his precious wife. Keep our dear friend and sister Clarissa safe and let no harm come upon her. God, I pray you also keep Miss Millie and her friends safe too. Let them win the victory and keep the freedom they've striven so hard to obtain. Please, don't have it stolen away from them. Let your Holy Spirit protect us. For in Second Corinthians 3:17, you said, 'Where the spirit of the Lord is, there is liberty." Ahh-men."

"Amen," everyone echoed.

Miss Ophelia sighed. "Well, I reckon' we'd better clean up now."

"We'll help too," Pearl and Margaret said, gathering the empty bowls in a stack.

While Miss Ophelia and the others cleaned in the kitchen, Mr. Poindexter and I reloaded our weapons. The rest of them in the kitchen followed Pastor Combs to the cellar, where cots were located and prepared for fugitives. This was where everyone slept at night—that is, everyone except me.

"Millie, go to sleep," Pearl whispered, lying on her cot across from me.

"All right," I said, but I couldn't keep my eyes shut to save my life. How could I sleep? An angry bounty hunter looking for us was still out there somewhere.

I took a series of breaths to calm my rapid heartbeat, clutching the pistol in my sweaty hand. We were going to face trouble again, and I wanted to be prepared for it any moment. Having anticipation running through my veins, a dread of knowing plunged in my gut.

Jack was coming to get us tomorrow.

33 *Heart of Courage*

EVERY COT WAS EMPTY and I panicked until I overheard talking and laughing in the kitchen. I sat up, put my father's pistol in my carpetbag, and exited the room to find out what was going on. Everyone stared back at me as I interrupted their conversation. Pearl and the others were sitting at the table eating flapjacks with maple syrup and scrambled eggs for breakfast. Some of them drank from steamy, pewter cup vessels.

"Good morning, everyone." I brushed a hand over my hair.

Miss Ophelia smiled. "Well, morning, Miss Millie." She studied my face, drying her hands with a dishtowel. "You're pink and flustered. Did you get enough sleep?"

"She's been tossin and turnin all night," Anna said, slicing her cake on her plate.

"Yes," Pearl said, "and holding her father's pistol."

Ophelia walked up and held me at arm's length. "You need not to worry, Millie. After breakfast, you and your friend will leave the church and go on your way to my cabin, which is far away in the forest. Pearl told me the whole story, and I'm letting her stay with me until she has the baby and gets on her feet. Now come and sit for something to eat."

I found a smile. "Yes, ma'am, and thank you." Pulling out a chair and joining the others at the table, I observed all of those sitting with me, realizing some people were missing. "Where's Mr. Carlson and Pastor Combs?"

"They've gone to check for bounty hunters around town," Miss Ophelia said, "but they and the Poindexters will be back later." She passed me the glass pitcher of syrup.

I forked a flapjack on my plate and drizzled it with syrup. Hearing the news about the Poindexters helped me feel better. I hoped they were coming back to live in Canada together with the rest of their friends.

Someone banged on the door, and my heart jumped.

"That must be Pastor Combs and Mr. Carlson," Miss Ophelia said, grinning. "I'll answer the door." She left the kitchen, and after a few minutes, rushed back to the room. "It's a strange man dressed in black. Looks like a bounty hunter. Everyone hide—hurry to the cellar!"

Jack Crenshaw. There wasn't doubt about it. It was him. Speechless, I gasped with fear and started to leaving like the others, but then I thought about what Anna said. We had been running for days on end and I was weary of letting terror paralyze me and steal my confidence and dignity. Although terrified and sweating, it was time to face Jack once and for all.

I stayed by the table with Papa's pistol in hand.

Pearl stared back at me. "What are you doing, Millie? We have to hide!"

"Your friend's right. It's no time to be a hero," Miss Ophelia said.

My eyes welled up. "No! I'm done hiding. It will never end until I face him. It won't stop for any of us." I glanced sheepishly at Pearl. "Hide if you must, but I'm staying here."

Pearl took a few steps forward but paused and walked back to the table again. "Then I'll stay too. I can't let you do this alone, Millie. It's me your Papa wants the most anyway."

"It's both of us, Pearl," I said, "you for the baby, and me to be a money trade-off to Chauncey McMillan for his selfish greed."

Another loud knock came. "Open up!"

I took a breath and straightened. "Let him in, Miss Ophelia."

"Are you sure?" Miss Ophelia wore an anxious look. "You don't have to do this, Millie."

I nodded and gulped. "Yes . . . it's all right."

Glass shattered, and a door thudded open.

Miss Ophelia gasped and widened her eyes, raising her hands to her ears. "Oh, my Lord, he broke in!"

"Where're you, girls? I know y'all in here somewhere!" Heavy footsteps marched toward the kitchen.

Pearl backed away and stood behind me. "I'm scared, Millie. I hope you know what you're doing."

"Everything will be fine. We're not going anywhere with him," I whispered over my shoulder to her. "We'll get through this. I promise."

Jack entered with his revolver. "There you are. Y'all gave my partner and me a chase for our money, but the game's over."

Like a protective mother, Miss Ophelia blocked us. "Why don't you leave them alone? They've done nothing to you."

"Get outta my way, woman!" Jack pushed Miss Ophelia onto the floor and marched toward us. He eyed Pearl with a cunning grin. "So, you're Master Crabtree's precious little jewel, huh? I came a long way for you, gal." He turned his attention to me again. "Your Papa promised me double for her return unscathed."

"Well, you aren't getting her," I said, revealing the pistol from behind my back.

Jack glanced down at the pistol and chortled, tilting back his head. "You can't be serious. Do you think I'm scared of you, missy?" He cocked his head and held out his hand. "Now, give me the gun and y'all come along with me. Your Papa's worried about you, both of y'all."

I clicked the hammer, gripping the pistol in my shaking hand. I'd already killed one man, and I wasn't confident I could do it again. But, if need be, I would do anything it took to keep our freedom and my sincere promise to my friend for her protection.

"We're not going back," I spat. "Not me or the others either. They're free in Canada now . . . we all are."

"Don't make me shoot you, girlie," Jack said. "Give me the gun!"

"No!" I yelled.

"Please, let them be!" Miss Ophelia got up from the floor with the help of a wooden chair.

Jack tucked his revolver in his holster and grabbed my hand, attempting to wrest the pistol away from me.

"Millie!" Pearl cried. "Millie, let it go!"

Whimpering, I held it with all my might and refused to release it. But with the slow turning of my hand, Crenshaw proved himself stronger than I. We wrestled with the pistol, pointing it downward. Then—a gunshot fired off.

Shock electrified me as I gasped and widened my eyes, convinced I'd been wounded. But I felt no pain—only a burst of fear and agitated energy.

Jack grunted and hunched his wide shoulders, his sunburned face filled with surprise. For a moment, he gripped my shoulder, and then he slid and dropped to his knees, falling facedown. A large, bloody stain was on the lower back of his black leather vest—shot from a short distance behind him.

I exhaled panicking breaths, startled by the incident. Then Pearl and I looked over and saw Mr. Poindexter standing across from us with his wife in the kitchen, lowering his shotgun.

"Are you girls all right?" he asked.

I panted and tossed my Papa's pistol on the floor. "I think so. I . . . I thought I'd killed him."

Mr. Poindexter sighed and then glanced from Jack's motionless body to me. His face fell. "God help me . . . I guess I needed to get revenge somehow. Our boarding house was wrecked and destroyed by the time I returned to Detroit—broken glass and things everywhere. Thank heavens Clarissa survived the attack. Nonetheless, if I'd come a minute later, you might've killed the scumbag. You're a courageous, young lady, Millie."

Holding back my tears, I sniffled and hinted a smile. "Thank you, sir."

"We'd better get the others," Miss Ophelia said.

Mrs. Poindexter took a slow breath and sighed with relief, but looked worn and exhausted from worry. "Yes, we should, Miss Ophelia. I'll follow you." She held the wide skirt of her evergreen day dress.

The two women left the kitchen and walked to the cellar.

"Well, I guess it's over, Pearl," I said between stifled sobs. "I told you . . . we're not going anywhere. You're free."

"Yes, free at last." Pearl smiled and sobbed. "I thank God and I thank you too, Millie. You're the best friend ever. I'll . . . I'll never forget you for this."

We hugged, overwhelmed with mixed emotions of happiness, sorrow, fear, and relief.

Shivers came over me. I turned my eyes away from the dead man lying on the floor and tried to appreciate the calmness that came from being free. No more running and hiding, no more hunger and starvation, no more seeking refuge from danger for days on end.

After Jack's death, there were no more worries for some time. Anna worked as a seamstress in a clothing mill downtown and Ozzie got a job as a fisherman on the docks. The two siblings stayed in touch as I knew they would, but lived in separate places.

I had lost track of the mother with her little girl and the others, but I believed they were doing well with their new lives. For more convenience, I became a boarder in Mr. and Mrs. Carlson's house in town. I had also gotten a job as a dishwasher at a hotel restaurant and took out a loan with the bank for the publication of my first children's story, *The Ruby Pendant*. Then one morning, I received a letter in the mail and was ordered to visit my home roots all over again.

Noah was in prison.

34 *Witness for a Trial*

THE TEMPERATURE HAD BECOME colder and the trees turned from rich, red-orange and brown to bare. Winter arrived in Canada and with pure white hills and the house rooftops dangling with icicles, Windsor was beautiful to behold. After spending time with Clarissa's parents, the Poindexters had started a new boarding inn close to where the Carlsons lived in their home. While the publication of my first children's short story, *The Ruby Pendant* was underway, I continued working at the restaurant to return the money I owed the bank. Meanwhile, Pearl lived with Miss Ophelia Vaughn, keeping her company.

I visited them sometimes for dinner, and the bigger her stomach grew, the harder it was to get past the thought of her birthing my half-sibling. Fortunately, the town doctor said she was healthy and coming along well.

Miss Ophelia always cooked three full-course meals every day and made sure Pearl ate regularly.

Sometimes Cecil, a young, strapping blacksmith who chopped firewood and did yard work for Miss Vaughn, joined them for suppertime. From their smiles, steady gazes, and lively conversation, I caught on he and Pearl were quite sweet on each other. Although Cecil was surprised about the baby, he still stuck around and remained her friend.

On a Tuesday morning, Mrs. Carlson gathered the mail from the post office and entered the living room of the house, sifting through letters.

"Anything for me?" I sipped my cup of chamomile tea and put it on the saucer. "I'm expecting a letter from Mr. Cohen, my editor."

"No," Mrs. Carlson said, frowning, "no Mr. Cohen, but you have a letter from the state court of North Carolina."

I gagged on the hot liquid in my mouth. "What?"

"Says so right here, addressed to you, Miss Mildred Crabtree." Mrs. Carlson handed me the letter.

I opened the small envelope, pulled out a note, and skimmed it silently:

Dear Miss Mildred Crabtree,

You're hereby summoned to testify before the commissioner to serve as a witness in favor of the defendant, Mr. Noah Shepherd, in the circuit court of North Carolina on Wednesday,

January 19, 1853, at noon. You've been given a month and a half for your arrival. The plaintiff, Mr. Wade Crabtree, has filed suit against Mr. Shepherd for conspiracy, stealing property, and violation of the Fugitive Slave Law of 1850. Failure to appear in court will result in a $100 fine or warrant for your arrest.

Sincerely,

Jonathan Curtis
Court Clerk

Processing what I'd read, I folded the note and sighed.

"What does it say, Millie?" Mrs. Carlson asked, concerned.

I rubbed my chin and glanced up at her. "I have to be a witness for a trial. Noah's in jail." I shook my head and covered my nose with my hand. "I can't believe it. My father filed a complaint against him."

I hadn't seen my father for several months, but only wrote to him. He claimed he accepted my decisions, but I doubted he wouldn't try changing my mind. I wasn't looking forward to going back to North Carolina, but I had to go for Noah's sake, regardless of the outcome of his sentence.

Entering my boarding room, I packed my carpetbag for my long trip to the South. Before I left for the night, I stopped by Miss Ophelia Vaughn's cabin in the woods and had dinner with her, Pearl, and Cecil.

"Are you scared?" Pearl's hazel eyes went round.

I spooned some sweet peas onto my plate and passed the bowl to Cecil. "A little, but you know, part of me is glad to see Noah again. I never said goodbye to him, Arthur, or Hubert. With Noah in prison, I hope the others are all right."

"Could you give him my thanks for his help?" Pearl said.

I smiled and nodded. "Certainly, I'm sure he'd appreciate that." I took a basket of buttered biscuits from Pearl and put one on my plate. "I'm afraid I'll say something wrong. I've never been a witness in court before, and especially not for a defendant."

"Whatever you do, don't lie," Miss Ophelia said. "Perjury is a crime and can lead to time in prison."

I licked my lips and gulped. "Yes, I know." Lying was illegal, but I also didn't want Noah's life to be at stake either. It wasn't because he was a heroic abolitionist who did good for the slaves or his encouragement of my writing, but I realized I was very fond of him. If he were sentenced to death, I doubted I'd be able to bear it.

"Best wishes to you, Miss Millie, and to Mr. Shepherd too," Cecil said.

I allowed a smile. "Thanks, Cecil."

We ate our food and changed the subject to my short story. I told the others I was waiting to hear back from Mr. Cohen and promised to let them know when it was published by the press. It would make a great bedtime story for children, and I hoped my future younger half-sibling would enjoy reading it as much as I enjoyed writing it.

After supper, I said my goodbyes to them and Mr. Carlson rode me to the dock.

Mr. Carlson waved. "Safe travels, Miss Millie."

"Thank you, Mr. Carlson. Goodbye." I walked into one of the fishermen's sailboats who took me across the river, starting my journey back down South again.

Knowing what could happen to Noah, I wanted to speak with him before it was too late. Maybe I was naïve, too young, or foolish to feel in such a way. Or maybe he wasn't the least bit interested in me. But he was a dear friend of mine, and over the journey to Canada, he held a special place within me. Before he lived his last hour on earth, I had to say what I had been too ashamed to mention before.

I had to tell him I loved him.

35 *Visiting Noah*

One month and a half later
MECKLENBURG COUNTY JAIL
Charlotte, North Carolina

FOR OVER A MONTH, I traveled back to North Carolina by carriage and boat, which was as challenging and exhausting as my first trip to Canada. When I finally arrived in Charlotte, North Carolina, nothing had changed at Crabtree Plantation. Those who were slaves continued working in the cotton fields under Mr. Jed's supervision, the overseer.

My father introduced me to his new wife Meredith, and I didn't like her one bit. She was a cocky, middle-aged woman. Her black hair was styled up on her head like a pile of coal stones, and her pale countenance was like chiseled marble—never did she smile.

Unlike Mama, she was the perfect woman for my father's conceited character. Over sweet tea and lemon cookies, we talked about my writing life in Canada. When the court case came up in our light discussion, I left the mansion, offended by Papa's callous attitude and his stubborn refusal to overturn Noah's conviction.

The next day, I rode with the district attorney Mr. Oliver Briggs to the jail where Noah was being held prisoner by the sheriff. Briggs was a quick-witted, slender, and middle-aged man, who was determined to do what he could for Noah. We walked into the jailhouse and stood in front of the sheriff's desk. A name tag of his surname "Townsend" was on the front of his desk. He was an overweight man with a thick, gray, curled mustache and pointy beard.

His clean, neat clothes of a white dress shirt and navy-blue button vest with matching trousers showed his exalted authority. Pinned onto his vest was a bronze star reading SHERIFF, faintly glistening in the dappled sunlight from his side window.

Reclining in his chair, he crossed his sausage-like arms and peered at me, gritting his teeth. "Now, what do you two want?"

"We're here to visit Noah Shepherd, your prisoner. I'm Millie Crabtree," I said.

"She's appearing in court as a witness for my client," Mr. Briggs added.

Sheriff Townsend released a loud sigh and furrowed his bushy brows. "Only relatives and legal officers can see the defendant. Besides, how do I know he won't coerce your testimony?"

"Noah's an honest man. He would never do that, and neither would I. You have my word." I placed my white gloved hands on his desk and leaned forward. "Please, it's important. I have to talk to him. It's urgent."

"All right, fine," the sheriff said, "but I want it in writing." He opened his side drawer and took out a slip of paper. After scribbling a notice, he pushed the paper to me. "Sign on the line, if you're willing."

I skimmed the paper and without hesitation sketched my signature.

"Where is he?" I surveyed the room for a jail cell, but only saw a half-filled bookshelf with Noah's violin case on one shelf and a ring of keys hanging on a wall hook.

Sheriff Townsend stood and led us through a wooden door. "Back here, ma'am."

Following the sheriff to the barred cell in the back room, we found Noah inside. He was sitting on the hard ground with his back turned, rocking and humming Mozart's piano concerto no. 21, pretending to strum his violin.

Flies buzzed around a tray of rotting, untouched food beside him, and a rat squeaked and dashed across the concrete floor. His red, curly hair and dress clothes were dirty, and his ruby suit jacket and fedora were on an unmade cot in the cell.

My heart broke from his poor condition.

"Five minutes. That's all y'all will get!" The sheriff exited and slammed the door.

I inched forward to the cell and gripped the cold iron bars. "Noah?"

"Miss Millie . . . how lovely to hear your voice." There was joy mixed with sadness in his tone as if he had been crying and didn't want me to know about it.

He sniffled and wiped his face with a hand, but didn't bother facing me.

I frowned, still holding the cell bars. "Why won't you look at me?"

"Oh, I don't know," Noah said. "I suppose I don't want to scare you."

"It's all right, son. She already knows what happened to you after I talked to her about the case," Mr. Briggs said.

Noah stood and held up a hand to his face. Scuffling his feet, he turned around slowly. As soon as I saw his battered face, it felt like someone had stabbed me in my chest. His right eye was barely open, and his left had a minor bruise under his lower eyelid. Dried scars were also on the bridge of his nose, above one eyebrow, and on one of his cheeks.

He looked as though he had been scratched up by a wild stray cat or beaten with a shovel. It made me want to love him more and embrace him in my arms. Noah was a sweet, warmhearted man, and he didn't deserve to be treated like an animal by my father and his friends ganging up on him at Crabtree Plantation.

"Dear God . . ." A tear trickled down my cheek.

"It was a pretty bad brawl," Noah said, "but don't worry, Millie. It's nothing. I'll be all right."

I turned to his attorney for more explanation.

"He was a lot worse before his wounds healed," Mr. Briggs said. "If the town sheriff hadn't intervened, they might've beaten him to death the night they caught him leading slaves off the land."

I faced Noah and studied him, intrigued. "What about Hubert and Arthur? Where are they?"

"Hubert was shot and killed during an assignment in South Carolina," Noah said and sighed. "And Arthur, he fell ill with a coughing sickness. Doctors don't know exactly what's wrong with him."

"Oh, no. I'm sorry about your friends and what my father did. I'll say whatever you want me to—"

"Don't," Noah interrupted. He walked to the caged door that barricaded him and grasped his hands over mine, clutching the iron bars. "Please, Millie. I don't want you to lie for me. Just be honest and supportive, and maybe the commissioner will go easy on me. No matter what, tell the truth, all right?"

I hung my head and sobbed. "I should, but I don't know if I can."

"Sure, you can. You went all the way to Canada," Noah said, smiling. "You can do anything, Millie." He reached his hand through the bars and raised my chin.

I blinked my tearful eyes and exchanged a wistful smile with him. "I . . . I love you, Noah. I couldn't help but to tell you how I felt before . . . I mean, if you die." I sniffled and lowered my eyes to the floor, blushing.

"Thanks, I'm glad you came, Millie." Noah sighed hopelessly. "I love you too. You're not as much of a child as I had thought you were before. You're a gifted, lovely young woman."

I lifted my head and touched his sad, injured face, seeing nothing but the fun-loving, redhead violinist I first saw on my eighteenth birthday.

Noah took my gloved hand from his cheek. He closed his eyes and kissed my hand firmly. "Goodbye, Millie."

"Goodbye, Noah," I said. "Pearl asked me to send her thanks for your help."

The sheriff swung open the door. "Time's up!"

Mr. Briggs gripped my shoulders. "We'd best go, Miss Millie. We've got a big day ahead of us."

I nodded and followed the attorney out of the jail cell room, glancing back as Noah raised a hand of farewell through the caged door.

The court session was tomorrow at noon.

36 *A Friend of a Friend*

ON THE DAY OF the court meeting, I awoke in my hotel room with a heavy pain in my chest. The talk between Mr. Briggs and me over breakfast yesterday was overwhelming. I explained the details about how I came to know Noah and him being an abolitionist. Wrestling with my thoughts, I tried to stay positive about the court situation.

But the more I shared with the attorney, the more it seemed my father had the upper hand. There was plenty of evidence against Noah, including his violin case and the route map and other items within it. Mr. Briggs prepared me for puzzling questions and advised me not to say more than I had to, so I avoid putting my own life in danger. Before we entered the courtroom, it was obvious all the defendant's side had was a prayer.

At noon, we rode in a stagecoach to the Mecklenburg County Courthouse where the meeting was taking place.

I didn't hear a word Mr. Briggs said to me, trapped in apprehension over the fates of Noah and I.

"Miss Millie?" Mr. Briggs said.

I drew a quick breath and looked over at him. "Yes? Sorry, I wasn't listening."

Mr. Briggs chuckled, glancing at his silver pocket watch. "Yes, I can see that. I said, 'Is there anything else you can tell me about the case?'"

I squinted at the sun beaming on my face. "Nothing that will change the outcome. Pardon me, Mr. Briggs, but our chances of succeeding in a state that condones slavery are pretty thin, don't you think?"

"Well, yes," Mr. Briggs admitted, "but on some occasions, abolitionists are spared in exchange for restitution or a fine of repayment. Let's hope the commissioner isn't utterly heartless and does the same for Noah. Perhaps he will after he finds out about the ill-treatment he's suffered from the hands of your father and his friends." The driver stopped us outside of the courthouse. People passed us and marched one by one into the stone, columned structure. Were all these people coming to watch the trial and a man sentenced to death?

"Let's go inside," Mr. Briggs said. "We don't want to keep everyone waiting." After the driver climbed down from the stagecoach, he opened the side door. The driver lent me his hand and helped me step down.

"Thank you, sir," I said.

"You're welcome, ma'am. Have a nice day." The driver

closed the door after Mr. Briggs and sat in the front seat of the carriage, waiting for out returned exit after the court session.

Mr. Briggs and I walked into the courtroom filled with chatting voices and recurrent coughs as everyone took their proper seats.

The audience of curious spectators waited for the commissioner and Noah, the indicted one. A group of all-white men packed the jury stand. Like a parliament of sitting owls, they stroked their hairy mustaches and beards and surveyed the area.

Some of them whispered remarks and glanced from me with the crowd of onlookers to Mr. Briggs sitting at the defendant's table. Standing around the circled balcony above us were the slaves of many masters, and like the women, they weren't able to take part in the final verdict. Their hopeless faces of desolation for a man they saw as a friend saddened me.

My heartbeat stopped as I saw my father walk up the aisle with his attorney, Chauncey, Jed; and Mr. John Weiss, another slave master and friend of my father. Under his arm in a side embrace was my stepmother, Meredith.

I sighed and turned away, but felt Chauncey eyeing me from the distance as he sat on the audience benches near the plaintiff's table.

The double doors banged shut.

I turned my head and watched as a brawny federal marshal pulling Noah along by his arm. Compared to the marshal, Noah looked like a little boy. The black chains of Noah's handcuffs shook and rattled as he took the walk of shame down the aisle to the defendant's table. The marshal plopped Noah in a chair beside Mr. Briggs. Indistinct voices mumbled about his presence. Some people in the audience gave him angry stares, and others shook their heads with concerned looks.

I jumped to my feet and held the edge of the audience bench in front of me. "Do you have to be rough with him?" I scowled at the marshal, but he said nothing and looked down his long nose at me.

"Are you all right?" I mouthed, studying Noah.

Noah gave a weak smile and whispered, glancing at me. "I'm fine, Millie."

The federal marshal cleared his throat and proceeded with the introduction in front of the commissioner's bench. "All rise! The court is in session. Commissioner Adam Sullivan enters as representative of Judge Hiram Jefferson."

Everyone stood from their seat as an old, droopy-faced man in his military uniform entered from a back room and sat at the centered high bench.

The federal marshal took a document from a young man at a side desk and put it on the commissioner's desk.

"Case two hundred and ninety-five, Shepherd vs. Crabtree."

"Thank you, marshal. Everyone may be seated," the commissioner said.

Except for the slaves, everyone else sat down.

"Will the defendant rise?" the commissioner said.

Noah and his attorney stood.

"Mr. Shepherd, you've been charged with conspiracy, illegally assisting slaves and stealing property. Hence, you've been suspected for violation of state law through the Compromise of 1850 Fugitive Slave Act. Are there opening statements from the plaintiff?"

My father and his attorney rose from their chairs.

"Yes, sir. I'm prosecutor Lloyd Dixon, representing Mr. Crabtree's case. My client is upset with Mr. Noah Shepherd. He allowed him into his home as a guest and treated him well, only for him to be a thief and steal his property. My client, his witnesses, and I will prove beyond a reasonable doubt Mr. Shepherd is guilty and an undercover abolitionist!" Mr. Dixon glowered and pointed at Noah.

The audience and jury gaped at one another and went into an uproar.

"Order! Order in the court!" The commissioner slammed his gavel on the block, calming down the noisy commotion. "Are there opening remarks from the defendant?"

Noah whispered in Mr. Brigg's ear.

"Sir, my client has chosen to waive his opening statement," Mr. Briggs said.

More mumbles arose from the audience.

The commissioner nodded. "Very well, I grant his request. Let us proceed with the trial."

"Thank you, sir. I'll begin with everything that was found on the culprit." Mr. Dixon showed the evidence in Noah's violin case, including the U.S. map marked with arrows of escape routes to Canada and a slip of paper written with code words. "Sir, as you can see these items are evidence against Mr. Shepherd. They're proof he's part of a conspiracy, a secret network known as none other than the scandalous Underground Railroad, which hides fugitives and transports them north!"

More whispers and mutters came from the jury and audience.

"I call my first witness to the stand . . . Mr. Wade Crabtree," the prosecuting attorney said.

Papa walked up and swore in by the federal marshal.

"Mr. Crabtree, what were you doing the night Mr. Shepherd trespassed your land?" Mr. Dixon laced his hands on the barred stand around the witness chair.

My father glanced from me and back to his attorney. "Why, I was celebrating my wedding with some friends. Miraculously, I had gotten another wife willing to tolerate my madness." He smirked at Meredith.

I lowered and shook my head.

Papa paused and continued. "We were dancing and drinking in the parlor of my mansion, but then Jed, my overseer, called me from outside."

"And what did your overseer say?" Mr. Dixon asked.

Papa knitted his brows. "He told me there was a redhead scum of an abolitionist in the slave quarters, talking about getting them free."

"And did you go outside to see for yourself?"

Papa nodded. "Yes, I did, and friends of mine at my wedding ceremony followed me. We saw Shepherd and some of my slaves running in a group together from the slave quarters, and many of my slaves got away."

"No further questions, Commissioner," Mr. Dixon said. "Mr. Crabtree, you may step down."

My father left the witness chair and sat back at the plaintiff's table.

Afterward, Mr. Dixon called his other witnesses to testify, but Briggs wasn't about to give the case away.

"Sir, may I cross-examine Dixon's last witness?" Mr. Briggs said.

"Proceed," the commissioner said.

Mr. Briggs held his hands behind his back and walked toward Chauncey in the witness chair. "Mr. McMillan, you stated you witnessed Mr. Noah Shepherd fighting Master Crabtree and Mr. Weiss on Crabtree Plantation. Did you also take part in the brawl?"

Chauncey shrugged. "What if I did?"

"Answer the question, McMillan," the commissioner said.

Chauncey cocked his head and sighed. "All right, fine. I was in on it too."

"Hmm, three against one? I hardly call that a fair fight," Mr. Briggs said, disturbed. "If Sheriff Townsend hadn't stopped it, it might've led to murder. Isn't it true Mr. Shepherd was unconscious?"

"Well, yeah," Chauncey began and snarled at Noah, "but he got what he deserved. He shouldn't have been on Crabtree's land, stealing property."

The audience roared and some of them raised their hands in agreement.

"Order!" the commissioner said, banging his gavel. "Order in the court! Order! Order!"

The commotion died down again.

Dixon jumped from his chair. "Sir, my opponent, Mr. Briggs is trying to make Noah out to be a victim when Mr. Crabtree is the *real* victim. He's suffered great debt and is still recovering from his financial losses. I ask his daughter, Miss Mildred Crabtree, to take the stand."

"I grant your request, Dixon, but after the defendant attorney has gotten a chance first to state his case," the commissioner said. "Miss Mildred Crabtree, please take the stand."

My stomach was tied in knots as I went over to the witness chair. At my request, I agreed to *affirm* to speak the truth.

The federal marshal held up his right hand. "Do you affirm to tell the whole truth and nothing but the truth, so help you God?"

"I do," I said, holding up my hand.

"What is she a Quaker or something?" one rude man blurted from the audience.

"Silence!" the commissioner said. "Miss Mildred's entitled to the right of affirmation, just as long as she tells the truth." He glanced at me. "You may sit down, Miss Mildred."

After the federal marshal walked away, I sat in the witness chair with my hands in my lap.

Mr. Briggs approached and stood beside the stand. "Now, Miss Mildred, you ran away from home. Is that correct?"

"Yes, sir," I said.

"And why did you leave home, Miss Mildred?" Mr. Briggs said.

I gulped and spoke up. "Because my father was going into a partnership with Master Chauncey McMillan. He was going to . . . exchange me for an arranged marriage, which is probably the case for half the women in this courtroom."

Some women gawked at me, stunned and offended I said such an impulsive statement, but the truth was the truth. Having little to no rights, women were property just as well as the slaves were.

"I wanted to fulfill my dream as a children's author and avoid living my mother's life," I added. "People think her heart sickness killed her, but it was the unhappy, restricted life she was living. Her dependent longing to please my father and her miscarriages carried her to her grave!" I dabbed my kerchief at my eyes.

Some commotion rumbled from the audience.

"And how do you know, Mr. Noah Shepherd, Miss Mildred?" Mr. Briggs said.

I drew a breath and hesitated. "He was the violinist who performed at my eighteenth birthday party. My father had musicians play music during the party for entertainment."

"No further questions, commissioner," Mr. Briggs said and took his seat.

"Sir, may I cross-examine now?" Mr. Dixon said.

The commissioner nodded. "Proceed."

As the prosecuting attorney came to me with his inquisitive face, I knew I was in deep waters now.

"Miss Mildred, some months ago, your father lost six slaves from his plantation around the same time you left home. Do you know anything about it?"

I glanced behind the plaintiff attorney at Mr. Briggs and Noah, who gave me slight nods. "I refuse to answer on the grounds that I might incriminate myself."

Mr. Dixon scowled and gripped the edge of the witness stand, closing in on me. "Was Mr. Shepherd responsible for their disappearance from Crabtree Plantation?"

My heart punched in my chest, clutching the arms of the witness chair in my sweaty palms, repeating my right to the Fifth Amendment and hoping it'll spare my and

Noah's lives. "I refuse to answer on the grounds that I might incriminate myself."

"Were there other slaves from your father's cotton plantation Mr. Shepherd helped escape to the North?" Mr. Dixon asked urgently.

I blinked and shook my head. "I . . . I don't know."

Mr. Dixon smirked and moved to my left side, speaking to my ear. He glanced at Noah and laced his hands on the stand. "Are you sure you aren't trying to cover for Mr. Shepherd because of friendship? Or maybe for love?"

"I told you I don't know!" I said, irritated.

Mr. Dixon growled and banged the edge of the witness stand. He clenched his teeth and pointed swiftly at the items on the plaintiff's table. "Does the evidence of the violin case belong to Mr. Shepherd?"

With hesitation, I paced my breathing and glanced behind the prosecuting attorney at Noah again. He sighed and inched up a closed-mouth smile, looking down at his cuffed hands.

I swallowed a hard lump and confessed. "Yes." Dread fell in my gut, knowing my one-word answer supported Dixon's claims, but what else was I supposed to say? Noah's eyes pleaded with me to speak the truth.

The audience made an astonishing ahh sound, and Mr. Dixon ceased to pepper me with anymore of his suspicious questions.

"You may step down, Miss Mildred." He smirked and grinned at me.

Disappointed, I surveyed the seated crowd of North Carolinians. "But please, wait, what about what they did? Mr. Shepherd was almost killed for crying out—"

"Step down, Miss Mildred," the elderly commissioner interrupted sternly.

Burdened and troubled by my defeat, I speechlessly scanned the stone-faced people in the audience and the jury stand and left the witness chair, taking my seat back in the audience.

The commissioner cleared his throat and wove his hands. "I've heard both sides with keen ears and have brought everything under consideration, but it's time to make a final decision. Are there closing remarks from the plaintiff?"

Mr. Dixon listened to my father whisper to him. "No, sir."

"Any from the defendant?" the commissioner asked.

Mr. Briggs nodded as Noah spoke to him and rose to his feet. "Yes, sir. My client wishes to speak a few words."

"Very well," the commissioner said.

Noah stood and observed the angry faces of the surrounding people. "I know you all hate me, but I apologize for upsetting you or being a threat to your way of life. Please, know I won't hold anything against you all no matter what happens."

He sighed and faced the commissioner. "Sir, I throw myself on the mercy of the court. Thank you." He sat down again.

Tears pooled in my eyes as Noah bowed his head, studying his chained wrists.

"All right," the commissioner said. "This meeting is adjourned for jury deliberations. The jury will exit to conclude a final decision. Afterward, I will declare the verdict." He slammed his gavel on the block.

The group of men on the jury left to debate their verdict in a back room.

I pushed through the audience and walked to the defendant's table. "What do you think, Mr. Briggs?"

The attorney crossed his arms and let out a slow breath. "I don't know, Millie."

"Neither of you worry about me. I'm prepared to take my death," Noah said.

"Don't talk like that, Mr. Shepherd," Mr. Briggs said, "you must keep hope."

"I'm going to get a quick drink of water." I started leaving out of the courtroom as Papa and the others on the plaintiff's side were leaving for a break.

Chauncey grinned and snagged my arm. "Well, long time no see, Miss Millie."

"Get your hands off me!" I frowned and yanked my arm from his grip.

"What's the matter? We're old friends, Millie." Chauncey stole a glance at Noah. "Don't tell me you've settled for that pathetic-looking, little abolitionist."

With boldness, I took a deep breath and craned my neck, looking up at him. "What if I did?"

Chauncey tilted back his head and chortled. "You've got to be joking, Miss Millie. He can't do anything for you. He's nothing more than a poor musician eating table scraps. Besides, if the jury goes easy, he probably can't afford to repay your father anyway. All he's good for is dangling on the end of a rope, which is what's gonna happen when the commissioner gives the verdict!"

I frowned and tried to slap Chauncey's face, but he caught my hand and gently kissed it.

"Good day, Miss Millie," he said and smiled smugly.

I pulled my hand away from him and changed my mind about getting a drink. Instead, I stayed with the others and sat on a bench behind the defendant's table, counting the minutes. When the verdict came, the jury returned to the courtroom. One man placed a slip of paper on the commissioner's desk and joined the rest of the jury in their stand.

"Case two hundred and ninety-five, Shepherd vs. Crabtree, as the charge of conspiracy and violation of state law under the Fugitive Slave Act. We, the jury, find the defendant guilty as charged," the commissioner said, reading the paper.

An uproar of celebration erupted from the audience.

The commissioner asked each of the men of the jury by number if it was his verdict and all of them agreed unanimously.

"Will the defendant rise?" the commissioner added.

Noah and Mr. Briggs stood.

"Mr. Shepherd, I extend my apologies for the assault you've endured and I reckon' you've suffered enough already from the hands of your adversaries. However, it's *still* illegal for anyone, whether negro or white to harbor fugitive slaves. Therefore, I sentence you to six months in prison. You also must pay restitution to Mr. Crabtree for his losses in the total of three thousand dollars. Court is adjourned." The commissioner banged his gavel for the last time.

I leaped up and hugged Noah's neck with a sigh of relief. But Papa and Chauncey weren't too happy with the sentence and neither was everyone else in the stands of the courtroom.

They were hoping for a lynching execution.

"Well," I began, sobbing, "at least your life was spared."

Noah nodded and cried. "Yes, for now. Promise you won't forget me. Friend of a friend?"

"I promise," I said and sniffled. "I'll never forget you."

The federal marshal thudded over to Noah and pulled him away, leading him out of the courtroom.

"Goodbye, Miss Millie," Noah said, looking back at me from the distance.

I smiled wistfully and waved. "Bye, Noah."

Then the doors in the middle of the aisle closed with a loud shut again.

It was the last time I saw him.

April 1861

EPILOGUE

THE DOCKS OF WINDSOR
Windsor – Ontario, Canada

AFTER THE TRIAL, I sailed back across the river and returned to Canada to continue building my life. By the spring of 1853, I had published *The Ruby Pendant*, my first children's short story. Mr. and Mrs. Carlson gave me a ruby brooch as a gift of celebration. Copies of the story and my photograph were printed in the weekly newspapers of negro and white publishers in Windsor. To my surprise, I had become the talk of many people over the neighborhood of Sandwich and in the nearby provinces of the country.

Over time, I had become known as a fellow Canadian like the others, and no longer a foreigner in a strange land. From time to time, I visited home in search of Noah, but I never found him. Some said he left farther South after getting out of prison, and others said he went on a musical tour through Europe. Unable to find out the truth, I had decided it was time for me to let go of false hope and move on without him. Pearl and Cecil grew fonder of each other and were married at the Savior Jesus Tabernacle Church by Pastor Combs. It was an emotional and wonderful ceremony, but tough times and restless tension over slavery came between them. Pearl spoke to me about Cecil's guilt of his parents and siblings, who were still in bondage in Louisiana. For him, living completely happy in peace wasn't possible, knowing they weren't free.

Now in Canada, Pearl didn't think the confrontation between the North and South was Cecil's business. But as other colored men, Cecil joined the black regiment to fight in the Civil War. The day he left, I visited the shoreline at the docks to see Pearl and Julian, my half-brother.

Cecil stood in his navy dress cap and gold-buttoned uniform, carrying his army rifle, a rolled blanket, and a bag of other equipment strapped on his back.

I approached as he and Pearl hugged and said their goodbyes to each other.

"I wish you didn't have to go," Pearl said. "I'm gonna miss you."

Cecil sighed and cradled her cheek. "I know, but it's something I feel I must do. Besides, a black man doesn't get no respect until he shows himself worthy of it."

"Will you write to me?" she asked.

Cecil smiled and kissed her. "Every day." He looked down at Julian, took off his gray wool cap, rubbed a hand over his hair, and placed the cap back on Julian's head. "Take care of your mama, ya hear?"

"Yes, sir." Julian grinned and straightened his cap.

Besides the lighter whiteness of his skin compared to his mother's, he showed no resemblance to my father and favored after Pearl. He was an endearing, young boy with pretty, light brown eyes and the demeanor of a handsome little prince. His curly, brown hair protruded around the edges of his wool newsboy cap, and he wore a cute gray dress suit with braces and a bowtie. Pearl always made sure the little boy was presentable like a gentleman.

Julian smiled and pointed at me. "Look! It's Millie!"

Pearl and Cecil turned their attention to me and waved.

"Hello," I said, "I just came to see Pearl and Julian, and wish you a safe trip."

Cecil gave another smile. "Thank you, Miss Millie."

"If you want, I'll help keep an eye out for Pearl and Julian while you're away for you," I added.

"Thank you. I'd appreciate it." Cecil glanced back at the other colored soldiers and the white colonel in the steamboat. He looked at us for the last time. "Well, I best be going now. Keep me in y'all's prayers."

"We will," Pearl said and embraced him again.

Cecil planted a kiss on her cheek. "Goodbye, Pearl. I love you."

"Love you too," Pearl replied as they broke away.

The three of us on the dock watched Cecil climb into the steam riverboat and give a salute and a wave. He didn't stop waving until he was far away in the distance. The whistle blew and thick gray clouds ascended from the smokestack into the vivid, multicolored sunrise.

I wrapped an arm around Pearl's shoulders. "You should try not to worry too much. How about we get some lemonade at my place?"

Pearl smiled at me. "Sounds good."

We walked down the platform of the docks when an old, bearded man called me.

"Excuse me, ma'am," he said, "Are you Miss Mildred Crabtree, the children's author of *The Ruby Pendant*?"

We paused and faced him, suspicious.

The elderly man held something wrapped in a brown package with an envelope tied to it.

"Yes, sir. I am. Is there something you want?" I said.

He cocked his head and studied my face. "A friend of a friend sent me these items. Mr. Noah Shepherd . . . he told me to give them to you . . . before he died."

"Died?" Shock overcame me.

The old man nodded sadly. "Yes. I'm so sorry, ma'am. He suffered a terrible horse accident."

"How did it happen?" I asked urgently.

The old man glanced aside a moment, and then back at me again. "I'm afraid his horse threw him off and he hit his head on a nearby rock. The doctor tried to help him, but he couldn't hold on for too long. He . . . seemed so downhearted during his last few days. I imagine he wanted to rest in peace." He released the package into my arms like a newborn baby. "This is for you. It was his dying wish." With tearful eyes, he inched up a pensive smile, his chin quivering.

"Uh, thank you, sir." I frowned and pulled out the cream envelope under the string tied to the package as the old man walked away from us down the platform. On the front of it was the phrase 'To Millie' in cursive handwriting. I glanced at Pearl in awe.

"Open it," she suggested.

I tore open the envelope, took out the note inside, and read it. Noah's smooth, eloquent voice spoke to me through the ink cursive writing:

Dearest Millie,

I'm aware you've been looking for me. I'm sorry for my unexplained disappearance after my prison release, but I've been busy gathering the money to repay your father. Most of it was my life's savings, and it's left me dirt poor. Therefore, I did the only thing I knew to do . . . I played my music and performed shows to make up for the rest of the cost. I wish things had been different between us, but I doubt you would've returned to the South if otherwise happened. Call me a fool, if you please, but getting captured was worth seeing your pleasant face again.

Your presence in the jailhouse was like a breath of fresh air. I've always been a wanderer since I left the orphanage, even before I joined the Underground Railroad network. Truth is, I never stayed still long enough to get to know a lady until I met you. I paid the restitution to your father, but I knew it wasn't enough for him. Your Papa wanted me dead. Well, he doesn't have to worry about that anymore. I've gone far, far away, and never plan to return. I couldn't bear seeing the pain in your eyes if something happened to me. I'm deeply sorry, Millie, but it's what's best for us. I only ask that you keep this gift and never forget me.

I will love and cherish you forever,

Noah

As I blinked, moisture blurred the words on the note in my gloved hands. I folded the letter and stuffed it back into the envelope. Then I pulled the string loose off the package and unraveled the brown paper wrapped around it. Inside was Noah's violin, engraved with his initials N.S. at the bottom of the instrument. I hugged the violin and closed my eyes tightly.

Pearl and Julian encircled me in their arms.

"Keep the memories, Millie," Pearl said. "That's how you keep him alive."

"I know." I hung my head and broke loose, willing myself to be strong.

With tears in her eyes, Pearl held me at arm's length. "Noah would've been proud of you, as I am. We've gone through low valleys and climbed some high hills along the way, but through it all, you kept your promise, Millie. You kept your promise."

"You did too, Pearl." I sniffled and gave a slight smile.

Pearl peered across the calm river. She faced me again. "I know how it feels to lose a man you loved and cared about, Millie. Even today, I've never forgotten Randy. He was a little stubborn with your father, but his heart was as pure as gold. I don't know what I'll do if something happens with Cecil too, but despite this, I'm here if you need someone. Nothing's changed that. You know that, right?"

"Yes, I know," I said and swallowed a lump. "Pardon me, you two, but I don't feel much like having company right now. Take care." I sniffled, smiled to keep from crying, and started walking on my way home.

"I'm . . . here if you need a friend, Millie," Pearl said again.

I froze, thought a split second of what she said, and then took a few more forward steps.

"I'm here, Millie," Pearl said with vigor.

Glancing over my shoulder, her face contorted with sorrow, her chin trembling. Was she reminding me of something, or was her call a plea for help? Since the day she married Cecil, a part of me felt like I was in their way, a shackle from Pearl's enslaved past. After all, what did she need of me anymore? As Papa said, she was my house servant at Crabtree Plantation, and now she was a free woman. But the memory of when we formed our blood pact as little girls came back to my mind. On that warm summer day, Pearl was barefoot in her sackcloth gown, while I wore my lavender day dress, both of us standing under a dogwood tree. After that day, we weren't only friends who had sealed a promise—we were sisters. Unable to hold the waterfalls from streaming, I yielded to her outstretched arms, thankful to have someone who related to my heartache and pain.

"You don't have to be ashamed of crying, Millie," Pearl said, sobbing and stroking my hair. "Crying . . . it helps the heart heal."

And I did.

Holding Noah's initialed violin, I wept bitterly for him, for my mother, for Hubert and Arthur, for Joseph and others who didn't make it to freedom, and for those who would die for other slaves to have it. Life was hard as a young woman on her own in the city, as it would be for Pearl without Cecil.

But despite the present, ongoing war, I believed God would sustain us. For our friendship remained intact through a kingdom of slavery, my father's ugly sin, and a long, perilous journey to the Promised Land. My past was gone and my future was unknown, but despite everyone I lost and all the tragic things that happened, I knew I still had a friend's love.

And she had mine.

AUTHOR'S NOTE

Historical fiction is no joke or easy task. A lot goes into crafting a fictional world based on a particular time period in history in order to make it realistic to readers, and I hope by the grace of GOD I did a good job with it after doing pretty thorough research based on the suggestions given me by my editor of this Christian and historical fiction novel, Diana Sharples.

I thoroughly enjoyed writing about my characters and the storyline in this book, as it's one of the darkest but most important times of American history. So, how did it all begin? You might be surprised to know, but my story *The Pact of Freedom* started as a murder mystery play I was attempting to write, then titled *The Killing of Wade Crabtree.* From there, it became a short story titled *The Pact.* This short story was about a slave master's wife named Harriet who murdered her abusive husband and helped free their slaves from her husband's plantation. As you can see, the concept of the story went through a stage of metamorphosis, as I changed up some things, made the lead character the slave master's daughter, and took the route of a coming-of-age type of historical fiction tale. I thought to myself. *What if a slave master's daughter was friends with one of the slaves and opposed slavery? What if she were against the traditions of the South and desired life outside of slavery? And what if like Angelina Grimke she saw slavery as a sin?*

I also found interest in the Compromise of 1850 and the Fugitive Slave Law, as I thought it'd be interesting if a slave master's daughter traveled north and assisted in freeing her father's slaves during this threatening time. I also thought it would be a good idea to write about the conditions slaves endured and their adventures to the North, inspired after watching a couple of classic slavery movies, documentary videos, and short films.

From there, I started to stretch the short story into a novella, and finally after some major edits, it became a whole full-length novel. Because of the main theme of *freedom* and the slaves escaping from their captivity, I then changed the title to *The Pact of Freedom*. With a title as such, I wanted the title to be symbolic to the story. *So, what is the pact?* Specifically, the pact is represented by Millie and Pearl's close friendship, their sisterly blood pact, and Millie's promise to help Pearl get her freedom, but it's also about three other situations.

Firstly, the pact of the Fugitive Slave Law within the Compromise of 1850, a federal law which gave white slave owners or their hired bounty hunters the right to recapture runaway slaves back into slavery. Secondly, the pact is represented by the collective mission of abolitionists to free African slaves against the law and persistently petition for abolition. And thirdly, the pact is represented by the money exchange between Master Chauncey McMillan and Master Wade Crabtree, which Chauncey offered to ask for Millie's hand.

All these situations involved the agreement between two or more parties, but as the story's ending suggests, Millie and Pearl's friendship symbolizes the concept of *the pact* the most. The young ladies were good friends who had suffered much during their journey with the others, but they truly loved and always looked out for each other, even despite their ethnic differences. *Love thy neighbor* is the second greatest commandment of GOD; yet, it seems to also be one of the hardest for many of us to properly do.

This commandment doesn't specify anything about race, color, gender, or creed, and likely for the simple reason that we all were created by GOD and based on his creating power are a part of one large human family. As it states in Acts 17:26, of one blood GOD made all nations of men despite our differences. According to the Holy Scriptures, we all also turn to dust when we die; hence, no ethnicity or anyone is better than the other.

This was a crucial point of the story, shown by all the caring station masters who treated the runaway slaves like human beings and not like wild animals. Racism in religion was another vital topic I chose to touch in this story. For years, religion has portrayed all the biblical characters and angels as "white people," while "black people" were seen as the Devil just because of the color of their skin. These are some of the most erroneous beliefs that ever existed, only causing the retaliation of black people from white supremacy and oppression to show themselves only as the "people of GOD."

However, I debunked both of these false ideologies, explaining that what matters most isn't the color of Jesus Christ, but his character and the example and pattern of good works he left for his disciples to follow. My religious leader, Pastor Gino Jennings, likewise teaches about this in the Truth of God program 1042-1044, which you might fine interest in, discussing how white slave masters misused the holy scriptures to manipulate slaves and make them feel interior to white people and that racism alone is a form of terrorism.

Although writing my novel *The Pact of Freedom* was a bit of a challenge, I intend to write a few other historical fiction novels Lord-willing someday in the future.

Thank you to all of my readers of this novel for taking the time to read this book. Please, don't forget to leave a review and tell your family or friends about it. May GOD bless you all for your reviews and contributions.

Peace be unto you,
M. L. Bull
February 17, 2024

P.S. If you want to join a true church that immensely follows God's Word in the Holy Bible, find out more about my church attendance at our church website www.truthofgod.com or visit First Church Truth of God Broadcast on YouTube.

ACKNOWLEDGMENTS

First and foremost, I'd like to thank my Lord and Savior Jesus Christ for the gifts of writing and imagination. I'm not the best speaker in the world, but when my pen touches paper or my fingers tap on the keyboard a sense of inspiration strikes and words flow from my complex mind onto the page.

As I mentioned in one of my personal writing quotes, "When I write I feel as though I'm chiseling at stone, building a sculpture." Writing is a creative venture I started as a young girl and what I hope to continue doing for many more stories and years to come.

Secondly, I'd like to commend my editor of this book, Diana Sharples. Thank you so much for your help and informative suggestions to do more research to enhance my story and lengthen my book from a novella to a full-length novel. It really made a big difference and gave the characters and settings more life based on the 1850s era. Thirdly, I'd like to thank Nikola Jankovic from Serbia for drawing the Underground Railroad map for my novel.

Even though you specialize in creating fantasy maps, I appreciated working with you, as this is the first time I ever put a map inside one of my books. Thank you for being patient and meticulous with creating the map, making all my requested changes to my liking.

Fourthly, I'd like to thank all of those who critiqued my book, *The Pact of Freedom* for me. All of your bits of advice were useful and helped with me making this novel what it is today.

Finally, I'd like to thank myself, my family, and all the former patrons of Monroe, North Carolina's Chick-Fil-A I served as the dining room hostess who I talked with about this book. Your encouragement and enthusiasm helped keep me motivated in completing of this novel.

DISCUSSION QUESTIONS

1. Why wasn't Millie sure whether she wanted to put her birthday flowers in water? Who does her flowers represent?

2. What and who made Millie a "branded traitor" to her own flesh and blood?

3. Seeing Missus Charlotte was a sickly woman, do you think Master Crabtree was always intent on taking advantage of Pearl, a mulatto house slave woman? Why or why not?

4. Why do you think Millie gave her friend Pearl her mother's pearl cameo brooch back?

5. What situations during the time era and in the storyline represents "The Pact" in the story?

6. Nina and Gerald are residents in Ohio. If you were a black, former slave during slavery time, would you rather live in a "free" state like Ohio or take the longer and perilous journey to Canada?

7. Along with Jack Crenshaw, Sal, a negro man worked as a bounty hunter. Do you think he was a free man? Why or why not?

8. What is loving thy neighbor as thyself?

9. What do you think would've happened to Millie if she had been caught helping her slave friends to freedom?

10. How did Millie change during her journey to Canada compared to her luxurious life back on Crabtree Plantation?

11. After reaching Canada, what did Millie realize about her father's bias notions and the meaning of true friendship?

12. Who were your favorite characters out of the station masters Millie and her friends sought refuge from during their journey to Canada?

13. Slaves were crucial wealth of slave masters, and Pearl is mentioned as Master Wade Crabtree's most expensive slave. Although threatened for her life, could Pearl have continued running for her

freedom unscathed if she hadn't stayed behind for
Randy? Why or why not?

ABOUT THE AUTHOR

Michaela L. Bull aka "M.L. Bull" lives in North Carolina, but is from Salisbury, Maryland on the Eastern shore where she was born and raised. She is the youngest of three daughters. She is also the founder and owner of Risen Halo Publishing, a Christian publishing company.

Presently, she writes Christian and women's fiction novels and stories based on characters who make changes in their lives through faith and determination, which she prays will create a positive influence and encourage readers to never lose hope through the adversities of life.

She is also an occasional blogger who writes about the mechanics of story writing and writing tips on her "The Brainstorm" writing blog of her author website, as well as past and present authors and poets of American Literature, commending them for their talented abilities and great accomplishments in the literary world. Her writing motto is: *Touching Hearts One Story at a Time*. Aside from writing, she likes playing piano, drawing, arts and crafts, watching classic TV shows, and creating her own book trailers for her stories.

The Pact of Freedom is her second novel.

FOLLOW M. L. BULL & RISEN HALO PUBLISHING

M.L. Bull:

BookBub: M.L. Bull

Twitter: @mlbullbooks

Pinterest: @mlbullbooks

Tumblr: mlbullsportfolio

YouTube: *Journey of a Christian Writer series* (writing channel) & M. L. Bull (author channel)

Risen Halo Publishing:

Twitter: @halo_risen

YouTube: Risen Halo Publishing

OTHER CLASSIC AND HISTORICAL BOOKS YOU MAY LIKE OR ENJOY

Uncle Tom's Cabin by Harriet Beecher Stowe

American Slavery: American Slavery as It Is: Testimony of a Thousand Witnesses by Angelina & Sarah Grimke & Theodore Weld

BIBLIOGRAPHY

Jones, Jae. "Traditional Clothes Worn By Slaves on Plantations in The South." Black Then: Discovering Our History. <https://blackthen.com/traditional-clothes-worn-by-slaves-on-plantations-in-the-south/>

History.com Editors. "Underground Railroad." HISTORY. A &E Television Networks. <https://www.history.com/topics/black-history/underground-railroad#what-was-the-underground-railroad/> Originally published: 2009, October. 29.

Ohio Prohibits Any Black Person from Testifying Against a White Person. EJI: A History of Racial Injustice. <https://calender.eji.org/racial-injustice/apr/01/>

Berkin, Carol. Robert W. Cherny, James L. Gormly, and Christopher L. Miller. "Sectional Conflict and Shattered Union, 1840-1860." *In Making America: A History of the United States*. 7th ed. Vol. 1: To 1877. 320 & 326. Boston: Cengage Learning, 2014.

"The Abolitionists: AMERICAN EXPERIENCE." Part 1 – Chapter 1. |PBS| Educational video, 10:16. 2013, January. 8. <https://www.youtube.com/watch?v=TcYivpmTYBM&t=1s/>

"The Abolitionists: AMERICAN EXPERIENCE." Part 2 – Chapter 1. |PBS| Educational video, 14:06. 2013, January. 8. <https://www.youtube.com/watch?v=YMd5G4RpFLk&t=5s/>

"The Abolitionists: AMERICAN EXPERIENCE." Part 3– Chapter 1. |PBS| Educational video, 12:39. 2013, January. 8. <https://www.youtube.com/watch?v=MILN_17KH6M/>U.S. Coins 1850-1909. American Numismatic Association. Colorado

Springs, Colorado. 2024. <https://www.money.org/money-museum/virtual-exhibits-hom-case26/>

THANKS YOU FOR READING!

Reviews are so important and more helpful for authors than customers' only purchasing their books. Please send an honest review on Amazon or other book retailers of my novel and let me know what you thought. If you enjoyed my story, don't forget to recommend it to your friends and family. It would be highly appreciated. Thanks, and God bless you!

www.ingramcontent.com/pod-product-compliance
Lightning Source LLC
Chambersburg PA
CBHW040514170726
48295CB00012B/200